HEARTFELT PRAISE FOR
DOROTHY GARLOCK
AND HER UNFORGETTABLE NOVELS

"Garlock is a master."   —*Booklist*

"A gifted writer."   —*Chicago Sun-Times*

"One of America's most endearing historical fiction authors."
—*RT Book Reviews*

TAKE ME HOME

"Garlock's lovely, sweet novel is a testament to the last great generation."   —*RT Book Reviews*

"*Take Me Home* has a unique perspective for a historical novel set during World War II."   —*FreshFiction.com*

UNDER A TEXAS SKY

"Garlock is a masterful storyteller who recognizes what her audience craves and consistently delivers a sweet, nostalgic read that conveys the reality and romance of the era…There is enough depth of emotion in *Under a Texas Sky* to satisfy her fans."
—*RT Book Reviews*

"Who could resist a romantic summertime read from the 'Voice of America's Heartland,' especially with 'Texas' in the title?"
—*Fort Worth Star-Telegram* (TX)

"The latest from romance doyenne Garlock mixes light suspense with traditional romance for an entertaining effect."
—*Booklist*

BY STARLIGHT

COME A LITTLE CLOSER

while Dorothy Garlock paints a vivid backdrop of 1946 Wisconsin."   —GenreGoRoundReviews.blogspot.com

KEEP A LITTLE SECRET

"Garlock is a master at developing characters through their actions and evoking settings so real they transport the reader back in time...All the elements that keep Garlock's fans coming back for more are here."   —*Booklist*

"Four stars...[Garlock] takes readers back in time with her simple prose and likable characters, making them able to believe they are witnesses to the story. Not only is Garlock a premier Americana writer, but she is one who touches chords in readers' hearts."   —*RT Book Reviews*

"Excellent...enjoyable and compelling...eminently readable... engaging characters, romance, suspense, and small-town America in an era gone by."

—TheRomanceReadersConnection.com

STAY A LITTLE LONGER

"Heartwarming...love blooms."   —*Publishers Weekly*

"Touching...[a] poignant, engrossing story of life, death, and second chances...Well written and swiftly paced, this story brings to life a time period that is seldom used in romance."

—*Library Journal*

"An emotional...profound Americana tale [with a] strong ensemble cast...fans will relish this terrific historical."

—GenreGoRoundReviews.blogspot.com

DOROTHY GARLOCK

Twice in a
Lifetime

GRAND CENTRAL
PUBLISHING

NEW YORK   BOSTON

Copyright © 2015 by Dorothy Garlock

All rights reserved. In accordance with the U.S. Copyright Act of 1976, the scanning, uploading, and electronic sharing of any part of this book without the permission of the publisher constitute unlawful piracy and theft of the author's intellectual property. If you would like to use material from the book (other than for review purposes), prior written permission must be obtained by contacting the publisher at permissions@hbgusa.com. Thank you for your support of the author's rights.

Grand Central Publishing
Hachette Book Group
1290 Avenue of the Americas
New York, NY 10104

www.HachetteBookGroup.com

Printed in the United States of America

RRD-C

First Edition: July 2015

10 9 8 7 6 5 4 3 2 1

Grand Central Publishing is a division of Hachette Book Group, Inc.
The Grand Central Publishing name and logo is a trademark of Hachette Book Group, Inc.

The Hachette Speakers Bureau provides a wide range of authors for speaking events. To find out more, go to www.hachettespeakersbureau.com or call (866) 376-6591.

The publisher is not responsible for websites (or their content) that are not owned by the publisher.

Library of Congress Cataloging-in-Publication Data

Garlock, Dorothy.
  Twice in a lifetime / Dorothy Garlock. — First edition.
    pages cm
  ISBN 978-1-4555-2728-1 (hardcover) — ISBN 978-1-4555-2727-4 (trade pbk.) — ISBN 978-1-4789-0414-4 (audio download) — ISBN 978-1-4789-3402-8 (audio book) — 978-1-4555-2725-0 (ebook)
  I. Title.
  PS3557.A71645T95 2015
  813'.54—dc23
                                        2015010927

For Anaïs
The peach of her father's eye

Twice in a Lifetime

Prologue

Sunset, Missouri
March 1945

Bᴇᴇs ʙᴜᴢᴢᴇᴅ ᴀᴍᴏɴɢ the early spring flowers. A gentle breeze rustled the boughs of tall evergreens and maples. Ted Glidden's dog, forever chained to his rickety house, barked angrily. But Clara Sinclair noticed none of these things.

She couldn't take her eyes off the black car.

The Oldsmobile had rounded the corner up the street at Wilson Avenue, coming straight toward her, and then slowed before parking against the curb in front of her house. Bright afternoon sunlight reflected off the car's window and hood, making it impossible for Clara to see who was inside. Standing on the porch, she leaned against her broom, absently brushing a strand of black hair from her cheek and tucking it behind her ear. She couldn't say why, but she felt uneasy.

From the open door behind her came the sounds of music and laughter. Her mother, Christine, was playing a spirited, happy melody on the piano as Clara's seven-year-old son, Tommy, sang; the boy's rendition of "Old MacDonald" was making his grandmother laugh. Clara had been humming along as she swept but had stopped when she noticed the car.

Clara fought the sudden urge to join them, to turn her back on the automobile, hurry up the steps, and lock the door behind her.

The car's doors opened and two men got out. The first was dressed in a crisply pressed military uniform. Medals decorated his chest. He glanced down at a piece of paper in his hand, then peered up at the house, his eyes taking in the large windows, the intricate lattice-work along the porch, the steep-pitched roof, and the fluttering American flag before finally coming to rest on Clara; he held her gaze for only a moment before looking away.

But it was the other man who shook her. He was older, his hair a snowy white that thinned toward baldness on top. He wore the dress of the clergy, the familiar starched white collar atop a black shirt, and had a well-read Bible in his hands. Unlike his military companion, his eyes found Clara's and didn't look away; the gentle smile he offered accentuated his many wrinkles.

Clara knew why they had come. Men like them had gone to Abigail Townsend's house two years ago, had traveled through a blizzard to Samantha Clinton's on Christmas Eve, had left Ann Tate crying inconsolably, and had changed the lives of countless other women in every state across the nation. These men acted not out of malice but out of duty.

And now they had come for her; the realization caused her heart to beat faster and an icy chill of dread to wash across her skin.

"Good afternoon, ma'am," the military man said as he took off his hat and slipped it beneath his arm. "I'm Captain Coulson of the United States Army." Nodding toward his companion, he added, "This is Father Booker with the Chaplain Corps." Up close, the clergyman looked as worn as his Bible; his eyes were red and rheumy, like those of a hound dog.

Clara nodded at each of them in turn.

The captain cleared his throat. "Are you Mrs. Joseph Sinclair?"

"I...I am..." she answered.

The look in the man's eyes softened. He took a deep breath. "Mrs. Sinclair," he began, "I must regretfully inform you that your husband, Private Joseph Lawrence Sinclair, was killed in action on Thursday, the fifteenth of March."

Clara's heart felt as if it had stopped beating. Her hands trembled. Tears filled her eyes. Even as she struggled to keep her knees from buckling, she latched on to the date the officer had given, not even a week past. That very day, she had received a letter from Joe. Sitting down at the kitchen table, she'd read through it again and again until she knew every word by heart. Her husband had written that he was being careful. He'd told her that she shouldn't worry, that nothing bad could happen to him so long as he had her and Tommy to come home to. Joe had promised that he would be back before she knew it, and that they would be a family again.

Over and over, he had written that he loved her.

"Private Sinclair died in service to his country," the military man continued. "It was a sacrifice that will never be forgotten."

But Clara was no longer listening. Her thoughts reeled, assaulted by memories: the moment she had first noticed Joe standing outside Bob Herring's grocery store; how nervous she'd been when he asked her to go with him to the movies; the way his lips felt against hers when he kissed her later that night. From those early, magical days, their life had spooled out just like the spools of film they'd watched, giving her a marriage, a home, and a child, all of it bound by love.

It had been perfect, a dream come true, but then the Japanese had bombed Pearl Harbor and everything had changed.

Like the other young men in Sunset, Joe had enlisted and gone off to war; after training, he'd sailed across the Pacific to fight against Hirohito and his army. At first, Clara had been bursting with pride; her husband was fighting for freedom, to say nothing of how handsome he looked in his uniform. But as time passed, the constant fear and worry threatened to overwhelm her. Many nights, she cried herself to sleep. Still, she managed to keep up a strong front, mostly for Tommy's sake. She clung tightly to the hope she found in her husband's letters and tried to share in his unshakeable belief that he would soon be home.

But now Joe was dead and Clara felt it in her heart, a sudden emptiness, as if it was her own life that had ended.

"Mrs. Sinclair?"

Clara blinked; both men were looking at her. "I'm...I'm sorry..." she managed, her head spinning.

"That's quite all right. I was just offering my condolences," Captain Coulson explained; he appeared uncomfortable, his eyes flickering away, as if he was still ill at ease with the responsibility that he had been given. "In times like this, it's been my experience that some measure of comfort can be found from a higher source." He looked toward his companion.

"My child," the chaplain began, "I know this is hard, but you must remember that the Lord works in mysterious ways. No matter what pain he would leave behind, the time had come for Joseph to return to His Kingdom, to make the journey home." His voice was soft and comforting; maybe under different circumstances, it might have been able to provide Clara with the solace she so desperately needed. "Let us read His words." Opening his Bible, the chaplain began to flip through the pages, looking for a particular line of scripture.

But Clara had already begun to walk away. Her rejection of the chaplain wasn't because she had no place in her heart for God, but rather because her pain was too great to fix. She was like a wounded animal, slowly but surely dying; all she wanted was to get away, to be alone.

When she reached the porch, Clara realized that she no longer held her broom; it must have fallen from her hands, though she had no memory of letting it go. Beyond the open door, her mother continued to play the piano as Tommy sang by her side; neither of them was aware that their lives had changed.

"Mrs. Sinclair?" one of the men asked. "Are you all right?"

Stepping inside, all Clara could see was Joe. He had built their house, working day and night one year from spring, through the summer, and on into winter, whenever he had time; Joe was in every nail that had been pounded and every doorway under which she walked. Her husband looked back at her from photographs sitting on the fireplace's mantel and hanging from the walls. He was even there in the toys scattered across the floor; they belonged to Tommy, their beloved son, the only real part of Joe she had left. All Clara saw was a reminder of what she had lost.

"Mrs. Sinclair? Are you sure that you don't need—"

Clara softly shut the door.

A heartbeat later, she dropped to her knees. The tears she'd managed to hold back now came like a flood, streaming down her face. Sobs heaved out of her chest, shaking her like a leaf in a storm. Despair, fear, and pain all dug their claws in deep. The future she had worked for, had prayed to come true, had staked everything on had been cruelly taken from her. Joe, her husband, the man she loved with all her heart, was dead.

When she screamed, the music stopped.

Chapter One

March 1954

So what happens now?"

"Tommy will go before the judge, and if Clarence isn't having a good day, there's a chance your son will be locked away for what he did."

Clara Sinclair's mouth went as dry as cotton. Her heart raced like a runaway train. Her hands clenched so tight they were white as bone.

"Jail? You . . . you can't be serious . . ."

"Like I said, there's a chance."

Frank Oglesby had been Sunset's sheriff for as far back as Clara could remember. He was getting on in years, now somewhere just past sixty, and beginning to show signs of his age: his formerly black hair was touched with white and thinning on top, his eyes were framed with crow's-feet and a dusting of age spots, and his uniform had grown tight around his stomach. But while Sheriff Oglesby might have begun to diminish physically, he still commanded the respect of his town. He was tough but fair, the sort of man who listened to both sides of an argument, no matter whether the person making it was poor or rich, white or black, educated or otherwise.

So when he said that her son was in trouble, Clara worried.

"The problem," the lawman continued, leaning forward to put his elbows on his desk, "is that this isn't the first time Tommy's slipped up."

"No, it isn't," she reluctantly agreed.

Ever since her husband had been killed in the war, Clara had noticed a change in their son. Whereas Tommy had once been a precocious, kind, and inquisitive boy, with the death of his father, he had slowly become withdrawn and argumentative. His grades at school had begun to suffer and, as the years passed, Clara noticed that fewer parents wanted their children to spend time with him.

When Tommy had become a teenager, his problems worsened. More than once, Clara had smelled alcohol on his breath. She suspected that some of the things she found in his room were stolen; when she confronted him about where he'd gotten the money to buy them, he laughed in her face. Finally, he had been caught kicking over fence posts on Homer Chestnut's property; fortunately, the old farmer had declined to press charges. But even then, Tommy had shown no remorse. Alarmed, Clara had desperately tried to reach her son, but no matter what she said, regardless of how hard she pleaded or even threatened, nothing made any difference. As a mother, she felt both helpless and hopeless. Now here she was, miserable in the early dawn hours, sitting in the sheriff's office.

"Are you sure that he did it?" she asked.

The lawman nodded. "As much as I can be without catching him in the act."

"Then you don't know for sure! Maybe he stumbled across it. Given time he might've come to you and told you what he'd found."

The sheriff's expression hardened; Clara imagined all the times he'd done this before, sitting at his desk, explaining to families that the one they loved wasn't as innocent as they believed.

According to Sheriff Oglesby, he'd driven his police car into the Sunset Cemetery around ten o'clock the previous night. A full moon shone brightly, so he'd shut off his headlights. One by one, tombstones had passed in the gloom until, unexpectedly, one hadn't. Curious, the lawman switched his lights back on and discovered Tommy Sinclair standing frozen in the beams. Lying beside him were the remains of a grave marker, broken into dozens of pieces; the sheriff had arrested Tommy for pushing it over. It was a deliberate act of vandalism, one that would surely ignite a scandal in town once word got out.

"What other explanation could there be?"

"He wouldn't have gone to the cemetery alone," Clara offered, grasping at straws. "You know who he's running around with these days. It could've been any of them. Maybe they started for the woods when they heard your car."

The sheriff shook his head. "Tommy was the only person I saw," he explained. "Besides, I asked your son if there was anyone else with him and he said that there wasn't."

Clara wanted to insist that Tommy was lying, that he was trying to protect someone, but she bit her tongue.

And I've got a pretty good idea who it is...

For the last couple of weeks, Tommy had been spending time with Naomi Marsh, the daughter of Wilbur Marsh, the owner of Sunset's roughest bar. Older than her son at nineteen, the girl was a troublemaker; Naomi smoked, drank, and had a mouth filthier than any trash can. But she was also beautiful; she had cavorted around with so many men that most folks in town had lost count. For reasons that escaped Clara, Naomi had developed an interest in Tommy; the boy had proven to be defenseless against her charms. No matter how much Clara protested, regardless of what she said or did to nip Tommy and Naomi's relationship in the bud, nothing had worked. Clara's growing fear was that Naomi would ruin her son. Now, even though Sheriff Oglesby hadn't seen her, Clara was convinced that the girl had been involved in what had happened at the cemetery.

"Would Judge Parker really send Tommy to jail?" she asked fearfully.

The lawman shrugged. "We'll have to wait and see."

"But he's just a boy!" Clara argued.

"Sixteen is almost a man. It certainly is in Clarence's eyes. Odds are, he won't show much leniency."

"But . . . but to lock him away . . ."

"Younger than Tommy have been sentenced for less. The judge believes that some time behind bars can do a wayward boy some good. He thinks it scares the crooked nail straight." Sheriff Oglesby paused. "In this case, he might be right."

Listening to the lawman, Clara feared that she had failed her son despite all her best efforts. She thought of Joe; what would her husband think if he could see the mess she'd made of her and Tommy's lives? Struggling to hold back tears, she bit down on her lower lip and turned to look out the office's lone window; outside, dawn had just begun to color the sky.

The sheriff noticed. Frowning, he pushed himself out of his chair and went to sit on the corner of his desk, right in Clara's line of sight.

"Maybe there's another way..." he said.

Clara looked up at him through wet eyes. She felt a flicker of hope flare in her chest. "What...what do you mean?"

"You were right about one thing. I *didn't* see Tommy push over that tombstone, so I can't say for certain that he's responsible. Maybe he would've come to tell me about it, maybe he wouldn't have. But because I happened upon him when I did, we'll never know, will we?"

Clara's heart raced. "But...but you said..."

The lawman sighed. "I know things have been hard for you, Clara," he replied. "Raising a child nowadays isn't easy. The Good Lord knows how much trouble I had with my own two boys. But to have to do it all by yourself, well, it doesn't seem fair to hold it all against you for how Tommy's turned out."

"I'm not looking for pity," she replied defiantly.

"That might be," the sheriff said, "but you should take it all the same. It's the only thing that'll keep your son out of jail."

He got up and fished a mess of keys from his pocket. When he looked back, the compassion in the lawman's eyes had vanished, replaced by a hardness that unnerved Clara.

"Once I've said my piece, we'll go to the cells, I'll let Tommy out, and you can take your son home. But let me be clear about something," Sheriff Oglesby said, his voice low. "This here is your son's last chance. The next time he screws up, whatever the reason, he'll stand before the judge and get what's coming to him. Your father was a good friend of mine and the whole town feels bad about what happened to Joe, but none of that will matter if Tommy can't keep his nose clean. I won't help him, or you, any more."

Clara was grateful for the tremendous favor she was being given, but the meaning of the sheriff's warning wasn't lost on her.

"Do we understand each other?" he asked.

She nodded, promising herself that this time would be different. No matter what she had to do, she would keep Tommy from trouble.

Now if only he would do his part . . .

* * *

Clara drove her pickup truck through the slowly awakening streets. The sun had just risen; its light streamed through the newly budded leaves of elms and oaks, painted weather vanes, and splashed across the steeple of the Methodist church. A young boy raced down the sidewalk on his bicycle, flinging newspapers onto porches and front walks. All in all, it had the makings of just another day in Sunset.

But inside the truck, all was not so serene.

Tommy leaned against the passenger door. He had rolled down the window as soon as he'd gotten in, planted his arm on the frame, and hadn't budged since they left the jail. He also hadn't said a word.

"What happened in the cemetery?" Clara finally asked; up until then she'd been too upset to speak. "What were you even doing there?"

Her son didn't answer.

Glancing at him, Clara was struck by how much Tommy looked like his father. Every year, his resemblance to Joe became sharper, stronger. He had the same thick, dark hair, though Tommy wore his a bit longer. He pursed his lips the same way when he brooded. There was the same curve to his jaw, the same high cheekbones. Tommy even had the same build, tall and lanky, a frame that he would someday fill out. Only his eyes, green flecked with gold, came from his mother. She noticed that his clothes, a worn pair of jeans and a denim button-down shirt, were wrinkled, probably from having slept on the jail cell's cot. Tommy absently pulled on a frayed string at the shirt's cuff.

Though the sheriff had been right, that at sixteen Tommy was almost a man, it was hard for Clara to see him as anything other than her little boy. She remembered how he had been as a child, in those years before his father died. He had loved to stand beside the piano and sing song after song for as long as his grandmother would play; now the piano was silent. Long ago, when Clara would stand at the sink doing dishes, Tommy would race into the room, shouting at the top of his lungs, rushing to grab her legs as he looked up at her with a smile that melted her heart; now it sometimes felt as if all Tommy wanted was to be alone.

No matter how hard Clara tried to fill the void created by Joe's death, to give her son the happiness he deserved, she never quite seemed to manage. In her worst nightmares, she never would've imagined that things would be like this.

And that made her angry.

"What do you have to say for yourself?" she pressed, slamming the heel of her hand into the steering wheel in frustration. "Answer me!"

But Tommy only yawned and kept staring out the window.

Glancing in the rearview mirror, trying to calm down, Clara took quick measure of herself. She looked exhausted; dark circles underlined her eyes, the result of having been up all night. Her skin was flushed red and marred by a few wrinkles. She'd haphazardly tied her long black hair behind her neck; a few loose strands spilled across her shoulders. Joe had once told her that she was the most beautiful woman he had ever laid eyes on; now, nearly thirty-six years old, she had a hard time believing that that had ever been true.

Clara slowed as they neared the intersection of Harding and Grant; there was such a dip in the road that driving through without braking meant she would bottom out the truck's undercarriage. Struggling with the gears, she managed to downshift in time to ease through. Twenty years old, the truck had a list of things wrong with it nearly as long as Clara's arm, but with money tight, patching its faults whenever one became too bad to ignore was the only option she had.

Turning onto Main Street, they passed the bakery, the post office, and Steve Clark, out washing the windows of his barbershop. Two blocks later, they saw the tavern that Naomi's father owned, shuttered and dark after the previous night's drinking; unlike the other businesses in town, the Marshland didn't show signs of life until after the sun had gone down. Clara watched her son as they drove past, expecting some sort of reaction, but he gave none.

They were almost home and she still hadn't gotten any answers.

"I can't believe you're going to just sit there and say nothing," she snapped.

"Why should I?" Tommy finally replied, yawning again as he ran a hand through his unruly hair; his voice wavered a bit, changing as he was from boy to man. "Besides, you're doing plenty of talking for both of us."

"I want to know what happened."

"No, you don't," he said, looking over his shoulder at
her; his narrow eyes were dismissive, as if she was the
child.

"Yes, I do," Clara insisted.

"What you want is for me to say something to make you
feel better, even if it's a lie."

"I want the truth."

Tommy gave a condescending snort. "Naomi says you
never let anything go, like a dog with a bone."

"Was she there with you?"

Tommy didn't reply, which was answer enough.

Clara's heart raced; her fears of the girl's involvement
had been well-founded. "Tommy, she's nothing but
trouble!"

"Naomi told me you'd say *that*, too. She thinks that the
reason you hate her so much is because you're angry she's
so much younger and prettier than you. Naomi says that
you don't want me spending time with her because you're
jealous she has a future to look forward to, while you're
stuck in this town. You've got nothing and no one to share
it with."

Clara was so upset, her hands were shaking even as
she squeezed the steering wheel tight. She pulled the truck
over, tromping down so hard on the brakes that the tires
squealed before bumping against the curb. Tommy didn't
seem the least bit put out, sitting there calmly as if they
were out for a Sunday drive. Glancing through the dusty,
cracked windshield, Clara realized they were only a block
from home.

"You almost went to jail because of Naomi!" she argued. "I don't want you seeing her again!"

"You can't stop me."

"As long as you're living under my roof, you'll do what I say!" she threatened, hoping it sounded more convincing to his ears than her own.

It didn't. "Then I'll move out," Tommy replied with a shrug.

Clara felt trapped. This was the way things were between her and Tommy; she pleaded with her son to change, while he mostly ignored her, argued when he didn't, and in either case kept right on doing as he pleased. The only choice left was to follow through with her threats. But should she actually kick him out of the house? What would happen if she did? She had long since convinced herself that if Tommy wasn't under her supervision, he'd be worse off. But what if she was wrong? What if Sheriff Oglesby was right? What if some time behind bars was the only thing that could fix what was wrong with her son? Clara shuddered. What would Joe think of what had become of his family?

"I wish your father was here," she said.

For the first time since Clara had seen him sitting in the jail cell, Tommy showed real emotion. "Don't say that!" he shouted, whipping around in his seat to jab a finger at her. "Every time things don't go the way you want, you say that. I hate it! He's dead and he's never coming back!"

Before Clara could reply, Tommy pushed open the door, jumped out, and slammed it behind him hard enough to shake the truck. She watched as he stalked down the street and right past their house. He never looked back.

As the minutes passed, Clara's heartbeat began to slow. The sun rose higher, and more of Sunset woke to a new day, but she still made no move to drive the short distance home. Instead, she sat and thought about her life, about how different everything was from how she'd imagined it would be; it was all upside down, backward, and inside out.

Whenever she thought about all that had been lost, a gaping hole that would never be filled, it hurt. But on this particular day more than any other, the memories were sharper, the pain more raw.

Today was the anniversary of Joe's death.

Chapter Two

CLARA PULLED INTO the driveway and shut off the engine; the truck shuddered as the motor ticked and hummed. She took another glance at herself in the rearview mirror, breathed deeply to try to steady her still rattled nerves, and got out.

The house had seen better days: its yellow paint was faded and flaking; on the far end of the wraparound porch, one of the eave spouts had come loose and hung precariously; the last time there had been a thunderstorm, the attic had sprung a leak, with water running down the bathroom walls; the flower beds were choked with last autumn's leaves, weeds poked their way through the cracks in the walk and driveway, and the grass was in dire need of cutting. Everything had decayed since Joe's death. Clara knew that her husband would have been ashamed; he'd always been so proud of his property, so meticulous in its care, that it would have devastated him to see it in such a state.

But inside was different.

Every week, Clara scrubbed the floors and staircase. Though the furniture was a bit worn and faded, she mended every frayed stitch and straightened every wobbly leg. She dusted the tables until they shone. But she took special care of the fireplace mantel. It was there that she kept her photographs of Joe. They marked every moment of their life together: their courtship, the day they were married, Tommy as a baby, and even Joe smiling proudly in his uniform. Just having them there, seeing him every day, made her feel like he was still around, as if he was watching over them.

The smell of coffee wafted from the kitchen. Inside, Clara found her mother, Christine, staring into the pantry.

"Good morning," Clara said. "You're up awfully early."

Christine nodded absently.

Clara went to the cupboard, grabbed a mug, and filled it with coffee. She sat down at the small kitchen table and looked at her mother.

To her daughter's eye, Christine Montgomery was still a beautiful woman. Her hair, a silvery white with only a few remaining streaks of black, swept over her shoulders. Though her face became more wrinkled with every passing year, it was as perfectly proportioned as a porcelain doll's; her green eyes, pert nose, and thin mouth were just where they should be. Even at such an early hour, at almost sixty years of age, she had an air of grace about her.

Still, something was clearly wrong. As Clara watched,

Christine took a hesitant step into the pantry, raised her arm as if she was about to grab something, but then quickly moved back, her face a mask of confusion.

"Mom? Is everything all right?"

"Of course it is," Christine answered with little conviction, offering a smile that never quite managed to reach her eyes. "It's just that since I was up, I thought I might make breakfast. I put on coffee and then opened the pantry, but that's as far as I got..." Gesturing at the door, she added, "I kept thinking that if I stood here long enough, it'd come back to me, but I'll be darned if I can remember what I wanted to make."

"Why don't we have pancakes?" Clara suggested, getting up from the table to gather the ingredients she would need.

"Now that sounds like a lovely idea!" her mother enthused.

Christine had always been one of the smartest and strongest women her daughter had ever known. When her husband had unexpectedly died in an automobile accident when Clara was a little girl, Christine had refused to let it keep her from living her life or raising her child as best she could. As Sunset's librarian, she had an encyclopedic knowledge and was ready and willing to help answer any question. A well-schooled pianist, she played in recitals, at church services, and at the town's annual Fourth of July picnic. She had plenty of friends, ladies with whom she gossiped, played bridge, and shared recipes. Everyone in town loved her.

But then, a little more than two years ago, something changed.

It began innocently enough; Christine complained that she couldn't find her house keys, or that she had forgotten the name of her cousin's youngest daughter. Clara hadn't paid her mother's memory troubles any mind. But then, one Sunday morning at church, Christina had repeatedly stumbled over a stanza she had played hundreds of times before. At her daughter's insistence she had gone to the doctor, but nothing had been found to be wrong. Still, the problems worsened; she blanked on the names of lifelong friends, repeated questions again and again, and forgot to pay her bills. Finally, last year around Christmas, Bob Herring had called Clara to say that Christine had been sitting in her car out in front of his grocery store for more than an hour; when Clara arrived, her mother burst into tears, fearfully admitting that she couldn't remember how to get home.

Slowly but surely, Christine began to distance herself from her friends, afraid that she would say or do something foolish. She quit her job at the library. She even stopped playing the piano. On the outside, she looked like the same person she had always been. But on the inside, Christine was withering away.

It was painful for Clara to watch. Eventually, with some prodding, she had managed to convince her mother to move in with her, as much for Christine's safety as her daughter's peace of mind. While making ends meet became harder than ever, there was simply no other choice.

"Did I hear the truck drive in?" her mother asked after she sat at the table. "I thought you were still in bed."

"I...had a few errands to run," Clara lied, thankful that she was getting some eggs out of the refrigerator and her back was turned; that way, Christine couldn't see her face.

"So early? What was it that couldn't wait?"

"Something for the bank..."

"Well, I just hope that Theo Fuller appreciates you," her mother said, taking a sip of coffee. "It's not often you find an employee so devoted to their job that they'd get up before sunrise on their day off!"

Clara had worked at the Sunset Bank and Trust since the war had conscripted most of the town's men into the service; after Joe's death, she'd stayed on. So while what she was telling her mother wasn't the truth, at least it was believable. But the lie was still distasteful; though Christine had confused Theo for Eddie Fuller, the man's son, who now ran the bank, Clara felt no need to correct her mother.

"What about Tommy? Is he still sleeping?"

"No, he...He left when I did..."

"That boy! Always up to something! The way he burns the candle at both ends, it's a wonder he sleeps at all," his grandmother exclaimed. "It seems like only yesterday he was racing down the steps on Christmas morning, wondering what Santa had brought him. Of course, he's almost grown up now. It won't be long before he leaves to start a life of his own." With obvious pride, she added, "With the job you've done raising him, I'm sure he'll end up right as rain."

Clara cringed; she had purposefully left her mother in the dark about Tommy's acts of mischief. Christine had enough problems of her own. For his part, her son behaved differently around his grandmother, more polite, more like the boy he used to be. Clara knew he cared deeply for Christine, that they had always been close, and that he, too, wanted to spare her more headaches, for which Clara was thankful. Still, right now, all she wanted was to talk to her mother about Tommy, to speak of her fears about what he was becoming, of how helpless she felt, unable to do anything to stop it. But she couldn't say a word.

When it came to Tommy, she was on her own.

Once Clara finished making breakfast, she sat down and ate, talking with her mother about the weather and other innocent topics, feeling both guiltier and more alone with every word. When she finished eating, Clara took her dishes to the sink and began to clean them.

"I'm going to take a bath and get dressed," she said. "I want to get out to the cemetery before the rain rolls in."

"The cemetery?" her mother asked, confused. "What for? Is today a holiday? We were just there to put flowers on your father's grave..."

Clara stopped scrubbing her plate. Her heart pounded and she felt tears rising, trying to overwhelm her already strained resolve. She took a deep breath in an attempt to compose herself. "No, Mom," she said as calmly as she could. "Today is the anniversary of Joe's death."

Christine's face fell. "Oh, sweetheart," she said, her

voice choking. "I'm so sorry. I should've known. It's just this muddled head of mine..."

Wiping her hands on a towel, Clara sat down beside her mother. She smiled, taking Christine's hands and giving them a gentle squeeze.

"It's all right. You shouldn't be expected to remember everything."

Her mother wiped away a tear. "How long has it been?"

"Nine years."

"I can't believe it. It seems like only yesterday when those men came and..." Her voice trailed away.

Clara forced another smile; she'd had years of practice acting the opposite of how she really felt. "It was a long time ago."

"It doesn't matter how much time passes," Christine said. "Your father's been gone for decades and there isn't a day that goes by that I don't think of him. Even if my memory isn't what it once was, I could never forget all he meant to me. So don't ever let go of Joe. Treasure your time together, even if it was short. Keep everything, especially Tommy, close to your heart."

Clara hugged her mother tightly. Over and over, she told herself to calm down, to keep her emotions under control; she fought back tears while quieting the thunderstorm raging in her heart. It had worked, at least for now.

But when she went to visit Joe, all bets were off.

Clara drove through the open gates of Sunset's cemetery and the truck bumped down the long avenue that divided rows of tombstones. The afternoon sun glinted off stone and weathered iron markers. In the oldest part of the cemetery, rusted fences cordoned off family plots, while a towering obelisk leaned to one side, a memorial to the Walker family, the first to settle there more than a hundred years earlier.

Turning off the main road, Clara meandered along the creek that bordered the cemetery. Sunlight gave way to shade as she passed beneath tall elms and maples. Gravel crunched beneath the truck's tires. On occasion, she had seen deer grazing here, their heads rising to watch as she drove past. It was a peaceful place, meant to soothe mourners as they came to visit those they'd lost.

But it had never comforted Clara.

In the years just after Joe had died, she had come often; she had stood in the pouring rain, wiped sweat from her brow, pushed away fallen leaves, and brushed snow from his stone. But now she visited only on the anniversary of his passing. Whereas once she'd sought answers to ease her pain and sadness, Clara had come to understand that the only things waiting for her here were more tears.

And she already had plenty of those.

Clara drove on as the road wound along the creek before finally climbing a short hill; when the truck crested it, she stopped.

Ahead, two men were pitching the pieces of a broken tombstone into a wheelbarrow. Immediately, Clara understood that this was the marker Tommy had been accused of knocking over. Fortunately, Joe's grave was in the opposite direction, so she wouldn't have to get too close; she imagined that the men would have been able to sense her shame, as if she was responsible.

For almost one hundred years, the men of Sunset had marched off to war. Many had died. In the oldest part of the cemetery, there were plots for soldiers who had fought in the Civil War, their simple stones faded by age and speckled with moss. There were graves for those who had gone off to the Spanish-American War, and for those who, decades later, had taken ships across the Atlantic to battle the kaiser during World War I. Joe was buried among the brave soldiers, sailors, and airmen who had died fighting Hitler and Hirohito. More recently, graves had been dug for Jeff Tjaden and Scott Cavanaugh, men Clara still remembered as boys, soldiers who had given their lives in Korea. She feared that someday soon there would be another war, off in some foreign land, and even more of Sunset's bravest would be laid to rest.

Clara sat in the truck with her hands on the steering wheel and stared at Joe's tombstone. His was the third in its row, carved out of dark marble. Even now, after so much time had passed, just looking at it filled her with intense feelings of loss. But still she came. Taking a deep breath, Clara grabbed the small bundle of flowers she'd brought, pushed open her door on squeaky hinges, and got out.

She wiped some leaves from the stone's base, pulled a dandelion from the ground—the weed just beginning to spread its small yellow petals, hungry for the sun—and placed her own bundle of flowers in its place. Clara put a trembling hand on the marker; the stone was warm, almost hot to the touch, but she didn't let go.

"Hello, sweetheart," she said softly, her voice nearly breaking.

In years past, Clara had told Joe all about her life, about her fears for her mother's ailing health, her money troubles, and especially her problems with Tommy. Unlike with her mother, she'd never held anything back during her graveside chats; Clara figured that Joe saw and knew all anyway, so there was no point in keeping secrets. She'd talked about what was happening in the world, from the dropping of the atomic bombs and the end of the war, to the outbreak of the conflict in Korea, to Eisenhower being elected president. She hummed the tune of "Too Young" by Nat King Cole. She tried to describe what it was like to see Gary Cooper in *High Noon* at the Palace Theater. She even told him about Jackie Robinson's debut with the Brooklyn Dodgers; Joe had been such a big baseball fan that she knew it would have mattered to him. She spoke as if they were sitting at the kitchen table, poring over the newspaper together or listening to the radio. She had laughed. She had worried. She had been afraid. She had cried.

But not today. Today she didn't know what to say.

After all the long years she'd spent missing her husband and struggling to care for her family and herself, Clara was tired, exhausted in both body and mind. In her weakest moments, she had even considered giving up, surrendering to her problems, but she knew that if Joe were alive, he'd be furious with her. He hadn't been a quitter, even during the worst of times. He would tell her to pick herself up and make things right, no matter what it took.

Sometimes, Clara wondered if Joe wouldn't have wanted her to find someone else, a man to love and help care for her. Over the last nine years, she'd had her share of suitors, men who were interested, but when they saw the sadness in her eyes they walked away. Clara had closed off her heart, burying it like she had buried Joe, never to allow it to love again. Her husband had been the man of her life. There could never be another.

She was alone and would stay that way.

"I . . . I miss you, Joe," she said as her hand ran along the top of his tombstone, the only caress she could give him now.

Tears fell down her cheeks. Clara had managed to hold them back when she'd spoken with the sheriff, through Tommy's outburst, witnessing her mother's forgetfulness, and during her drive to the cemetery. But now, she no longer had the strength.

"Help me, sweetheart," she sobbed, sinking to her knees in the grass.

Now, when she really needed an answer, all she heard was silence.

Chapter Three

DRAKE MCCOY RACED toward the turn, then eased off the accelerator, one hand downshifting gears while the other whipped the steering wheel to the left. Tapping on the brakes, he sent the car drifting, deftly holding it steady as dirt and rock sprayed. The engine roared and the tires screamed as he strained against his seat belt. Finally, he was through the curve, hurtling into another straightaway and stomping back down on the gas.

Through it all, he never stopped smiling.

The small track was just to the west of town; Drake wasn't even sure of the place's name, only that it was one of hundreds like it scattered across northern Missouri, and that it had a tavern where he'd rustled up some action. The track had seen better days: weeds filled the cracks in the pavement in front of the rickety grandstand; the paint on the outbuildings was faded and chipped; and rainwater had eroded part of the grade buttressing one end, making it harder to navigate. Worse, the track had been laid out with the straightaways running east to west, meaning that drivers would be staring straight into the setting sun. Normally these things would have bothered Drake, but not today.

Today was easy money.

Confident, Drake took a quick look into his rearview mirror. The other car was fading fast. The driver had entered the turn too high and was now struggling to stay on the road; he had to slow dramatically, falling farther behind with every passing second.

So Drake took his foot off the gas.

In the many years Drake had been taking money from drivers foolish enough to bet that they were better than him, he'd learned a valuable lesson: never whoop them *too* badly.

Drake whizzed past the grandstand. His friend and mechanic, Amos Barstow, watched impassively, his arms folded over his chest. Beside him were four or five other men, friends of the driver Drake was currently leaving in the dust; he had only gotten a quick glimpse, but he could see that none of them looked happy.

Most times Drake raced, it was like today; he was either on his own or had one other person along, while his opponent would be a local, a loudmouth, surrounded by friends, his pride on the line alongside his money. Usually, they drove fancy cars, new but without much substance, and looked at Drake's four-year-old black Plymouth as outdated. They were braggarts who wouldn't know how to spell *humility* if you spotted them six letters. That often made them sore losers. If they were beaten so badly that they were embarrassed, there could be problems; once, in Arkansas, Drake had had a gun pulled on him. Now, both older and wiser, he found it better to let his opponents lose with their dignity intact.

Barreling headlong into the next turn, Drake made it seem as if he was struggling to hold the road, which was tricky; it couldn't be *too* obvious that he was shrinking the distance between the cars. By the time Drake was back on the opposite straightaway, the other driver was much closer.

And I bet he's starting to think he just might win this thing…

But he was dead wrong. The bet had been for ten laps, so that meant there were only two to go. Drake would let the other car hang around, never drawing much closer, making for a good showing, but when it was time to cross the finish line, he would be first.

Drake smiled again. No matter what his life was like off the racetrack, he had always found peace behind the wheel. Most people would be terrified by the deafening noise, the bumpy rides, and the ever-present danger of a crash, but Drake was filled with a sense of calm. The inside of a racing car felt like the place where he belonged, almost as if it was home. Here, everything made sense.

Suddenly, violently, Drake was jolted out of his thoughts when the other driver rammed his rear bumper. The force of the blow caused the steering wheel to fight him, the Plymouth loose on the dirt track, trying to escape, but Drake held on, his hands a strangling vise, and fought it back under control.

"Now why in the hell did you have to go and do that?" he asked into the rearview mirror.

The rube wasn't going down without a fight. At the next turn, one of the last, he took the more dangerous route and tried to pass Drake's car on the left, to the inside of the track; at high speed and with such a tight angle, his chances of success were slim. Still, the odds didn't appear to dissuade him any.

"You better watch what you're getting into..." Drake warned.

Having been in this position hundreds of times before, Drake refused to budge; he had seen less-experienced drivers shrink in the face of impending contact, but if he wanted to win, he couldn't give way.

Sure enough, seconds later the Plymouth was once again battered. The other driver's bumper rubbed up against Drake's rear wheel. The car bucked hard and the sound of grinding metal was deafening; he could only imagine the look on Amos's face. Risking a quick glance back, Drake saw a shower of sparks. Regardless, he hung steady, determined not to give an inch.

You're not going to get me that easy!

Roaring into the final curve, as the grandstand and finish line came into sight, Drake cut the corner tighter than he normally would, shrinking the other driver's space further. Such a move left his competitor with few choices: he could either back off and concede victory to Drake, or he could push himself into an even more precarious situation, a dangerous one, a position that could easily end in a crash.

Not knowing better, and with the pressure of his friends looking on, Drake knew exactly which choice the man would make.

Danger, and damn the consequences.

With his accelerator pressed to the floor, the other driver plowed recklessly forward, once again brushing up against the Plymouth. Neither man would surrender an inch, determined not to be the loser, as they hurtled toward the rapidly approaching finish line. Drake grinned as he held the shaking wheel, his heart pounding in his chest, sweat dripping down his face as he tried to force his opponent farther to the inside. Wooden poles had been spaced at regular intervals along the track, many now leaning and worn, in as much of a state of disrepair as the rest of the place, and it wasn't long before the other car smashed into one, then another, and then more. They exploded on contact, sending showers of splinters flying; one broken pole cracked the car's windshield. Eventually, the barrage became too much for the other driver and he spun out of control, shooting up a cloud of dust before eventually coming to rest pointed back the way he had come.

Drake crossed the finish line first, the winner.

He was laughing the whole way.

"I told you to be careful!"

Amos Barstow stormed past Drake and knelt beside the

Plymouth, inspecting the damage. When his hand touched the deep dent in the rear panel, he winced.

"That's what I was doing," Drake insisted, raising his hands, palms out. "But when the other guy gets it into his head to try to pass on the inside and there isn't room to do it, I'm gonna get hit. What was I supposed to do? Lose?"

"Fixing this might cost us more than we won!"

Drake shrugged. "Take it up with the other guy if he ever manages to get off the track, though I doubt he'll be in the mood to talk."

The other car looked to have stalled. The driver was under the hood, swearing so loudly they could hear him at the grandstand.

"If you'd done what I told you to do, that bum wouldn'ta been within half a lap," Amos grumbled, wiping sweat from his brow with a handkerchief.

"What are you talking about? I won the race."

The mechanic frowned. "I seen you take your foot off the gas, all 'cause you're worried 'bout tryin' to make that chump look good." Giving the dented bumper a rap with his knuckles, he added, "And this is what it got us."

Drake chewed the inside of his lip. Amos knew him as well as anyone. Hell, he knew him better. They had met eight years earlier, just after the war, when Drake got back behind the wheel. Amos had bounced around tracks for decades, tinkering with engines and making them run harder and faster than they'd ever gone before. Now closer to sixty than fifty, almost fifteen years older than Drake, Amos was thin, with sandy blond hair that looked white in the sun. Sweat slicked his forehead, wetting his shirt against his skin. Grease stained his fingers and filled the deep wrinkles that creased his hands, a testament to his work and passion.

"Every one of these dents is 'cause you were takin' risks you ain't got no reason chancin'," Amos continued. "What's wrong with us embarrassin' that boy, winnin' some money, and then hightailin' it outta town?"

"What would be the fun in that?"

"Fun," the mechanic echoed dismissively.

While Drake found happiness behind the wheel of a race car, caked in choking dust or dripping with sweat as he whipped around a track or down a lonely road, walking a dangerous, fine line, Amos's love of cars was different. To Amos, automobiles were puzzles in need of solving. Under the hood, with a tool in his hand and the bright light of a work bulb illuminating the guts of an engine, was where he found happiness. If there was a problem, he fixed it, replacing broken parts and busted hoses, adding grease, water, or oil. When there wasn't an issue, he created one: a challenge to drive faster, to push himself and the car to greater heights. Drake was the beneficiary, putting Amos's handiwork up against drivers in Illinois and Mississippi, Kansas and Oklahoma, Arkansas and Missouri. Together, they managed to eke out a living running sanctioned races around tracks, winning their share of trophies and prize money, and then supplementing their income by running against braggarts who thought their skills would match up. After all the years they'd spent together, the bond between the two men was strong, greater than friendship; Drake sometimes felt as if Amos was the father he wished he'd had. Still, that closeness didn't mean the mechanic wasn't testy whenever Drake brought back a damaged car.

"It's gonna be hell to knock out these dents," Amos grumbled.

"What are you complaining about? Would you rather I get hit up front? At least the engine isn't busted up."

"I'd rather you didn't get hit at all!"

As he and Amos bickered, Drake kept an eye on the other driver's friends. They appeared uncomfortable, put out that the car they'd backed had come up short. They kept looking back and forth between Drake and their bested companion, still swearing a blue streak out on the track; it was telling that not a one of them had moved an inch to help him.

"Which one's holding the money?" Drake asked.

"The mousy-lookin' one in the checkered shirt," the mechanic answered, not even looking up from the damaged car.

Before the race had begun, they had agreed to have one of the men hold the forty dollars wagered; now that he'd won, Drake wanted his earnings.

"I'll be right back."

"You best be more careful than you was racin'," Amos said.

Flashing a good-natured smile, Drake walked over to the men. Right away, it was obvious which one held the money. He was a runt of a man, short, all bony shoulders and elbows. His eyes were narrow and wild, looking everywhere but at Drake; just as Amos had said, he looked like a rodent.

"So, fellas," Drake began. "Now that the race is over, I reckon it's time for me to collect my winnings."

"Well, I...I, uh..." the mousy man mumbled.

"I wouldn't give him nothin', Garrett," one of his companions suggested; neither of the other men was much more remarkable than the money holder, disheveled in appearance and dress, clearly lackeys, not leaders.

"Just wait till Caleb gets here," the other said.

"Listen here, Garrett," Drake insisted, raising his voice enough to grab the man's full attention. "You watched the race, didn't you?"

Garrett nodded dumbly.

"So you saw me cross the finish line first, right?"

Another nod.

"Then there shouldn't be any problem giving me the money. I was the winner, after all." Drake had seen enough situations like this one to know that the sooner he got his money and took off, the better. Once men like this started thinking, bad things happened.

But a sudden honk meant that it was too late.

Drake turned to see the other driver finally leave the track. He braked his dented car to a sudden stop, kicking up a cloud of dust. The driver's-side door flew open and Caleb got out. The man was red with fury, his face covered in sweat, his clothes and hands filthy from working beneath the hood. "Don't give that son of a bitch a dime!" he shouted.

As Caleb stalked toward them, Drake noticed that each of the man's friends took a small step back, all of them cowed in his presence.

Drake moved closer.

"The deal was winner takes all," he explained, once again trying on his easy smile. "The way I see it, that would be me."

"I didn't lose," the other man growled.

Caleb reached Drake and stopped, staring at him with barely restrained rage. Almost twenty years younger, he was half a head taller, his arms thick with muscle, his body tense with the energy of youth. There was little doubt in Drake's mind that the man was used to getting his way, bullying those around him into doing his bidding; to be shown up so badly had wounded far more than his wallet.

To the younger man, Drake figured he looked like just another obstacle to be bowled over. At forty-two, he wasn't physically imposing, but he carried himself well. Trim, he still had plenty of strength. His dark hair was cut short and flecked with silver across the temples. There were a few lines on his face, but whenever he smiled they vanished. It was only in his eyes, autumn brown touched with green, crinkled with a flock's worth of crow's-feet, that he saw his true age; some mornings he had trouble recognizing himself in the mirror, as if a stranger was looking back at him in the glass. But though he was no longer a young buck, Drake McCoy wasn't easily intimidated.

Especially when it came to racing.

Drake chuckled. "Must have been my imagination then, crossing the finish line while you were pointed in the wrong direction."

"I didn't lose *fair*," Caleb explained. "You cheated me."

"How do you figure?"

"You knew I was trying to pass you," he argued, spittle flying from his mouth, "so you smashed into my car to keep me from winning."

Drake shook his head; this was hardly the first time he'd had to listen to a driver make baseless accusations to cover up his shortcomings. Caleb's Chrysler was first-rate, not long off the assembly line, cherry red with white trim, a far prettier sight than the Plymouth. But Drake knew that it was what was under the hood, as well as who was behind the wheel, that really mattered. Caleb had come up short, and since it would've been hard to put the blame on himself or his car, he pointed his finger at Drake.

"You hit me first."

"Bullshit," the other man spat.

"Come on, now," Drake replied, trying to calm things down before they got out of hand. "Losing is never easy, but—"

Caleb interrupted by pushing his chest, hard, forcing Drake back a step.

"You callin' me a liar?" the bully demanded.

"All I'm saying is that—"

Another shove came, but this time Drake held his ground, which only served to infuriate Caleb further.

Glancing over, Drake saw that Amos had stood up from the rear of their car, a wrench in his hand; if it came to it, the mechanic would be there to back him up. He also noticed that Caleb's buddies had all moved closer, as if they could sense what was coming, drawn to it like moths to a flame.

"Cheaters don't deserve no money," Caleb announced as his hand tightened into a fist and a sneer worsened his already rough features. He was nearly trembling with anger. "The only thing you got comin' is a beating."

Drake could have laughed; what sort of fool announced what he was going to do before he even threw the first punch?

He ducked nimbly, Caleb's fist sailing harmlessly over his head; if it *had* landed, there was little doubt that he would have been knocked cold. Unfortunately for Caleb, the bigger man was now completely exposed. Quick as a flash, Drake pivoted on his front foot and drove his fist as hard as he could into his opponent's stomach. Caleb collapsed in a heap, rolling over onto his side, holding his midsection as he gasped for air.

The fight was over before it had even really begun.

Drake walked over to where Garrett and the other men stood in stunned disbelief. While before they had been gaining confidence with every loud, threatening word Caleb uttered, now all their faith had vanished; they resembled mutts cowering in the face of a new alpha dog in the yard.

"My money," Drake said, holding out his hand.

Quick as a flash, Garrett dug into his pocket and pulled

out a crumpled wad of bills that he then jammed into Drake's palm.

"Much obliged," Drake said with a wink.

He got into the Plymouth—Amos was already in the passenger's seat—and turned the key in the ignition. All the while, he watched the men in the rearview mirror. Caleb tried to get to his feet but failed, crashing back down into the dirt, while everyone else stood around, impotent.

"Nothing with you is easy," Amos said. "Always got to be a show."

Drake laughed. "And you had the best seat in the house."

With that, they drove off toward the next forgettable town and the next opponent willing to bet he was faster.

Chapter Four

Even after all these years, I still can't quite wrap my head 'round the fact that I got me the same name as the fella on this here coin."

Clara smiled. Ben Franklin stood on the other side of her teller window at the Sunset Bank and Trust, holding a new half-dollar between his fingers, raising it so the late morning sunlight caught the silver, making it shine.

"Every time I march on in here and plop down my coins," he said, waving at the pile Clara was busy counting, "there he is, starin' back."

"If you want, I could flip them over."

"Nah," Ben replied with a grin. "Makes me feel like I'm famous."

And in some ways he was. For decades, Ben Franklin's family had raised pigs on their land south of town. An enormous man in both size and spirit, Ben also had a booming voice that could be heard a block away. His overalls, which strained to hold his girth, were often covered in pig manure, creating a smell so potent that plenty of folks, when they understood he was coming their way, quickly headed in the opposite direction.

But not Clara. For almost ten years now, she had waited on him at the bank; he was there most every day. Whenever the Franklin family made a transaction, butchering a hog or selling eggs from the chickens they raised on the side, Ben brought whatever money they earned down to the bank the next morning; stood bright, cheerful, and fragrant in Clara's line; and made a deposit. While others wrinkled their noses, Clara enjoyed his company, odor and all. Today, only one day removed from the anniversary of Joe's death, that company was especially welcome.

"Sometimes I wonder what that old cuss woulda thought of me," Ben said, still staring at the coin. "Reckon we woulda got along?"

"No doubt in my mind," Clara answered with a smile. "As smart of a man as he was, I bet you would have taught him a thing or two."

"Signin' the Declaration of Independence, sailin' off to France, and discoverin' 'lectricity—why, ain't none of that holds a candle to raisin' hogs!" he declared before bursting into laughter at his own joke.

Even though she'd heard this gag, or at least one like it, dozens of times, Clara couldn't help but join in.

It was at times like this that Clara felt grateful for her job. In the beginning, her reason for working at the bank had been to help the war effort; most of Sunset's men had gone into the service, leaving behind jobs in desperate need of being filled. But it hadn't taken long for her to fall in love with it. She soon knew everyone in town. People who were happy or sad, rich or poor, young or old. She knew about births and deaths, who was to be married, as well as which couples' relationships were in trouble.

But that familiarity cut both ways.

When Joe had been killed, all of Sunset knew. To make matters worse, in the weeks and months after, her heart aching, struggling with her grief, Clara had had to face her friends, neighbors, the whole town as they stood before her and offered their condolences. Everyone meant well, but it still brought back the agony of her loss again and again. The same was true for her mother's health and Tommy's rebelliousness; though no one ever came out and said anything, it was obvious that they knew all the same. Still, it wasn't as if she could quit to save herself the shame and scrutiny; her family desperately needed the money her job provided. Besides, there was plenty to enjoy, particularly people like Ben Franklin.

She had just said her good-byes to the pig farmer when Agnes Durant, one of her fellow tellers, approached and said, "Eddie wants to see you in his office."

Clara's stomach knotted. Unfortunately, she had bigger problems at the bank than the occasional smell of manure.

Clara stood outside Eddie Fuller's office, waiting for a sign to enter. The bank president sat behind his enormous desk, talking on the telephone. Through the open door, she caught snippets of conversation that were occasionally punctuated by nervous-sounding titters of laughter.

Eddie's father, Theodore, had been the founder of the Sunset Bank and Trust and one of the most respected men in town. Theo had run things both profitably and fairly, believing that business agreements should be honorable for all parties. His son was but a pale shadow of the man. Theo had brought Eddie into the family business hoping that with some experience he might come out of his shell, might lose some of the awkwardness that handicapped him. But no matter how much his father coaxed him along, no matter how many chances he was given, Eddie hadn't changed much. Eventually relegated to a corner desk, he had sat silently, like a piece of furniture, waiting for another opportunity.

Then, two months ago, Theo had unexpectedly died.

A few days after his father's casket had been lowered into the ground, Eddie had installed himself in the bank president's office; Clara had watched him stand silently in the middle of the room, a box in his hands, looking completely lost. Whatever hopes people had that Eddie would seize his father's mantle were quickly dashed. Long-standing customers grumbled about Eddie's incompetence. Desperately trying to right a listing ship, undoubtedly feeling his authority threatened, he had fired Roy Washington, an employee for nearly twenty years. Through it all, he flashed his trademark weak smile.

Glancing up at her, Eddie cupped his hand over the receiver and motioned for Clara to enter. She went inside and sat down as he resumed talking.

"It's like I've been telling you, Fred," Eddie began, pausing to glance at Clara. "Things are changing around here. You can either get on board this speeding train now, while there's still time, or you can watch from the depot as we rocket down the tracks without you."

Clara struggled to keep from frowning. Eddie's bragging sounded ridiculous to her ears. She wondered whether anyone was even on the other end of the line; it'd be just like Eddie to make another misguided attempt at impressing her.

For years, ever since she had started working at the bank, Clara had understood that Eddie fancied her. It had begun with long, lingering looks as she stood behind her teller window; these had been easy enough to ignore, but soon after, he had become bolder, telling her jokes without a sliver of humor, inappropriately complimenting her on her clothes, her hair, noticing even when she changed her shade of lipstick. Though Clara certainly never encouraged his advances, she was wary of turning him away too brusquely for fear of losing a desperately needed job. One day, a couple of years back, Theo had caught Eddie dithering on as Clara stood silently beside him and called his son into his office; Eddie must have gotten a stern talking-to because he hadn't said a word to her for months, though he'd still spent most of his days staring at her from his desk.

"Listen here," Eddie continued. "Now that I'm in charge, if there's something you want done, I'm your man."

Looking at Eddie, Clara wondered what any woman could possibly find attractive about him. He was short and pudgy; the rolls of his neck mushroomed up over the top of his stiffly starched shirt. His eyes were wide and always wet. His sparse hair was combed across his head, making his oncoming baldness all the more obvious. His chin was weak, almost nonexistent, as if it had fallen off by accident. Worst of all, his lips were always dry and cracked, an ugly feature made worse when his tongue, fat and pink, darted out to wet them.

His personality was equally unappealing. Though he was around Clara's age, he seemed younger, more innocent, sheltered. Simply put, he didn't know how to interact with others. He laughed loudly at his own jokes, interrupted conversations, and forgot names, dates, and important figures. Unlike his father, whose willingness to listen made him a pillar of Sunset's business community, Eddie was distracted, often staring blankly at the person across from him as if he hadn't been paying attention.

"That sounds great! Together, we'll both make loads of money!" Eddie boasted before wrapping up his conversation.

With the phone back in its cradle, Clara sat quietly and expectantly, but to her surprise Eddie didn't say a word. While she hated the sound of his high, nasal voice, she found the deepening silence to be equally uncomfortable.

With a show of fanfare, Eddie opened a silver box on the corner of his desk and took out a cigar. He cut the end, put it in his mouth, snapped his lighter to life, lit it, and inhaled a deep drag. Almost instantly he coughed, a harsh bark that shattered whatever illusion he was trying to create. Embarrassed for him, Clara offered a weak smile. Undeterred, Eddie came around to the front of the desk. He sat on a corner and his pants, a tighter fit than they should have been, hiked up awkwardly at the crotch. Disgusted, Clara looked away.

"You don't like me much, do you?" he asked.

Momentarily taken off guard, Clara wasn't sure how to answer; she knew that the truth probably wouldn't do her any good. Finally, she settled on "I haven't always enjoyed the attention you've given me."

Eddie nodded as if he understood. "For a while, I blamed myself for the misunderstanding between us," he explained solemnly. "But the more time passed, the more I realized that it was actually my father's fault." Sneering, he added, "That old blowhard kept us apart."

"He...he was a good man..." Clara stammered.

"No, he wasn't," Eddie disagreed, pausing to give his dry lips a long lick. "Nothing I ever did was good enough for him. Every suggestion I made to strengthen this bank was rejected. Whenever I wanted to speak with someone about making us all richer, he told me to be quiet. It was always 'Do as I say,'" he explained sarcastically. "Well, now he's gone and I'm in charge. From here on out, things are going to be different."

If Clara hadn't been in such dire financial straits, if her family's survival hadn't hinged on her job, she would have wondered if the smart move wasn't to follow Roy Washington out the door. Eddie was delusional. Theo had built the Sunset Bank and Trust into something special; now his incompetent son was going to knock it all to the ground. In the days, months, and years to come, it would surely ruin him, as well as the lives of many others in Sunset. But no matter how badly Clara wanted to tell him how wrong he was, she couldn't bring herself to do it.

"He was wrong to interfere," Eddie reasoned.

Unsure of what he was talking about, Clara asked, "With what?"

"Us," he answered, pointing at her with his index finger, himself with his thumb, and wiggling his hand back and forth.

Clara could only stare as the sickening feeling in her stomach grew stronger.

"If he'd have stayed out of it, you would've fallen for me by now, like Juliet for Romeo," Eddie continued, punctuating his claims with a strange snort of laughter. "If he hadn't banished me to that damned corner desk, I'd bet every damned cent this bank has that you'd feel the same for me as I do you."

"I...I don't..." she muttered, her head swimming.

"I love you," he proclaimed; hearing it so bluntly horrified her.

"Eddie, I can't...I don't..."

He licked his lips, then asked, "Do you want to be happy? *Truly* happy?"

Still stunned, Clara nodded; her thoughts raced as she

tried to come up with a way to reject Eddie without offending him. "Of... of course I do, but..."

Eddie went behind his desk. Piles of paper were spread across his blotter; he shuffled through them until he found the one he wanted.

"It says here that you and your late husband," he read, pausing to give Clara another awkward smile, "borrowed the money for your house back in '37."

"That sounds about right..."

Clara remembered those days well; she and Joe had been married the summer before and wanted a place of their own. Unfortunately, money was hard to come by. Her mother, having long struggled to make ends meet after her husband's death, had nothing to spare. Joe's parents were even worse off. Instead, they'd taken out a loan from Theo Fuller to build a roof over their heads; by the time the house was finished, they owed the bank a pretty penny. But all their plans for repaying what they'd borrowed had ended with Joe's death. Now, though money was tighter than ever, Clara had diligently kept up the payments, refusing to default, which made Eddie's words all the more mysterious.

"From the look of these numbers," he said, peering at her over the top of the paper, "it seems you still owe plenty."

"I do, but... but I've always paid on time," she replied.

"What if I told you that I could make this debt of yours disappear," he said, letting go of the paper, which fell back into the pile on his desk.

"I . . . I don't understand . . ."

Eddie leaned forward onto his elbows, licked his lips, flashed his goofy smile, and then said, "Marry me."

Clara recoiled, flinching as if someone was about to strike her; it embarrassed her to have reacted that way, but she couldn't help herself. She waited for Eddie to laugh, to confess that he was joking with her, but he just stared expectantly, as if waiting for an answer. His delusion frightened her.

"Eddie, you've got the wrong—"

"As Mrs. Edward Fuller, you'd want for nothing," he interrupted. "Everyone in town would smile as you walked by, acknowledging you as the beautiful, important woman you'd be. After the wedding, you, your son, even your mother would all move into my home." Eddie's eyes were aglow with excitement for the fantasy he'd woven out of his imagination. "It would be perfect," he proclaimed.

Clara took a deep breath, trying to steady herself.

Incredibly, there was a teeny-tiny part of her that found Eddie's offer alluring. If she became his wife, her financial troubles would be over. Poring over her ledgers, trying to find the money to pay for clothes, groceries, the electric bill, or her mother's trips to the doctor would be a thing of the past. It wasn't that she wanted to be rich, just not so poor.

But Clara knew that marriage was about *far* more than money. She and Joe had never been well off, scrimping and saving for a few luxuries—a washing machine and a new icebox—but the love they shared more than made up for whatever was lacking in their bank account. Every passing year brought them new riches: the house was one, the pickup truck another, and on the day Tommy was born, Clara felt like the wealthiest woman alive. It was love, not dollar bills, that paid for their life together. To marry Eddie just for his money would have been an insult to Joe's memory, and *that* she would not do.

"Eddie, I can't marry you," she declared.

For an instant, the banker's smile faltered, but he quickly recovered, bringing it back to its usual intensity. "You say that now," he replied, pausing to lick his lips, "but given enough time, I'm sure you'd come to realize that—"

"No, I wouldn't," Clara said, daring to cut him off. "I can't marry someone I'm not in love with. I just can't."

Eddie's expression reflected his desperation. "All I want is a chance to—"

"I'm *never* going to be in love with you."

As soon as the words left Clara's mouth, she regretted them. Eddie's reaction was immediate; this time, when his smile disappeared, it stayed gone. His eyes narrowed, his cheeks flushed a deep red, and his lower lip trembled. Clara knew that she'd both angered and embarrassed him.

"You're turning me down? You're rejecting *me*?!" Eddie snapped, his voice shrill enough to make Clara worry that other people in the bank could hear.

"I'm sorry, Eddie, but—"

"If you don't care about what I can give you," he said, spittle foaming on his dry lips, "maybe you'll give a damn about what I can take away!" Furiously, Eddie snatched back up the paper detailing Clara's house loan, crumpling one of the corners in his clenched fist. "What if instead of making this disappear," he spat, "I took your home and everything in it?"

Clara was too stunned to answer. Nothing could have prepared her for this side of Eddie Fuller; she'd never seen him so angry. She wondered if it had been there all this time, lurking just beneath the surface, waiting years to be let out; his father's death had apparently unlocked the door.

"But...but I told you..." she finally said. "I've always paid on time..."

"So what?" he answered with a sneer. "Do you think I can't alter the ledgers to make it look like you've fallen behind, and that it was only because of my father's generosity that you were allowed to skate by? Just like that," he explained with a snap of his fingers, "you'd be out on the street."

"You...you'd do that...if I didn't agree to marry you?" Clara nearly shouted, her voice laced with panic, her heart racing.

But then, bizarrely and faster than flipping a light switch, Eddie's anger vanished and his familiar, dopey smile returned.

"Now, now," he soothed. "Don't go getting all worked up. I wasn't saying that I was *going* to do that, only that I *could*."

Clara reeled. Her troubles were already bad enough without this. Eddie was blackmailing her, plain and simple.

If she didn't give him what he wanted, if she didn't agree to become his wife, he would take away everything.

Still smiling, Eddie came back around the desk and knelt down on the floor in front of her. Clara worried that he was going to formally propose, like something out of a trashy romance novel, but he just took her hand and stared at her; when he licked his lips, it made her want to retch.

"Never mind all that loan business," Eddie told her, acting as if he wasn't the one who'd brought it up, using it against her like a weapon.

"All right..." she muttered.

"What we need is a new start," the banker continued, giving her hand an insistent squeeze. "I'm sure that the next time I come over to talk with—"

Eddie's ramblings were interrupted by the ringing of his telephone. After he had answered, settling back into his chair and propping his feet on the desk, Clara took it as her cue to leave; if Eddie tried to stop her, she didn't notice.

All the way back to her teller window, her head swam.

How am I ever going to get out of this mess?

Chapter Five

U P, BUDDY. It's your turn to drive."

Drake slowly blinked his eyes as he swam up from the depths of sleep. He leaned against the Plymouth's passenger-side door, a wool blanket draped over him for warmth. Music played faintly on the radio, some scratchy jazz, a trumpet braying out a long, lonely note. When he didn't immediately move, Amos reached over and gave his shoulder an insistent shake.

"I'm not kiddin' here. The road's growin' faint and I'm havin' trouble keepin' my eyes open," the mechanic said.

"Yeah, yeah, give me a second," Drake replied.

He sat up and swiveled his head, trying to get the kinks out of his neck while he looked out the window at the countryside. The sun hadn't yet risen in the east, but it was painting the underside of a flock of clouds a dull orange and red. It had gotten cool in the night, so fog clung to the ground; it hung above small creeks and huddled among trees.

"Where are we?" Drake asked.

"Just passed through Colton, a wisp of a place if there ever was one," Amos answered. "Wasn't a single light on in the whole town."

"That's because they've got the good sense to be in bed instead of driving the back roads to nowhere," Drake said, then yawned. "Why didn't you pull over and get some shut-eye?"

Amos shrugged. "Wasn't tired, least not then." He looked at Drake and smirked. "Besides, what with the way you snore, a dead man couldn't get any rest."

Drake laughed. He'd always marveled at the older man's stamina: even after a long, hot day at the track, Amos could stay up for hours, playing pinochle and drinking with other drivers and mechanics, sweating bullets as he tinkered under the hood, or, like now, driving countless miles in the middle of the night. But later, when he did finally lie down, it'd be nearly impossible to wake him until he got his sleep. If Amos was at the end of his limits, it was best that they switch places.

"Besides," he explained as he pulled off the road and onto a spur cut into a stand of evergreens, "I've got to take a leak."

"By all means, then," Drake said. "I wouldn't want you to wet your pants, especially when you're sitting behind the wheel."

Amos dug around in the backseat, grabbed his coat and a roll of toilet paper, and then disappeared into the woods.

Drake got out and stretched his legs. The air was crisp, almost chilly, and he felt refreshed. When he'd been younger, he could have jumped straight out of bed and into his car, then raced for hours, but now he needed some time to get his wits about him.

"You're turning into an old man," he muttered to himself.

Lately, Drake found himself thinking a lot about age. He wasn't young anymore; getting behind the wheel, racing against drivers half his age, choking on dust, and sweating like a hog were beginning to take a toll on him. He knew he couldn't keep doing it forever, that there would come a time to hang it up, but he'd been running on fumes for years and still won enough money to make it worth his while.

He'd been born in Iowa, the second son of a pig farmer, an overly religious man whose day began with the coming of the sun and ended with its going. Music was forbidden, as were books other than the Bible; Drake always wondered if his father detested smiles, too, since his face was always twisted into a frown. His mother, a woman who had come from Norway when she was a little girl and therefore never felt comfortable speaking English, was more lively. But she was too cowed by her husband to protest when he took off his belt and whipped his stubborn son for disobeying him. Drake's older brother had no reservations about spending the rest of his life knee-deep in pig shit, but Drake refused to accept that his world would never extend much farther than the fence line at the edge of his family's property.

Drake had vowed to leave someday, even if he'd had no idea how.

The answer had come unexpectedly. He was fifteen, his desire to get away so intense that he could scarcely stand to be in his father's presence, when he'd first experienced the joy of riding in a fast car. A friend's older brother had returned from his successful new life in Chicago driving an automobile unlike anything rural Iowa had ever seen. It was a Ford, brand new and dazzling to Drake's eyes, no matter that it was caked with dust from the dirt roads. It was obvious that its owner had only come home to brag about his new life, but Drake didn't care; he couldn't take his eyes off the car.

Finally, he'd gotten a chance to ride in it. Sitting in the passenger seat, Drake was wide-eyed as they roared away, the driver whooping like a banshee, zigzagging dangerously across the road while kicking up an enormous cloud of dust. Drake's heart had pounded in his chest not from fear, but exhilaration. Right then and there, before the ride was even over, Drake knew what he wanted to do with his life. A few months later, he packed a bag, snuck out of the farmhouse in the middle of the night, and took the first train he came across.

He had drifted south into Missouri and eventually settled in Hampton, a little place that barely deserved the speck it took up on a map, finding work in a garage. Drake knew a fair amount about engines from fixing his family's tractor, though he quickly learned that it wasn't the same under the hood of the latest automobiles. Still, he proved to be a quick study. The garage's owner, a kindly old man named Dave Eichelberger, took Drake under his wing, patiently correcting what he did wrong while also encouraging him to learn as much as he could. He even let Drake drive his own car, a beat-up Packard that was frustratingly difficult to start. At first, Drake choked the engine, slammed too hard on the brakes, and blew out his fair share of tires. But it didn't take long before he found that he had some natural ability behind the wheel. He soon longed for more and more horsepower, to go faster and then faster still.

His first race had been the thrill of his life. Again, it had been Mr. Eichelberger who'd prodded Drake to enter, finding him a car to drive and paying his entry fee. Sitting behind the wheel, the engine rumbling, the steering wheel vibrating in his hands, waiting for the checkered flag to drop, was something he would never forget. The race had been a blur—someone had bumped him from behind and he'd finished in tenth place—but Drake hadn't once stopped smiling. He kept at it, learning the tricks of the trade, getting steadily better until he started to win more than he lost. Somehow, the years had brought him from then to now.

Drake dug around in the Plymouth until he found an apple he'd bought at a roadside stand. He bit into it, crunching noisily; juice ran down his chin until he wiped it away with the back of his hand. For a long while, he was content to eat, watching how the rising sun blossomed across the treetops, colored the gently stirring leaves, and warmed the air. It hadn't risen high enough to shine off the car or the small trailer that carried their tools, but it grew lighter by the second. The arrival of morning set the birds to chirping.

When Drake finished eating, he tossed the apple's core into a bush and started to wonder what was taking Amos so long. The thought crossed his mind that his friend had gotten lost or stumbled onto trouble. He considered shouting out to him, but then held his tongue.

A man's private business is his own...

Instead, Drake again rummaged through his things until he found a worn paperback novel; *Tarzan and the Leopard Men* by Edgar Rice Burroughs, one of his favorites. Leaning against the Plymouth, he licked his finger, turned the pages to where he'd left off, and began to read. Once Drake had escaped the restrictive life imposed by his father, he had discovered books and the joy they could bring. He enjoyed tales of all kinds: cowboys and their wild adventures in the Old West, pirates who sailed the seas in pursuit of treasure, New York detectives who searched for the one elusive clue that would solve a murder, glimpses of a future filled with flying cars and green-skinned men from Mars, and especially tales of an abandoned baby raised by apes to become the king of the jungle. He liked to immerse himself in another time and place. When he read, Drake embraced the solace and quiet, so very different from the loud, dangerous life he led. Normally, he could escape for hours at a time.

But not today...

Drake put down his book; he'd read the same line three times and was too distracted to follow the story. His thoughts whirled. Not for the first time, he asked himself just how much longer he was going to travel backcountry roads in the middle of the night and live out of his car, always looking for another race to run or sucker to fleece. He wanted more, longed for something different, something he had trouble naming but knew was out there all the same, calling to him. He was getting older; most men his age had long since settled down, taken the opportunity presented to them by the G.I. Bill to get an education, buy a house, find a beautiful wife, and raise a couple of kids, with a dog for good measure.

But not him. He was getting into a fistfight with a muscle-bound hothead over a handful of wadded-up bills.

Occasionally, Drake wondered if it wasn't already too late. Maybe while he'd been busy speeding one way, life had been racing in the opposite direction and he would never catch up. He'd tried to broach the subject with Amos a couple of times but had never gotten very far; for the mechanic, racing was his life, and he couldn't understand why Drake didn't feel the same. So here he was, still driving and still wondering what else was out there, what he might be missing.

Drake shoved his book back into his duffel bag, but once his hand was inside, he paused. Digging a little deeper, he touched the thick wad of money he had secreted away, safely out of sight. The cash represented most of his savings; there was more, a couple thousand he'd deposited in a small bank in Illinois. He had never been comfortable with the idea of someone else holding his money, for it to be out of his hands, and he worried that if he ever found himself in a situation where he needed it, it wouldn't be there. Drake knew it was risky to have it on him, that he could be robbed, get in an accident, or have some other calamity befall him. So he remained careful and cautious at all times; not even Amos knew it was there.

But some days he questioned what he was saving it for. Since leaving Iowa, Drake had had no contact with his family. He'd never met a woman he felt strongly enough about to want to settle down. There had been no property, no business venture he'd wanted to invest in. So instead, whenever he won a race, he just put his winnings with all the rest, and waited for...

"Beats the hell out of me," he muttered.

Once again, Drake began to wonder about Amos. He understood that a man needed his privacy, but this was getting ridiculous. But then, just as he was about to shout, his friend stumbled from between two bushes. He looked a little dazed.

"What the heck happened to you?" Drake asked. "I was starting to wonder if you hadn't run off on me."

"Not yet," Amos grumbled. "Just took a while to find the right place. The brush back there has more bugs than a dead fish."

Drake laughed. "I wouldn't have thought you'd be so choosy. Makes you sound dainty, like some society gal who powders more than her nose."

Amos scowled. "Fancy yourself a comedian, huh?"

They shared some food and a cigarette but little conversation before getting back in the car. Amos looked out on his feet; his eyes were glassy and he couldn't stop yawning.

"You get all the rest you need," Drake said as he turned the key in the ignition and the engine roared back to life. "I'm good to go."

"Wake me when you want to stop for lunch," Amos answered, bunching up his coat into a makeshift pillow and settling against the door.

"You got any particular place in mind?"

"I was aimin' for this little town called Sunset," the mechanic replied, then stifled a yawn with the crook of his arm. "Keep headin' west and watch for signs. I ain't been there in ten years, but I remember it was a nice place right along the Missouri. Who knows, we might even be able to scrounge up some action."

"Sunset it is." Drake pressed on the accelerator harder than he normally would have and the Plymouth shot back out onto the road, spraying gravel and causing Amos to curse.

They were off.

Amos leaned against the Plymouth's door as the car raced down the road; Drake, happy to be back behind the wheel, paid no mind to potholes or the rocks pounding against the undercarriage. Most times, the mechanic might have complained, but not now. Slowly, he slid down the slippery slope toward sleep, dreamily giving himself over to the morphine he had injected into his arm.

After they'd stopped, Amos had retrieved his coat, as well as the drug hidden in its inner pocket, and gone into the woods, lying that he needed to empty his bladder. Once he was far enough away to be sure he wouldn't be followed, he found a secluded spot and rolled up his shirtsleeve. Pulling out a length of rubber tubing, he tied off his arm, raising the veins at the crook of his elbow. Next, he inserted a needle into the dark glass bottle, drawing out the milky liquid, carefully measuring the right amount—too much and he wouldn't be able to make it back to the car. Seconds later, he was flooded with the sweet relief that he so loved and had to steady himself against a nearby tree.

Amos Barstow was an addict, through and through.

Morphine had a hold on him; it was an insatiable animal that demanded to be fed. He had known many others like him: drunks who crawled back inside a whiskey bottle in the early church-time hours of a Sunday morning, gamblers who would've bet their children's shoes that the next roll of the dice would come up in their favor, and old men who still chased every skirt they saw. They were all the same, all addicts, all slaves to their demons, no more able to quit than to sprout wings and fly.

Though sometimes the morphine sure made it feel like he *could* fly.

It had begun innocently enough. Two years ago, while working on a car, Amos had had an accident; trying to yank a stubborn bolt loose, his wrench slipped, resulting in a deep cut that ran the length of his forearm. His doctor had prescribed morphine to dull the pain. Generously, he'd given the mechanic a bottle, warning him to use it only when needed. At first, Amos had done as instructed, but the dreamy way the drug made him feel, with all his pain and worries blissfully floating away, soon became a lure he couldn't resist. So he started to use it more often. When the first bottle was empty, he bought another. By then, it was too late. He was caught in a snare and couldn't get out.

Amos had tried to quit countless times, usually in the sickened aftermath of a bad dose, full of heartfelt promises that this time would be different, that his will was strong enough. But then the shakes would come, the sweating that left his shirt plastered to his skin, and the paranoid feeling that he was being watched. He would get the chills so bad that even in the middle of summer, covered in a wool blanket, he couldn't stop shivering. In the end, he'd always been too weak. He had come to accept that morphine had its claws sunk in too deep for him to ever get away. No matter where he went, no matter what he did, the need to get high was coming, calling to him...

Unfortunately, morphine wasn't cheap, nor was it easy to find. In order to get it, Amos had resorted to lying, stealing, and on one regrettable night in Burlington, violence. The desire made him a lesser man; as a matter of fact, it was the reason they were driving to Sunset. All through the night, Amos kept expecting to see headlights come roaring up behind them, for his luck to finally run out. That was because the last time he'd been in St. Louis, he'd hooked up with Ronald Woods, a small-time drug dealer who went by the nickname Sweet. Amos had used Sweet a few times before, and while the thug was crude and violent, a fledgling businessman who wanted to be much bigger, his product was good and cheap and came without questions. But then, one night a month back, Amos had seized an unexpected opportunity and stolen from Sweet...

He'd been on the run ever since.

Amos glanced at Drake through one half-closed eye; his friend spun the radio dial, searching for something worth listening to through a fog of static. The driver was a good man, his closest friend, but he knew nothing of his mechanic's addiction. Amos took enormous pains to hide it, and had so far succeeded in keeping it a secret. Unfortunately for Drake, ignorance didn't mean he wasn't also in danger; Sweet Woods would see guilt by association.

Guilt gnawed at Amos. Beneath his gruff exterior, despite the way they traded barbs, he felt a real affection for Drake. They were friends and business partners, but their bond ran deeper than that; though Amos wasn't *that* much older than his driver, he reckoned that Drake was the son he'd never had. He felt humiliated that he had put them in danger but helpless to do anything about it.

What choice did he have? He couldn't tell the truth. Amos needed Drake if he wanted to make money, funds that he had to have in order to keep feeding his habit. So far, the only solution he'd come up with was to stay far from St. Louis, to not let Sweet get too close, and to never remain in any one place for long; doing so would protect him and Drake both. Sunset was in the middle of nowhere, completely forgettable. They could stay for an afternoon, run a race, win some money, and then move on down the road, staying ahead of trouble. He had enough morphine to last him for a while, at least until he could find another dealer. It would all work out. It had to.

When he finally surrendered to the drug's embrace, Amos felt as safe as a newborn baby in its mother's arms.

Chapter Six

Ronald "Sweet" Woods popped a butterscotch candy in his mouth, rolling it around on his tongue. He stood in the open doorway of an abandoned barn; the whole frame sagged, looking like it might fall over in a strong wind. High above, the sky was awash with stars, far more than he ever saw in the city. Absently, he hummed a tune he couldn't quite remember, the sound mixing with the whimpers and cries behind him, a melody occasionally interrupted by the raw, thudding sound of heavy fists.

Before him, a town settled down for the night. Lights still shone in houses, but dinners had long since been eaten, radio shows listened to, and children tucked into bed. The sun had set hours before; a chill filled the air. Sweet couldn't remember the name of this godforsaken place, but for most of the town's residents, the day was done.

Sweet's was just beginning.

Turning around, he saw a man tied to a chair; rope crisscrossed his chest, securing his arms and legs. Drool hung from his busted lip, a mixture of saliva and blood; it dangled for a moment, swinging like a pendulum, before breaking loose to drop onto his leg. Sweat plastered his greasy hair to his forehead. He was missing some teeth, but Sweet wondered if they hadn't been gone long before he'd gotten his hands on the man.

"Let me see him," Sweet said.

Malcolm Child stood beside the bound man, his fists bloodied from carrying out his boss's orders. He was a huge presence, tall, shoulders as wide as most doorways, the muscles of his broad chest straining against his shirt. An ugly scar zigzagged down his cheek, the tissue almost white, the memento of a bar brawl years earlier. As quiet as he was intimidating, Malcolm was a constant presence at Sweet's side, his enforcer, entrusted with carrying out the most violent of orders. Now, he did as Sweet commanded and grabbed a fistful of the man's hair, yanking his head up.

"What's his name?" Sweet asked, mostly out of curiosity.

Malcolm shook his head.

Sweet stepped closer. "Tell me," he demanded.

Slowly, the man looked up; one eye was watery, barely focused, while the other was already swollen shut from being struck. His jaw hung open, slack; his tongue slid out over cracked lips, causing more bloody spit to fall. When he still failed to answer, Malcolm gave him a violent shake.

"Ga— Garrett," he managed.

"All right then, Garrett. Start again from the beginning."

The battered man took a deep, wheezing breath, wincing from the pain it caused, and looked imploringly at the stranger before him.

Sweet Woods was a small man, short in stature and thin as a rail; standing beside Malcolm, he barely came up to the brute's armpit. Even though he was in his midthirties, his round face was pockmarked with acne scars, a remnant of the boy he had once been; the flatness of his dishwater-gray eyes, the way he slicked back his dark hair, and the sneer that curled the corner of his mouth spoke loudly of the man he had become. Recently, he'd begun to wear fancier clothes, suit coats and neckties, his shoes shined so immaculately that he could see his reflection in them. Sweet had chosen the new wardrobe because he wanted to look more like someone with money, someone who commanded respect; it didn't matter that the collar scratched his skin or that the shoes gave him blisters. He wanted to project the image of a man who shouldn't be fucked with.

The gun tucked into his waistband didn't hurt, either.

"They…they come into the…the Tipsy Dog…the tavern…the day before…yesterday…" It was the same place where Sweet had surprised Garrett, tossing him into the back of his car and bringing him to the secluded barn.

"Who were they?" Sweet pressed.

"There was just the…two of 'em…one was older than

the other...he was the mechanic...and the other one... he done the drivin'..."

"What were their names?"

"I...I don't recall...them ever sayin'..."

Sweet was convinced that they were talking about Amos Barstow, the bastard he had been tracking for more than a week through the no-name towns of northern Missouri. The mechanic was one of hundreds of people who came to Sweet to buy drugs and put down a bet on a horse race. Barstow had been indistinguishable from the others, just another face holding a wad of money.

Until the son of a bitch stole from him.

He still wasn't sure how it'd happened. Like a half-dozen times before, Sweet had met with Barstow to sell him morphine. They had almost finished when a flunky who ran numbers for Sweet barged in complaining about some missing receipts. In the time it had taken to fix the problem—a threat of grave bodily harm had finally done the trick—Barstow had made off with three bottles of morphine and a bag holding a couple hundred dollars cash. On top of that, the mechanic seemed to have vanished into thin air. Even after Sweet put the word out, offering a reward to whoever brought him Barstow's whereabouts, no trace had been found.

It was bad enough that Sweet was out his stuff, but the real problem was that it wasn't his to begin with. Sweet had been given the drugs and cash by Curtis Webber, a bigger fish in the criminal pond that was St. Louis. Sweet was to sell and otherwise distribute it, skimming a small amount off the top to keep for himself. After Barstow's theft, Sweet had had to return to his superior with his tail tucked between his legs and come clean about what had happened. He'd expected there to be severe and immediate consequences. Instead, Curtis had calmly explained that if Sweet didn't get back what had been stolen, if he didn't cut Barstow's throat from ear to ear, not only would he lose any chance to advance in the underworld that ruled the city, but he would soon find himself dead, floating in the river, food for the fishes.

Sweet understood immediately. This wasn't a job for his men. He had to do it himself. After all, more than his product had been taken; Barstow had also robbed him of his pride.

"What kind of car did they drive?" he prodded.

"It...it was a black...Plymouth..." the bound man answered. "It didn't...look like much...but the way that fella drove...it was fast as all get out..."

That fella was Drake McCoy, Sweet was sure of it. He had never met the driver, but word was he was aces behind the wheel and had been working with Barstow for years. Their play was simple: between seasons on the racing circuit, they drove around the countryside winning money from fools like Garrett. While Sweet couldn't have said for certain whether McCoy was in on Barstow's theft, in the end, it didn't matter; when he finally got hold of the mechanic, if McCoy was with him, he'd suffer the same fate.

"Which way were they headed?"

"I...I don't...don't know..." Garrett replied, his breathing labored. "They...done left the track...and headed south, but there...ain't no knowin' for certain... after that..."

Sweet pulled the pistol from his waistband and squatted in front of Garrett so that the man could take a good look. He turned it around in the faint light of the lone bulb that dangled overhead, a dull shine off the dark steel. "I suggest you think hard 'bout the details," he said. "If I was to think you were keepin' something from me..."

"I ain't! I swear it!"

"Can't say I'm convinced," Sweet said as he cocked the pistol's hammer and raised it so that it was level with the bound man's eyes.

Garrett shook in terror, causing blood and sweat to splatter the ground at his feet. For an instant he strained against his restraints, his body shaking like a leaf, before he fell limp, unconscious.

Sweet lowered the gun and stood.

"You should cut his throat now and be done with it."

Sweet looked into the deeper, darker shadows at the back of the barn. Jesse Church leaned lazily against a beam, absently picking at his fingernails with a switchblade, his hat pulled down low over his face. Unlike Malcolm, Jesse was tall and lanky; though he was far less imposing physically, it didn't mean he was no less dangerous. While his fellow henchman was adept with his fists, Jesse preferred his knife; he had slid it between the ribs of many a man, especially those who crossed his boss.

"No sense in leavin' a tongue to wag," Jesse said matter-of-factly.

Sweet shook his head. "We kill him and we'll have the cops looking for us. Besides," he said, giving Garrett's lolling head a knock, "he's gonna be scared of his shadow for the rest of his life after this. He won't talk."

Jesse shrugged, Malcolm nodded, and the matter was settled.

Leaving Garrett tied to the chair, the three men walked out to their car, a brand-new forest-green Cadillac Sixty Special. Jesse dug around in the glove compartment and came out with a map that he unfolded across the hood. Flicking a lighter to life, he held it over the paper so they could see.

"He said they went south," Jesse commented.

"Only when they left the track," Sweet replied. "Problem is, there ain't no way of knowin' for certain whether they continued that way or not."

"So which way do we go?"

Sweet peered at the map. Roads branched out from where they stood in every direction. Following the routes that led north, south, and west took them to dozens of small towns: Dawson, Merchant Falls, Bougainville, Sunset, Clarion, the names went on and on. To randomly pick a direction might lead them on a wild goose chase, but what choice did they have?

"South first," he answered. "We'll do like we done here,

ask around to see if anyone's seen 'em. If we run into a dead end, we'll backtrack and try another road. Eventually, we'll find 'em."

And when they did, Sweet would kill them.

Eddie Fuller pulled the stopper out of a decanter of scotch, winced as he took a sniff, and then poured two fingers' worth into his glass. He swirled the amber liquid around and around, then took a deep swig, closing his eyes tight as it burned painfully down his throat and into his belly. He'd never been much of a drinker, nothing more than an occasional glass of wine, but he was going to learn.

After all, it was what powerful people did.

Standing at the window, Eddie looked out over Sunset, long since quieted for the night. His home was a towering Victorian, built by his father atop the ridge running west of town, which offered a magnificent view; most days, he could see the houses and businesses clustered around Sunset's center, beyond that to the docks jutting into the river, boats chugging down the wide waterway, and finally to the thick woods on the opposite bank. It was the nicest vantage point in town.

The same could be said about the house. It was huge, with a dozen rooms, including a library, servants' quarters, and a small greenhouse off the kitchen. Eddie had grown up under its roof, and no nook or cranny held any secrets from him. As a boy, especially after his mother's death, he had ranged from cellar to attic, roamed up and down the grand staircase, hidden in closets, rummaged through pantries, and even ridden the dumbwaiter. The large grounds encompassed several acres and were as familiar as the back of his hand. He hadn't ever had many friends, so with so much time alone he had developed a strong imagination. Theo Fuller had lived one life under the house's roof, Eddie another.

But now his father was gone, and it was all his...

The few rooms that had always been off-limits to him, forbidden places like his father's bedroom and den, were now open. So Eddie entered them. He inspected drawers full of papers, thumbed through treasured mementos, played antique phonograph records, and even tried on a few of his father's favorite suits, posing in front of the full-length mirror. He started smoking cigars and drinking hard liquor. After years spent in the shadows waiting for his chance, he could finally step into the light.

But oddly enough, he still wasn't happy. In fact, he was restless, uncomfortable, out of sorts, and even a little scared. Even with all that had fallen into his lap, something was still missing.

Fortunately, it didn't take Eddie long to figure out what it was.

Clara Sinclair.

The first time he'd laid eyes on her, Eddie had been smitten; Clara wasn't the type of woman who would've been considered a knockout, but to his eyes, Hollywood starlets paled in comparison. He had marched over to her teller window and started talking about anything he could think of: the weather, the new Perry Como song, even ruminations about how many people touched any one particular piece of change. It was nonsense, but looking at her, seeing just how captivating she could be, he couldn't help himself. He felt certain that Clara must have felt the sparks rocketing back and forth between them, but amazingly, she appeared put off, even a bit embarrassed. She never uttered more than a few words.

Which only made him want her all the more.

Just like that, Eddie was infatuated. He watched her from across the bank, memorizing every strand of her hair, the way her face lit up when she smiled at a customer, the cut of every outfit in her closet. Every chance he had, he approached her, complimenting her work, her shade of lipstick, even what she'd brought for lunch, anything that might strike up a conversation between them, but he never managed to crack her frosty exterior. Eventually, it became such an obsession that he pressed her more often, more insistently, until finally his father noticed and hauled Eddie into his office.

"Stay away from her," Theo had warned, his face creased with a disapproving scowl. "She's got enough troubles in her life without you chasing after her like a puppy. You look like a fool."

Chastised, Eddie retreated to his desk and did as his father asked. But being barred from speaking to Clara only drove his unrequited feelings to even greater heights. His daydreams grew in intensity; he imagined the two of them married, the talk of the town, living in the house on the hill surrounded by their children, and happier than he would ever have imagined possible.

Then his father died and he no longer had to hold back his feelings.

Over and over, Eddie replayed his talk with Clara. It hadn't gone quite how he'd imagined. Telling her that he loved her and that he wanted to marry her had been liberating, as if a great weight had been lifted from his shoulders. But her reaction had been disappointing, to say the least. Listening to her, understanding that she was rejecting him, had lit a fuse inside Eddie, sparking an explosion that had surprised him almost as much as Clara. He hadn't intended to use the money she still owed on her house against her; he'd only wanted to show her what she stood to gain by becoming his wife. But later, after she'd gone, he saw how useful the threat of taking her house was. All his life, squirming beneath his father's thumb, Eddie had been powerless.

Now, *he* had the power.

Eddie poured another drink, this time adding an extra finger's worth. Raising the glass, he offered a silent toast to his future.

He swore that he would court Clara the right way. He would make her see what she'd been missing all these years. Then, when he officially proposed, offering her a ring adorned with the biggest diamond he could find, she would fall into his arms and tearfully accept, realizing just how wrong she had been.

That day would be the happiest of both their lives.

But then again, if she remained stubborn, if Clara refused to acknowledge what was best for her, Eddie would use the loan on her house against her.

Either way, he would get what he wanted. He was tired of being denied.

This time, when he swallowed down his drink, it felt good.

Chapter Seven

Naomi Marsh closed her eyes, tipped back her head, and let a moan rise in her throat, enjoying the feel of Tommy's lips against her skin. She sat on a scarred workbench in his garage, deep in the dark shadows, as the afternoon sun blazed down outside, an unusually hot day for spring. He was sweaty, a mixture of heat and passion. They faced each other, Tommy standing, Naomi's legs spread so that he could come closer. She twisted her fingers into his hair, fanning his desire, feeling it exhaled in hot, ragged breaths.

"That's nice," she murmured.

Tommy's lustful longing wasn't surprising; Naomi had taken great pains to make him feel the way he did. She was almost twenty, just three years older than him, but she was far more experienced in the ways of the world, especially when it came to the desire of a man, or in this case, boy, for a woman. Everything she did, every word she said, was calculated to get his attention: the way she batted her dark green eyes; the lipstick that colored her full mouth a candy-apple red; how she tossed her long black hair over her shoulder; the words she whispered in his ear; the rhythmic way she moved her hips when she walked, a sexy metronome meant to hypnotize him. But it was especially in the way she dressed: heels, white pants that hugged her curves like a second skin, a sleeveless black blouse unbuttoned far enough to allow a glimpse of cleavage. Add it all together and Tommy could have ignored his lust for her no more than he could shut off the sun.

"Naomi…" Tommy groaned as he slid his hand up her thigh, across her waist, rising toward her breast.

"Naughty boy," she scolded, moving his hand away.

"But I can't stand it anymore," he complained, his breathing ragged and his face flushed.

"Everything in due time, sugar. Don't you worry none, the day you want so bad ain't that far away. For now, just keep on doin' what you were doin.'"

Like a well-trained dog, Tommy went back to kissing her neck.

Naomi smiled. The power that she wielded was potent. She wanted Tommy hanging on her every word, obedient, even a little bit frustrated, bottled up like a volcano ready to erupt. She couldn't have said why it was this way, not exactly. Tommy was handsome and doting, though imma- ture. The truth was, she had no reason for turning him down. It certainly wasn't because she was a virgin. At a young age, when most girls were growing into their bodies, she had understood that her looks could get her anything she wanted, so long as she was occasionally willing to give something in return.

So far, with Tommy, she hadn't had to offer much.

It had become a game to her, though Naomi would have struggled to explain why she played. Because the hold she had on Tommy was intoxicating, she supposed, though she worried that might be slipping a bit.

The night at the cemetery when she'd knocked over the tombstone, drunk from the bottle of whiskey she'd stolen from her father's tavern, Tommy had been reluctant to cut loose, worried that they were going to get caught.

"Quit bein' such a goddamn kid," she had slurred.

"We shouldn't be here," he argued.

"Maybe I oughta find me a man who ain't gonna worry 'bout gettin' into trouble. There's plenty who'd be happy to take your place..."

Tommy had protested loudly; it was because they were arguing that they hadn't heard the sheriff's car, so when he flicked on his lights, the broken tombstone lying at their feet, Naomi had momentarily frozen. Next thing she knew, she was running. She expected Tommy to be right behind her, but when she burst through the honeysuckle bushes at the wood's edge, she was alone. Glancing back, her eyes blurry from the liquor, she watched him give himself up. Then she left without a shred of remorse. Fortunately for her, he'd held his tongue and not spoken a word about her involvement. Naomi could only imagine how angry his mother had been to find out that her precious son was in jail.

I sure wish I could've seen that…

Petty as it was, a small part of the reason Naomi was still with Tommy was because it drove Clara Sinclair crazy.

She knew little about the woman; as a kid, she'd stood in front of Clara's bank window when her father made an infrequent deposit. She'd always seemed to be nice enough. Like everyone else in town, Naomi knew that Tommy's father had been killed in the war and that Clara had never remarried.

But when Tommy had told her that his mother didn't want him spending any time with her, that Clara thought she was trashy, the gloves had come off.

Naomi figured that Clara was jealous. She had good reason to be; rather than waste her looks, Naomi planned on using them to get ahead. The second she got the opportunity, she was going to go to New York or Hollywood, someplace where she could be as famous as she deserved to be, and become a movie star or a singer. Maybe she would model clothes or jewelry, her face up on a billboard. Wherever she went, rich men would fall all over themselves, desperate to give her whatever she desired. Everything about Sunset, including Tommy Sinclair and his mother, would be faded memories; even their names would eventually be forgotten.

But until then, she'd keep on having her fun.

"Kiss me," she said; he readily obliged.

But then, just as Naomi began to wonder if she hadn't

been too hasty in keeping Tommy's hands from roaming, his mother's truck wheezed into the drive and parked outside.

Naomi stiffened; though she took pleasure in rankling Clara, that didn't mean she wanted to come face-to-face with her. But surprisingly, when she made to move, Tommy held her in place.

"She can't see us in here," he said.

In the end, it didn't matter; Clara never looked in their direction, but instead headed for the house. Moments later, the screen door banged shut behind her.

Naomi exhaled, embarrassed to find she'd been holding her breath.

"You'd probably better get going," Tommy said.

"I can stay awhile longer," she replied, her voice dripping with honey. "Now that she's gone, we can get back to what we were doing."

But when she put her hands on his chest, Tommy took them away.

"I haven't talked to her in a while," he explained, glancing at the house. "If I don't show my face now and then, she gets a little nuts."

"So let her," Naomi said with impatience.

Tommy chuckled uneasily. "That's easy for you to say. You're not the one who has to deal with her guff."

Naomi watched him closely, her eyes narrowing. Once again, she wondered if Tommy wasn't going soft on her, if her control over him wasn't slipping.

She may not have wanted to be with Tommy Sinclair

forever, but when the day came for it to end, she wanted to be the one who walked away.

"Fine," she finally said, hopping down off the workbench. "But I'll see you later, right?"

"Yeah," he answered, still distracted.

Naomi grabbed him by the chin and turned his face to hers. "I'd better," she warned. "I hate being disappointed."

Tommy said his good-byes to Naomi, pulling her close for one more kiss before she slipped out the garage's side door. He wiped her lipstick from his mouth, took a deep breath, and then crossed the yard toward the house, steeling himself for another unwanted and unwarranted lecture.

Ever since his mother had gotten him at the jail, Tommy had done his best to avoid her, sneaking into the house late at night after she'd already gone to sleep, then rising before her, even if it meant arriving at school so early that the janitor hadn't unlocked the doors.

So far, so good, but like he'd told Naomi, he still needed to see his mother every now and again, even if the thought filled him with dread.

Through the kitchen's open window, Tommy heard a voice; it was his grandmother, surely talking with his mother. He could only imagine what would be said the second he walked through the door...

Where have you been?

Stop throwing your life away!

Naomi doesn't care about you, not the way you think she does!

What would your father say if he could see you now?

Tommy gritted his teeth. Even the way he carried himself was defensive; his hands stuffed into his jeans, his shoulders slumped as his eyes looked down at his feet. He was sick of all the questions and complaints. His mother's words, her accusations, stung.

She didn't understand. He and Naomi were in love. Whenever Tommy was around her, when he stared into her eyes, when he listened to the sound of her voice, and especially when he kissed her, he knew there was no one he'd rather be with. The more time they spent together, the more convinced he was that Naomi Marsh was the girl for him. He had even entertained the thought of proposing, of asking her to become his wife. Sure, they were young, but his own parents hadn't been much older when they'd gotten married. It could work. Their love would overcome any obstacle.

What about all those other men she's been with?

The cruelest of his mother's charges echoed in Tommy's head. She spoke of rumors around town that Naomi was loose. But he didn't believe it. If Naomi was so immoral, why had she refused to sleep with *him*? It was just another lie meant to keep them apart.

Maybe Naomi was right. Maybe his mother's increasingly desperate attempts to ruin their relationship were because she was jealous. For the first time, Tommy entertained the thought that Clara wasn't just envious of a younger, prettier woman, but of *her own son*. After all, he'd found true love, something she had lost with the death of his father. Maybe it was more than she could bear.

Tommy pulled open the door, the hinges screeching, and entered the house. He braced himself, expecting the worst, but he was surprised to find his grandmother alone, sitting at the kitchen table reading a book.

"Hey there, partner," she exclaimed warmly.

"Hi, Grandma," he mumbled as he made his way to the refrigerator, grabbed himself the fixings for a sandwich, and sat down opposite her. As he began to make his lunch, he listened closely for the sound of his mother's footsteps coming down the hall. But by the time he took his first bite, he'd heard nothing.

"Where's Mom?" he asked, curious.

"Upstairs, lying down," Christine explained. "She was complaining about a headache and I thought that a little rest over her lunch break might make it go away." She sighed. "I keep telling her that she's working too hard down there at the bank, but she doesn't listen. But I suppose that's just the way it is between parents and their children. Everyone's too darn stubborn."

Tommy paused midbite and looked at his grandmother. He wondered if what she'd said wasn't a dig at him; he couldn't recall the last time he'd taken his mother's advice. But Christine had already turned her attention back to her book, a dog-eared paperback she'd been hauling around everywhere with her lately. He read the title: *Strangers on a Train*, by Patricia Highsmith. The cover was dark, with a strangely drawn couple.

"Is it any good?" Tommy asked.

"I suppose so," Christine answered wearily, setting the book down and rubbing her eyes. "The problem is that every time I pick it up, I can't remember what I've read, which means I have to go back and do it all over again. I swear, I've read the same twenty pages a dozen times now."

Tommy nodded sympathetically, but that was all he could offer. His grandmother's health troubles bothered him. Like his mother, he had noticed their onset slowly, a misplaced item here, a forgotten name there, but now the deterioration was obvious. He wondered if the day wouldn't come when he would walk in the door, just like this very afternoon, and she would stare blankly at him, as if a stranger had entered the house. He felt helpless, like the child he'd once been, unable to provide comfort, so instead he kept eating as the silence dragged on.

"I suppose it can't be too bad," his grandmother finally said as she picked her book back up. "Why else would I keep reading it day after day?"

Tommy laughed uneasily; he was almost thankful when he heard his mother coming down the stairs.

When she entered the kitchen, she stopped suddenly, staring at him; her expression briefly showed relief, but quickly hardened. "You're home..."

"I got hungry," Tommy replied with a shrug; his eyes roamed from his mother, down to his plate, across the table to his grandmother, and then he started over again, uncomfortable, unable to settle on anything for long.

His mother looked exhausted, almost haggard. Tommy

wondered if he was the reason she looked so out of sorts, even if she was worrying for nothing.

No matter how tired his mother appeared, Tommy still expected her to light into him, to demand to know where he'd been, to ask about Naomi. Instead, she got herself a plate, sat down across from him, and began to make a sandwich of her own. For a moment, Tommy was reminded of better times, summer afternoons when he was a boy, when the three of them, his grandmother included, sat around the kitchen table just like this, laughing, singing songs, and enjoying one another's company. But then his father had been killed. Ever since that day, no matter what Tommy said or did, he could never completely wipe the tears from his mother's eyes.

"Do you have any plans tomorrow night?" his mother asked.

Tommy shrugged. "Not really."

"Well, I was thinking that it might be nice if we went to the movies. There's a new Lucille Ball picture coming to town. It could be fun."

Some of Tommy's fondest memories were of sitting in a seat at the Palace Theater, captivated by the flickering images up on the big screen. If he was well-behaved, he might have gotten a bag of popcorn. It had been a chance for them to get away from their troubles, at least for a while. Maybe it *would* be fun. But before he could agree to go, his mother spoke again.

"Would Naomi want to come along?"

Just like that, Tommy was overcome with anger. He

couldn't believe it; here was his mother, once again sticking her nose where it didn't belong. He stood up quickly, the legs of his chair scraping the floor as it was forced back, almost tipping over. He was suddenly so furious that he couldn't even speak. Instead, he glared. For her part, Clara seemed so genuinely shocked by his reaction that Tommy wondered whether he was mistaken, if her suggestion had been innocent. But he shook his doubts away. It was too late to back down now.

"Tommy, wait..."

But he was already moving. He rounded the table and was outside, the door slamming hard behind him, a loud crack in an otherwise quiet afternoon.

Chapter Eight

CLARA BACKED OUT of the driveway, ground the truck's stick shift into gear, and started back toward the bank. Though she knew it was pointless, she looked up and down the sidewalks, peered between houses, and glanced in all her mirrors, hoping for a glimpse of Tommy. But he was nowhere to be seen. Once again, despite the best of intentions, things between them were a mess.

How does this keep happening?

The night before, Clara had lain in bed, staring up at the ceiling as the hours slowly ticked past, thinking about what she might do to patch things up with her son. In her heart, she knew that Naomi was a terrible influence on Tommy, that if he continued to be with her, she could lead him down a dark path. But so far, her warnings had fallen on deaf ears. So instead of trying to push Naomi farther away, Clara had decided to bring the girl closer. She imagined that if they spent some time together, eating dinner, sitting on the porch, or going to the movies, the tavern owner's rowdy daughter would eventually slip up and do something to finally show Tommy that she wasn't worthy of his affections.

But when she'd extended the invitation to Tommy, he had taken it all wrong. Clara supposed she only had herself to blame; after all, every other time she'd talked about Naomi, she'd dragged the girl down. Her son was young, immature, and hotheaded; he took the mere mention of his girlfriend's name as a threat to their relationship.

And so he'd stormed off, putting more distance between them.

Clara turned onto Main Street. Wind whipped through the open window and stirred her hair. When she pressed on the accelerator, she felt the truck sputter before doing as she asked. Normally, Clara would have grumbled about the continuing decline of her vehicle, but her thoughts were elsewhere.

"Since when doesn't he like Lucille Ball?" her mother had joked after Tommy's angry exit.

Somehow, Clara had managed a smile. But she could see that Christine was as confused and worried as she was.

Still, she hadn't said another word about Tommy, even though she wanted to ask her mother for advice. Not after what had happed the night before.

While she had been lying in bed, trying to figure out what to do about Tommy's infatuation with Naomi, Clara had heard a noise in the hall. At first, she assumed that it was her son, returned from God knew where; he hadn't been home when she'd gone to bed, another reason for her frustration. Thinking that it wouldn't hurt to take a quick peek, Clara had cracked open her door to discover that the source of the sound was her mother.

Christine was in the bathroom. She had turned on the light, the bulb flickering slightly, but she didn't move, just stared at her reflection in the mirror. Clara figured it was just like when she had stared into the pantry; somewhere along the way, her mother had forgotten what she was doing. But this time, instead of coming to Christine's aid, she shut her door, careful not to make any noise. Over time, Clara had come to the conclusion that whenever she intervened, when she steered a conversation back toward its original destination, brushed away her mother's forgetfulness, or simply did something for her, more of Christine's pride was chipped away. After all, it wasn't as if her mother didn't know that her mind was slipping. To burden her further, to tell her of her troubles with Tommy, wouldn't be right; so instead, Clara kept it to herself.

The closer she got to town, the busier things became. People walked Sunset's sidewalks beneath a bright, clear afternoon sky, many of them returning from lunch. When she stopped at the town's lone traffic light, the truck's engine sputtered and the steering wheel shuddered in her hands. Within a matter of minutes, Clara would walk through the front door of the bank.

And right back into another of my problems...

Ever since her meeting with Eddie, Clara had been walking on eggshells. Standing at her teller window, she forced a smile on her face and tried to act as if nothing was wrong; it was rare that she succeeded. Try as she might, she couldn't keep from glancing at the door to Eddie's office, wondering when he was going to come out, saunter over, and make another unwanted advance, expecting her to go along with it. The consequences of refusing him terrified her.

But so far, surprisingly, Eddie hadn't done a thing.

He greeted her just as he would any other employee, awkwardly remarking on this or that, a little innocent small talk before retreating to his office. But Clara knew that it was all a ruse. Someday soon, Eddie Fuller was going to repeat those terrifying words he'd uttered in his office.

He was going to propose marriage.

But when it happened, what was she going to do? If she refused him, Clara knew she could lose everything. Tommy, her mother, all of them would suffer. Giving in to Eddie would be hard, but it was a small price to pay for—

Clara was startled by a loud bang from beneath the truck's hood. Immediately, clouds of hissing steam billowed out, making it impossible to see. The pickup sputtered and then slowed; it was all she could do to pull over in front of Freeman's Bakery, where the engine finally stalled.

Clara trembled. This was the last straw. It was all too much: her problems at work, with her mother, with Tommy . . . It had been building since Joe's death, an accumulation of troubles, like grains of sand that had become a mountain too steep to climb. And so, right there in the

middle of Sunset, the afternoon sun shining brightly, she
put her face in her hands and cried.

Drake stifled a yawn as he drove into Sunset. He had followed the road that led west, skirting the winding river,
hemmed in by thickets of trees occasionally broken by an
abandoned field. Slowly, the landscape had become dot-
ted with ramshackle houses. The first signs announcing the
coming of town were a relief. Up ahead, Drake noticed a
few taller buildings, a church steeple, and a rusty water
tower. He took it all in but wasn't impressed. It was like
countless others he'd been through over the years; in the
end, it was just another dot on a map.

"This is the place you were so dead set on?"

Amos yawned so hard his eyes shut; he'd slept like the
dead for hours, stirring only when Drake gave him a good
shake. "It ain't without charm."

Giving the town a closer look, Drake could see some
of what the mechanic was talking about: a woman held
hands with a young boy of about three and the two of them
sang as they walked down the sidewalk; resting against his
broom, a shopkeeper cleaned his glasses with his apron;
flowers bloomed in window boxes up and down the street,
their colors brilliant in the sunlight. In a way, it reminded
Drake of Hampton, the Missouri town he'd settled in
shortly after leaving home.

Maybe this place isn't so bad after all . . .

Driving past the post office, Drake pulled the Plymouth
over in front of the Sunset Hotel.

Amos looked at the weather-beaten sign with confusion. "Why are we stoppin' here?"

"To get a room." Seeing the other man's frown, Drake added, "Don't tell me you're already thinking about leaving."

"I hadn't planned on spendin' the night, that's all."

"Well, too bad. I'm bushed. You might not mind sleeping all wedged up against the window, but my neck is killing me. I need a bed."

Amos opened his mouth as if he wanted to say more, but didn't. Instead, he glanced over at the side mirror, looking back the way they'd come.

"What's the matter?" Drake asked.

"Nothin'..." the mechanic answered with a shake of his head.

"Look, we spend the night, get rested up, have a bite to eat at what passes for a diner around these parts, and then get back on the road." Smiling, he added, "Who knows, maybe we can even scrounge up a little action. There's got to be someone in Sunset who thinks he's got a fast ride."

Amos nodded in agreement, but Drake could see that his thoughts were elsewhere. The two men got out of the car.

"Go grab us a room," Drake said. "I'm going to stretch my legs, take a look around."

The older man took a couple of steps toward the hotel but then turned around, reached inside the car, and grabbed his jacket. Before Amos finally went inside, he paused and took one last look back up the road.

What the heck has gotten into him?

Drake stifled a yawn as he squinted up at the sun, enjoying the feel of its heat against his skin. He nodded politely to an older couple as they walked by; the man touched the brim of his hat in friendly greeting. He was just about to go for a walk, to maybe ask around for a good place to eat, when he heard a loud bang. Across the street, on old pickup truck wheezed over to the sidewalk. Steam billowed out from under its hood, a familiar sight in Drake's line of work. Seconds passed. Drake figured that the driver would get out and take a look, but the door stayed shut.

Then he noticed a woman sitting behind the wheel.

She was crying.

Drake looked up and down the street. He expected to see someone coming to her aid, but surprisingly, he seemed to be the only person who'd noticed. He thought about ignoring her, about going back to the hotel and helping Amos unload their things, getting a bit of rest. After all, it wasn't his problem. But something, an unfamiliar feeling, wouldn't let him turn away.

"Aw, hell," he said, and started across the street.

Clara gasped in surprise at the sudden, unexpected sound of knocking on the truck's roof. Her head flew out of her hands to find a man she didn't know standing at the window. He leaned casually against the truck, wearing an easy smile. He looked tired, his dark hair mussed and his cheeks peppered with stubble. Looking into his brownish-green eyes, Clara felt something stir inside her, like the unmistakable flickering of a flame, small but undeniable.

"Are you all right?" he asked, his voice deep, his eyes narrowing in an expression of concern.

"I was...I was just..." She struggled to answer, wiping tears from her cheeks.

"Do you need any help?"

"With what?" Clara asked, her head still muddled.

The stranger smiled. "With your engine."

"Oh, that." She had so many troubles weighing down on her that, for a moment, she hadn't been sure what he meant. She felt embarrassed by how she must look and didn't want to impose on him. "No, its fine...I'll just..." she stammered.

"It's no bother. Let me take a look."

He reached inside the cab, his arm brushing against Clara's leg, sending a shiver racing across her skin, and gave the hood's release a yank. She could only stare as he walked to the front of the truck, waved his arm through the still billowing steam, and raised the hood.

Clara was dumbstruck. She didn't know what to say or do. Who was this man? Why was he doing this? Should she get out of the truck? Should she tell him to stop, insist that she would take care of it on her own? But then again, what was wrong with accepting his help? She was more knowledgeable about fixing things now than she had been when Joe was alive, but she knew she couldn't repair the truck's engine, nor did she have the money for a mechanic.

Feeling helpless, Clara stuck her head out the window. The stranger had moved back to her side of the car, tinkering under the hood. He reached into his back pocket and removed a handkerchief; she noticed the corded muscles of his forearms. When he leaned back and wiped his brow, she quickly pulled her head back inside the truck's cab, not wanting to be seen. Glancing into the rearview mirror, she saw that her cheeks were flushed.

"Here's the culprit."

Clara had been so lost in thought that she hadn't noticed the stranger return. Once again, he startled her. She found him holding a broken hose, both ends drooping limply.

"These things can take a heck of a beating, but there always comes a point when they give out," he explained with a chuckle. Looking over the old truck, he added, "You're lucky it didn't happen sooner."

"Thank you," Clara told him, genuinely meaning it, before quickly turning away. There was something about his eyes, about *him*, that made her feel a little self-conscious. "I'll call the garage and see if they have a replacement."

"I've got a better idea," the stranger said.

Stepping away from the car, he looked back up the street. Clara followed his gaze to the Sunset Hotel, where an older man stood on the sidewalk turning around in confusion, as if he was trying to find someone. The stranger put two fingers in his mouth and gave a short but loud whistle; his companion saw him, waved, and trotted over.

"I wondered where the heck you'd gotten off to," he

said when he arrived, a little out of breath. "Afternoon, ma'am," he added politely to Clara.

"We still have any radiator hoses in the trailer?"

"Maybe a couple," the older man answered, scratching the back of his head as he glanced under the pickup truck's hood. "But what with how hard it might be to find 'nother one, I don't know if we oughta—"

"Go get one," her rescuer said.

"Now just hold on a second, Drake. What happens if we—"

"We'll make do, Amos," he said, his voice rising a bit. "She needs it more than we do right now."

Amos looked over at Clara and forced a thin smile. Sweat beaded on his forehead; he wiped it off with the back of his arm. "All right, then," he grumbled before sauntering back toward the hotel.

"You didn't have to do that," Clara said. "I don't want to put you out."

He smiled easily. "You're not. Amos is something of a worrier. He hoards parts like they were made of gold. I practically have to beg for a new fan belt."

"Why are you traveling around with parts you can spare?"

"I race cars for a living," he said. Holding out his hand, he introduced himself. "My name's Drake. Drake McCoy."

"Clara Sinclair." She gave him her hand, so small that it almost disappeared inside his; when he let it go, he left streaks of grease behind.

"Sorry about that," he apologized. He turned his hands

over in the bright sunlight. "Sometimes I wonder when they were last well and truly clean." Drake grinned. "Maybe I shouldn't have said it quite like that. You're going to think it's been years since I took a bath."

"Oh, no," Clara replied. "I wouldn't have thought it had been *that* long. A couple of months, tops..."

Her joke made them both laugh.

Suddenly, as if someone had snapped their fingers in front of her face, Clara realized that she was no longer upset, that instead of crying, distraught from bearing the weight of all her problems, she was smiling.

She was enjoying Drake's company.

Daring to risk his notice, Clara took a good, long look at him. His features were strong, if a bit rugged. His jawline, in need of a shave, resembled those of Hollywood's leading men, while his mouth was almost delicate, curving at the ends so that it always looked like he was about to smile. His eyes were warm and inviting; even his crow's-feet just added to his charm. She guessed that he was around her age, maybe a little older, somewhere in his early forties.

If she were being completely honest with herself, Clara would have admitted that she found him handsome. She was so certain she was blushing that she didn't dare look in the mirror for fear it would only make it worse.

Fortunately, just as she began to wonder what to say next, Amos returned with a hose and a bucket nearly sloshing over with water.

"I suppose you're expectin' me to put it in," the older man growled.

"I can do it," Drake answered.

"Never mind," Amos huffed when Drake tried to take what he was carrying. "I'll do it better and faster than you, anyway."

Once the mechanic went to work, Clara, having regained her bearings, said, "You're a race car driver..."

Drake nodded, running a hand through his dark hair. "My father wanted me to be a farmer, but I was only ever good at driving fast."

"It sounds exciting."

"Some days. Others, I wonder what it would be like to do something different, something slower, where I could help people."

Clara frowned. "I work at a bank and there's rarely a day that goes by that I don't find myself staring out the window, daydreaming about doing the same thing, only in reverse." Suddenly, she caught herself, self-conscious that she was revealing too much to a man she'd only just met. Changing the subject, she asked, "So what are you doing in Sunset?"

"We're just passing through," Drake answered, nodding toward his partner. "One night at the hotel and then we'll be on our way."

An unexpected pang of disappointment raced through her. "Well, I'm glad I had a chance to meet you," Clara said. "And not just because of my truck."

Drake chuckled. "Me, too." He paused, looking as if he was weighing his next words. "As a matter of fact, I'm thinking that maybe we could—"

But before he could finish, Amos slammed down the

truck's hood, interrupting him. "That oughta do it," the older man declared. "Filled up the radiator while I was at it." Looking at Clara, he said, "Give it a try."

She turned the key and the engine shuddered to life.

Amos laughed loudly. "I think all I did was put a bandage on a limb in need of amputatin', but she'll keep goin' for a little while longer."

Clara thanked them both for all they had done, but she found her eyes lingering on Drake a little longer, as if she was waiting for him to finish what he'd been saying, but he remained silent.

Finally, she stuck out her hand. "It was nice to meet you."

Drake smiled. "Are you sure you want to do that?"

She shrugged. "I'm already dirty. What's a little more grease?"

They shook hands; when she made to let go, Drake held her hand a heartbeat longer, but Clara didn't mind.

When she finally drove away, now plenty late in getting back to work, wondering if Eddie would be angry with her, her eyes kept darting to her mirror. Drake stood in the middle of the road, watching her.

She wondered what he was thinking.

Chapter Nine

CLARA COLLECTED THE PLATES and dishes, the glasses and silverware, the bowls and pans that still held what was left over from dinner, and brought them to the sink. Her mother washed them, Christine's hands deep in the soapy water; those she'd already cleaned were drying on a towel beside her. Music played on the radio, an old-timey ballad, a man's voice crooning in the kitchen and out through the open window into the early evening.

"*If you're heading for a sunny honeymoon*," her mother sang softly.

Clara frowned as she gathered the last items: Tommy's unused setting. Christine said he hadn't been home since their misunderstanding that afternoon. Clara had waited, their dinner growing cold, but finally gave up. She imagined he was sulking somewhere, probably with Naomi whispering more nonsense in his ear, forcing the gulf between Tommy and his family even wider. Clara worried about her son, but until he returned home, she didn't know what more she could do.

"How were things at the bank?" Christine asked.

"Pretty slow," Clara answered, forcing a smile; this was the second time her mother had asked that question. "Eleanor MacGregor wanted me to say hello. She says you're overdue for a visit."

Clara wondered if her mother would remember her mentioning the greeting from one of her oldest friends, then worried that the realization might embarrass her. But Christine replied, "That was nice of her," and Clara understood that their earlier conversation had been forgotten.

Outside, the sun was slowly setting. A pair of boys raced down the street, riding a contraption they'd built out of an old apple box, loose boards, and some scavenged wheels. The symphony of birdsong steadily quieted for the night, with only a few intermittent calls. For Sunset, it was just another day coming to an end.

But for Clara, it had been anything but ordinary.

It had been headed for ruin; the outburst from Tommy, her mother's continued confusion, her worries about Eddie Fuller, and finally the truck's breakdown had left her ready to give in to despair.

Then Drake McCoy had shown up...

When she'd needed help the most, Drake had given it, had even gone out of his way to do so, and Clara had found herself enjoying his company, his smile, especially the way he made her laugh. Back at the bank, standing at her teller window, she had found herself thinking of him, wondering what he was doing, what it was like to race a car for a living. Still, her daydreams had turned sour; watching him fade from sight in her rearview mirror was the last she would ever see of him.

Then, to make matters even worse, she'd thought about Joe.

She remembered all the years they had spent together, how passionately she'd loved him. She recalled how delighted they had been when she first learned that she was pregnant, how nine months had felt like forever, how everything had changed for the better one September morning when Tommy had been born. She thought of their dreams, how she'd believed they would all come true.

Shame had flushed Clara's cheeks. That she'd been so happy in another man's company, that she found him handsome, made her angry at herself. Was she some silly teenager, swept off her feet because a man gave her a little attention? Drake had helped her, she had thanked him for it, and that's all it was. Fortunately, Eddie had stayed in his office all afternoon, leaving her plenty of time to think.

"How come you never go out on any dates?"

Clara was so dumbstruck by her mother's question that she nearly dropped the plate she'd been drying.

"What . . . what did you say?" she stammered.

"I was just thinking that it's a shame you spend so many nights home with me, when you could be at the movies, dancing, or whatever it is young couples do these days," Christine explained. Showing her daughter her soapy hands, she added, "Anything would be more exciting than this."

Clara didn't know what to say. Two days earlier, just before she'd put flowers on Joe's grave, her mother had told her how important it was to hold on to the memory of her dead husband, to cherish their time together and never let it go. At first glance, Clara assumed that this was just another example of her mother's deteriorating memory, but the more she thought about it, the more she wondered if the two ideas, to not forget Joe but still be open to meeting someone else, couldn't coexist. Either way, she didn't want to talk about it.

"There's not much interest in a widow slowly but steadily making her way toward forty," Clara said, hoping that would be the end of it.

"Why would you say such a thing?" Christine asked, a touch of fire in her voice. "You're still one of the prettiest girls in town! You're friendly and kind; anyone who walks into that bank of yours would attest to that! What man *wouldn't* be interested in you?"

Clara thought of Drake. It had been a long time since someone had spoken to her the way he had. She remembered how he'd *looked* at her, his body leaning against the truck, and how that attention had made her feel. She could still see him standing in the middle of the street, watching...

"Well, no one has come along yet," Clara said as she took another wet dish from her mother. "So even if I was of the mind to—"

Before Clara could say another word, she was interrupted by a sudden, insistent knocking at the front door. She looked at her mother; neither of them was expecting anyone. Clara went to answer; on the way there, she realized that she'd forgotten to dry her hands so she wiped them on her skirt.

Someone stood outside, but with the thin curtain covering the door's glass and the murky light of dusk, she couldn't tell who it was.

But if she was surprised to have a visitor at such a late hour, she was stunned by who she found when she opened the door.

It was Drake McCoy.

"You keep pacin' like that you're gonna wear a hole in the floor."

Drake stopped and looked at Amos; the mechanic lounged on his bed, one hand behind his head, the other holding the folded-up newspaper he'd bought that afternoon. An open beer bottle sweated on the nightstand.

"I've got a lot on my mind, is all," Drake answered.

"The only thing you oughta be thinkin' 'bout is gettin' up bright and early and headin' on down the road."

Drake didn't answer. He still thought it strange that Amos had been so intent on reaching Sunset, only to now be chomping at the bit to leave, but Drake's attention was elsewhere, on someone in particular.

He couldn't stop thinking about Clara Sinclair.

Ever since he'd watched her drive away, Drake had replayed their every moment together. The things she had said. The way she'd blushed. The sound of her laugh. And especially how she had looked, her beauty...

Whenever he closed his eyes, he saw her smile, the perfect curve of her cheek, the way she pushed loose strands of her dark hair behind her ear. But he was drawn to her eyes, marveled at how they pierced him, that when she looked at him he felt like the luckiest man in the world just to have her attention.

You sound like a damn kid, he'd chided himself more than once.

It had been a long time since Drake had met a woman who so completely captivated him. There had been a few over the years, companions who lasted only a short time, long enough to give each of them that fleeting something they needed. He had always been a nomad, more married to his work than to any relationship. But somewhere in the back of his mind Drake had always figured that someday he would meet the right woman, the one who would put a halt to his wanderings, someone with whom he could settle down and make use of the money he'd been saving for so long. Clara Sinclair stirred something in him, even if he'd only known her for minutes. He even wondered if he hadn't misjudged her, if she wasn't as interested in him as he was in her. Regardless, he knew that if he left town without seeing her again, it would eat at him for a long, long time.

"I'm going out," he said, heading for the door.

Drake had expected Amos to give him more grief or, at

the least, to ask where he was going, but he didn't look up from his paper. "Have fun."

Downstairs, Drake asked the woman behind the front desk for a phone book. Flipping through the pages, he quickly found Clara's listing, memorized her address, and then inquired about directions. Minutes later, he was walking down the street on which she lived. The early evening was cool as a breeze rustled the trees. Two boys laughed loudly as they raced down the sidewalk, riding their homemade contraption. In the little light left to the day, he peered closely at the numbers tacked beside doors or painted on mailboxes and soon found Clara's home.

Staring at a house that had clearly seen better days, Drake wondered if he wasn't about to make an ass out of himself. Maybe Clara would be happy to see him, but maybe she wouldn't. He couldn't say for certain whether she was married; he had noticed that she wasn't wearing a ring, but maybe it was sitting on the dresser. He was taking a chance.

But Drake hadn't come this far to chicken out. He *wanted* to see her, to hear her voice. He had to know for certain, one way or the other. Just like when he was racing, there were times to be cautious, but there were also moments when the only thing to do was to floor it and see what happened. This was one of those times.

He took a deep breath and started for the door.

Clara stared at Drake, her mouth falling slightly open. He seemed to sense her surprise; his eyes softened and a smile slowly spread across his face. As if he'd done it a dozen times before, he leaned against the door's frame. "Sorry to drop by like this," he said. "I hope I'm not interrupting anything."

"No . . . it's fine," she stammered. "I was just cleaning up after dinner . . ."

"That's good," he answered with a nod. Absently, he ran a hand through his hair, a habit she found charming. "I've been thinking about you."

"You have?" Clara asked.

"Ever since I watched you drive away, I wondered if you had any more trouble with your truck. I'd hate to think Amos hadn't fixed it right."

"It hasn't died on me yet, but I'm not holding my breath for tomorrow."

Drake chuckled at her joke, a genuinely happy sound.

Clara smiled, too, though her head was muddled. Drake was the last person she'd expected to find at her door. He wore the same clothes as when they'd met, a worn blue button-down over jeans, but he had shaved; without his whiskers, his face was cleaner, his features more pronounced, especially the shallow dimples when he smiled. The end result was that she found him even more handsome than before; embarrassed that it might be obvious, she looked away.

But then, struggling with what to say next, she heard the faint sound of footsteps behind her.

Clara was certain that it was her mother coming to see who was at the door; the last thing she wanted was to have to introduce Drake. Thinking quickly, she grabbed her shawl from the coat tree and hurried onto the porch, shutting the door behind her.

"Let's go for a walk," she said.

Drake smiled. "That sounds like a good idea."

On the sidewalk, Drake nodded back toward her truck. "That's a '35, isn't it?" he asked.

"I'm not exactly sure, but somewhere around there," Clara answered; unspoken was her memory of the day Joe bought it slightly used, how he washed it in the driveway, the hours spent under its hood, tinkering with the engine, making sure it ran right, all the little details she'd neglected over the years.

"You might find this hard to believe, but that year and make is considered something of a classic," Drake explained. "Still, when they're that old, there's no shortage of things that can go wrong with them."

"I'd like to take better care of it," Clara admitted. She looked at her home and softly added, "I'd like to take better care of a lot of things these days..."

"I think you're doing just fine," Drake offered.

Clara forced a smile. She hesitated and then said, "My son helps when he can."

Even in the growing darkness, she saw that her revelation surprised him, though it didn't show on his face for long. "How old is he?"

"Tommy is sixteen going on thirty," Clara said with a short laugh. "Seems like only yesterday when he was running around in short pants."

Drake nodded. "When I was around that age, I was hell on my folks. I wanted to be anywhere other than where I was, under their roof, abiding by my father's rules. It's a tough time in a boy's life. We think we have all the answers, but we don't."

"I wish I had some of my own. It's been hard raising him by myself."

This time, Clara didn't see Drake's reaction, but she did notice his lack of a reply, too polite to ask the questions he must surely have.

Instead, they walked silently. The curtain of evening had fully descended, with only the faintest hint of light on the western horizon. The streetlamps began to switch on; they moved from one bright circle to the next. They passed the overturned boxcar the boys had been playing with, its wheels silenced for the night, its owners inside and getting ready for bed. In almost every house they walked by, lights were on as families settled down for a late dinner or to listen to a radio show. The wind had picked up a notch, carrying with it a chill, making Clara pull her shawl a little tighter around her shoulders.

"We can head back if you'd like," Drake told her.

"I'm fine," she answered. "I don't do this as much as I should. I used to..." Clara hesitated, suddenly uneasy about saying more.

But in the end, I don't really have anything to lose...

"My husband and I used to go for walks, in the years before he died," Clara said matter-of-factly, laying herself bare, just as she'd done about Tommy.

"In the war?" Drake asked, his eyes fixed straight ahead. Clara nodded. Her heart raced.

"I was in the army," he told her, sharing a part of himself, as if in exchange for what she'd offered him. "I was a mechanic. I fixed just about anything that had an engine. Jeeps, tanks, transport trucks, motorcycles, you name it. My unit was stationed in England, then followed the invasion into France, and finally on to Germany." Drake paused, as if searching for the right words. "I saw a lot of good men die and often wondered about who they'd left behind, their families and friends. When I finally came home and saw women wearing black, flags hanging at half-mast, I knew."

Clara fought back tears.

Drake stopped walking. He turned to look at her, his gaze steady yet sad. "I'm sorry for your loss."

"Thank you," she managed before walking on, knowing that if she didn't, she would break down; she didn't want him to see her cry.

In the years since the war had ended, Clara had met other veterans: soldiers, sailors, and pilots, men who had once been Joe's age, men like Drake who'd fought for their nation and for freedom. When they'd earned their victory, bleeding and dying on foreign soil, they had returned to their former lives, to children, to wives, to their homes and businesses, putting all they'd seen behind them. Most were restrained when they spoke about it, choosing their words carefully, just as Drake had done. They were heroes, yet humble.

The two of them walked beneath the moon as it slowly traced its arc across the sky, surrounded by an endless number of twinkling stars. It didn't take long for Clara to be put at ease, relaxed in Drake's company. He told her about where he had grown up, about how different the flat farmland of Iowa was from Sunset. They shared jokes, tried to remember the lyrics to a song that had been popular when they were younger, and wondered whether it was birds or bats they saw swooping between the trees. It was so easy for her to be with him, watching how he smiled beneath the streetlights, hearing the joy in his voice; Clara found herself smiling and laughing right along with him, captivated by the stranger who had unexpectedly entered her life. But that was the thing; it didn't *feel* like Drake was a stranger. Being with him, listening to him talk, sharing his company, was comfortable, as easy as if she had known him for years. At the same time, it was exhilarating, exciting, something different from the everyday doldrums her widowed life had become. She was having such a good time that she was surprised when Drake stopped back in front of her house.

"Here we are," he said.

Gently, he reached out and took her hand in his own; it was the first time he'd touched her all night. Clara allowed it, his skin warm against hers, welcoming. She looked up into his eyes.

"I had a nice time tonight," he said.

"Me, too."

Drake smiled a bit sheepishly. "I suppose this is as good

of a time as any to admit that I wasn't completely truthful earlier."

"About what?" Clara asked.

"I didn't really stop by to check on your truck." He paused, his eyes roaming across her face. "I came by because I couldn't bear the thought of never seeing you again."

Clara's pulse quickened.

"All afternoon, I couldn't get you out of my head," he continued, inching closer, his free hand reaching out to remove a few strands of hair from her face, his thumb sliding softly across her cheekbone. "I kept thinking about where you were, what you were doing. So I decided to come looking for you, to see you again. I thought about all the things we might say. The laughs we might share. By the time I knocked on your door, I had it all played out in my mind."

"Was it what you thought it would be?" Clara asked, her voice little more than a whisper.

Drake shook his head. "It was better."

Slowly, he leaned toward her. Clara knew what was about to happen; though decades had passed since her first kiss, she could remember how she had felt, her heart pounding as butterflies fluttered in her stomach. She felt the same way now. Instinctively, she closed her eyes and waited for his lips to find hers.

But then, before they could touch, she stepped away. In that split second, something inside Clara changed.

I can't do this. I just can't . . .

Surprisingly, before Clara could begin to apologize,

Drake did. "I'm sorry," he said as he allowed her hand to slip from his. "That was too forward of me."

"It's not you..." she insisted. "It's...it's just..."

But words failed her. How could she begin to explain herself? It wasn't because of Tommy. It wasn't because her mother might have been watching or because she'd only just met Drake. It wasn't even because of Joe, or their marriage vows, or that only a couple of days before, she'd put flowers on his grave, mourning all she had lost. It was *each of these things* and more, a flash flood of emotions. It made no difference that she was attracted to Drake, that he was charming and funny, or that he was clearly interested in her.

She couldn't kiss him. She wouldn't.

Not here. Not now.

Not ever.

"I'm...I'm so sorry," Clara managed as tears filled her eyes. Sadness and ache rose inside her like a wave. In moments, she would be overwhelmed, racked by sobs; worst of all, she'd look as foolish as she felt.

So instead, she ran.

It was a blur; toward the house, stumbling up the stairs, and reaching for the door, all while Drake called her name.

Unlike that afternoon, when she couldn't take her eyes from the mirror, watching him, this time Clara didn't dare look back.

Chapter Ten

*T*HIS IS GONNA BE *one hell of a good day…*

Amos Barstow pulled a pack of cigarettes from his breast pocket, tapped one out, lit it, and took a deep drag, holding the smoke in his lungs until it burned before blowing it out. Early-morning sunlight streamed through a tangle of trees, dappling the ground and warming his skin. Most mornings, he imagined that he would have heard plenty of sounds: leaves rustling in the soft breeze; squirrels chittering as they dug up the nuts they'd buried last fall; water gurgling in a nearby stream.

But today he couldn't hear a thing over the loud, growling roar of a pair of car engines just itching to be let loose.

Drake sat behind the wheel of the Plymouth, his face impassive, his eyes fixed on the long stretch of dirt road in front of him. They were a couple of miles from town; to get there, they had gone past weathered barns, many with neglected fields and cars rusting away at the ends of long drives, before entering into thick woods. Ahead of the Plymouth, the road ran for a couple of miles before narrowing into a covered bridge that spanned a small creek.

"Your driver ready?"

Amos turned to see a man approaching; he looked as worn as a gnarled log, his age hard to determine, though it was unquestionably old, with wrinkled, unfashionable clothes and a cane that helped with a limp. Earlier that morning, in Sunset's only diner, they had struck up a conversation over scrambled eggs, one that had soon turned into a wager: first one across the bridge wins fifty dollars cash.

"As rain," Amos answered, nodding at Drake. "Yours?"

"My boy's itchin' to go," the man replied confidently, as if he already knew the outcome, almost as if he felt guilty about it.

If there's gonna be anyone cryin' when this is over, it sure as shit ain't gonna be me...

A brand-new Chrysler New Yorker hardtop idled beside the Plymouth. Though he tried not to show it, Amos was impressed. It was gray-blue in color, with sleek curves, shiny chrome, a one-piece curved windshield, and whitewall tires. As good as the car looked on the outside, he was all too aware of what was under the hood; its Hemi V8 engine had the highest horsepower output of any model around. Still, Amos wasn't the slightest bit worried. Even if someone had a fast car, they still needed a driver capable of making it go. When he peered into the Chrysler, Amos had to stifle a laugh; behind the wheel sat a boy the spitting image of his father, only younger and dirtier, a country bumpkin who, even if he was the best around these parts, was just the sort of punk Drake ran rings around. While Amos's driver might try to make it look competitive, a trait the mechanic hated, there was no way he would lose. It was easy money.

"Lotsa luck to ya, fella," the other man said before heading over for a few last words with his son.

Only one of us is gonna need it.

In his head, Amos was already counting his winnings. Within the hour, with another wad of cash split between them, he and Drake would finally drive out of this godforsaken town. Looking at the map that morning, Amos had already settled on Arrow Landing as their next destination, another backwater, forgettable place. No matter what it took, he needed to stay one step ahead of Sweet Woods; the alternative was too gruesome to consider. With a bit of luck, Amos would manage to keep himself and Drake safe; if he used his head, the drug-dealing thug would never get within fifty miles of them. If they could run long and far enough, somehow, someday, he would come up with a solution. So far, they'd been lucky.

Unfortunately, another problem loomed on the horizon.

Amos was almost out of morphine. The night before, he had been glad Drake wanted to go for a walk. No sooner had he stuck his head out the window to watch his friend saunter off down the sidewalk than he was digging in his coat pocket for his drugs. Seconds later, when the needle slid effortlessly into his vein, he was on his way to paradise; in fact, he'd barely had enough time to put away his paraphernalia before the morphine's haze descended. When next he woke up, Drake had come back and the sky outside the windows was pitch black.

Although Sweet was undoubtedly still out there, Amos remained one step ahead. Soon, he'd be on the road with money in his pocket and enough morphine to last a couple of days longer. The sun shone brighter by the minute. Amos smiled.

This is going to be one hell of a good day…

This is one of the worst days of my life…

Drake sat behind the wheel of the Plymouth, but his mind was far away. Absently, he pumped the car's accelerator, the engine rumbling beneath him, while his hands strangled the steering wheel. He hadn't even glanced over at the other car when it pulled up beside him; its driver kept echoing him, his own engine growling like a caged animal desperate to escape. But even though Drake knew he should be concentrating on the race, visualizing the road that stretched out in front of him, he couldn't.

All he could think about was Clara.

Once he'd finally made it back to the hotel, Drake had lain awake for hours, staring at the cracks in the ceiling, consumed by what had happened. Over and over, he had sifted through their time together as if it was a haystack and he was in search of a needle. But no matter how hard he looked, beginning with knocking on her door and ending with his clumsy attempt to kiss her, after considering everything that he might've done differently, he hadn't found any answers.

"How you feelin', champ?"

Drake jumped; he'd been so busy thinking about Clara that he hadn't heard Amos approach. The mechanic leaned against the Plymouth, one elbow sticking through the open window, smiling like a cat about to pounce on a canary.

"Good...I'm good..." Drake answered distractedly.

"That's what I wanna hear," Amos said enthusiastically. "One thing, though," he continued. "This road ain't the straight shot they want us to think it is. Up ahead, 'bout three-quarters of the way to the bridge, it curves a bit to the right. As I'm sure you noticed, they put you on the left."

Drake nodded, hearing little, his head still a mess.

Amos kept talking. "They think they got an advantage, so we're gonna let 'em go on believin' that. All you gotta do is make sure you're in the lead when the road slants. By then, that kid will be so far behind you that it won't matter one red cent which side you started on." Nodding at the other driver, he added, "Just look at that cocky son of a bitch."

The kid was young, probably half Drake's age. Acne marred the corner of his mouth. His hair was greased back in a style he'd probably copied out of a magazine or the movies. While Drake watched, his opponent glanced his way, nodded, and then gave a smile without an ounce of respect in it. Amos was right; the kid *was* cocky. Still, Drake didn't hold that against him. Years ago, back when he had started racing, he'd probably looked the same, in over his head but too stupid and stubborn to know better. The realization embarrassed him slightly.

"Dumb rube," Amos spat, shaking his head.

As if in answer, the other driver revved his engine.

"Don't pay him no mind," the mechanic continued. "He ain't worth the gas they filled that fancy car a his with. That jackass'll be chokin' on your dust 'fore he gets into third gear.

"But I want you to remember somethin'," Amos added, his tone changing, becoming more serious. "I don't want none a that garbage you pulled last time. You don't gotta make it look good. You whoop that boy, we get our money, chuckle while that country bumpkin wonders what the hell happened, then we leave this town."

Drake nodded absently.

That morning, after breakfast, Amos had laid out his plan. Once they won the race, they would head down the road.

And Drake would never see Clara Sinclair again...

Everything had been going so well, better than he could have hoped. Their conversation. Her laughter. The final moment of anticipation, sure that he was about to kiss her. But then, somehow, it had fallen apart. Now, the final image he would have of Clara was of her running from him, shutting him out. Once he left Sunset, Drake knew he would long wonder if had he done something different, gone after her, maybe they would have—

"You listenin' to me, Drake?"

He shook his head. "Yeah...yeah, I heard you," he managed.

"All right, then," Amos said, giving his driver a slap on the arm. "Next time you see me, I'll be countin' our money. This race is gonna be easier than takin' candy from a sleepin' baby!"

Unfortunately, Drake wasn't quite so sure...

Once both cars were at the starting line, the man with whom Amos had made the bet walked out twenty paces in front of them holding a striped handkerchief. He looked at each driver, waiting until he received an acknowledgment they were ready; Drake raised two fingers from the steering wheel. Both engines rumbled beneath their hoods. Finally, the man raised his makeshift flag high above his head, then plunged it toward the ground as fast as he could. The race had begun.

Drake pressed down on the accelerator and felt the Plymouth leap forward, but he was shocked to see that the other car had gotten off the line first; clearly, the Chrysler had plenty of horsepower. In a matter of seconds, both automobiles had rocketed past the older man, his handkerchief once again flying while he energetically whooped and hollered, cheering on his son, as they sped down the road. Behind them, the starting line had already disappeared in a thick, billowing cloud of dust.

It's going to take more than a fast start to beat me...

Calmly, Drake increased the Plymouth's speed. He had done it thousands of times before, one hand gripping the steering wheel tightly while the other rested on the stick, waiting for the precise instant when the engine roared, straining for more, before effortlessly shifting into a higher gear.

But today, something was wrong.

Drake tried to shift the car from second to third, but his usually steady hand faltered and the gears ground together; he had to force it where he wanted it to go. It hadn't taken long, a couple of seconds, but his opponent took advantage, increasing his lead to half a car length.

The road was rock and hard dirt, a track Drake usually favored. Fortunately, it'd been some time since it had rained, so there were no puddles to watch for or mud to deal with. Still, now that he was behind, he felt as if the trees had inched closer, their trunks whipping past just outside his window.

Drake cursed himself. This was all because he'd been distracted, thinking about Clara. In racing, even the smallest of errors could be the best driver's undoing. He tried to concentrate, to get back what he had lost, but even as he did so, the Chrysler widened its lead.

"Come on, damn it!" Drake shouted, urging himself on.

Suddenly, up ahead, he saw the curve in the road that Amos had warned him about, although it looked different than the mechanic had explained; it slid so dramatically to the right that, as Drake hurtled toward it on the left, he worried he would have to brake to keep from smashing headlong into the trees. Worse, he hadn't heeded Amos's advice; instead of being comfortably out in front, he was behind. Consequently, as he entered the curve, he took his foot off the gas and grabbed the wheel with both hands. The tires protested loudly while the trees whipped closely by, but somehow he managed to stay on the road. Once it straightened, he stomped back down on the accelerator; unfortunately, the kid had taken advantage of his better positioning, as well as Drake's caution, and had furthered his lead.

Drake bore down on the other car. So far, the other driver hadn't managed to get a full car length ahead; if he had, he could have drifted back and forth in front of the Plymouth, making it almost impossible for Drake to gain ground. Still, Drake had no margin of error; if he made one more mistake, the race would be over.

And so, slowly but steadily, Drake inched closer. Glancing up, he saw the other driver's reflection in the Chrysler's side mirror; the kid's skin was slicked with sweat, as if holding such a slim lead was making him nervous. With every passing second, Drake cut the distance between them.

As long as I don't run out of road, I'm going to catch him...

But unfortunately, that was exactly what was happening.

Up ahead, Drake saw the bridge. It was just as Amos had described it; narrow, with room for only one car to go through at a time. To win, Drake had to cross first. If there was ever a time for him to make his move, this was it.

But the Chrysler's driver knew it, too. Gunning the car's

powerful engine, the kid held his lead; the closest Drake managed to get was to draw his front wheels even with his opponent's side door. But Drake understood that the other driver wasn't going to back down; he would force them both to crash if it meant fending off his challenger. To avoid an accident, one of them had to give way.

"Aww, hell," Drake growled.

Jamming down on the brakes, he sent the Plymouth skidding sideways. Holding tight to the wheel, he let the car turn, eventually bringing it to a shuddering halt a hundred feet short of the bridge. Helplessly he watched the other car barrel across, the punk kid honking the Chrysler's horn in triumph.

Drake had lost.

"What in the hell happened?"

Drake drove them back toward town. Amos hadn't said a word since Drake had returned to the starting line, though even a blind man would've noticed how angry the mechanic was. The Chrysler's driver and his father had celebrated loudly as they counted their winnings; to Drake, it felt like having salt rubbed in an open wound.

"I got beat," Drake answered, hardly believing it himself.

"Don't give me that bullshit!" Amos barked. "That kid weren't nothin' and you know it! Didn't I tell you how the road curved, that he was on the inside, and that you needed to get out in front if you were gonna beat him 'cross that bridge? Was I talkin' to myself?"

Amos pounded his fist angrily against the Plymouth's dashboard, and then he cursed because it hurt more than he'd expected.

"I'm sorry," Drake offered, and meant it. "I was distracted."

"What kinda sorry excuse is that?" Amos asked disdainfully. "The only thing you shoulda been thinkin' 'bout was the money we stood to win. Now it's our pockets that're empty and those two rubes is crowin' like roosters!"

"I just . . . I've got a lot on my mind."

Amos opened his mouth as if he was going to keep on ranting, but he stumbled. "Wait, wait, wait," he finally said. "Hold on a second, now." His head turned slightly to the side, his eyes narrowing, staring hard at Drake. "Is this 'cause a that dame we helped yesterday? The one with the broken-down truck?"

Drake didn't answer. His eyes never left the road.

"Is that where you went last night?" Amos kept prying. "Is that where your walk took ya? Over to some lonely broad's place?"

"Watch it now," Drake answered, his temper rising.

The mechanic threw up his hands. "Aw, hell and high water!" he exclaimed. "If somethin' goes wrong under the hood, that's on me, but when my driver's tomcattin' 'round, there ain't a damn thing I can do 'bout it!"

Drake wanted to argue against his friend's claim but found he couldn't; the truth was that it was his fault they had lost, because he'd been thinking about Clara.

So instead, they rode on in silence.

Finally, Amos sighed. "What's the use in stayin' mad 'bout this?" he asked rhetorically. "It ain't like complainin' is gonna change anything. Let's just call it water under the bridge, get back to the hotel, grab our things, and skedaddle on down the road. That way, we can find another—"

"We're not leaving," Drake blurted, giving voice to something that had been building inside him ever since Clara had rejected his advances.

"What are you talkin' 'bout? This morning, we said—"

"*You* said," Drake interrupted, correcting him. "You're the one so hell-bent on getting out of here. What for? Why the hurry?"

Amos stared out his window. "I...I just don't see the point of stayin' in this little nothin' of a town for long," he answered. "Men like us, we gotta go where the action is, where we can make a bet, although now, what with losin', we ain't got enough money for another."

"I do," Drake answered matter-of-factly.

"What's that?" Amos asked, turning toward him.

"Don't worry about money. Even with what we lost today, I can cover us next time."

"You got that kind of cash on you?"

Drake nodded. He still had most of his savings in the bottom of his duffel bag. He'd never told Amos that he had the money, but desperate times called for fewer secrets. The truth was, he wanted another chance to see Clara; he didn't care what he had to give up to get it.

Amos nodded, taking it all in.

"Maybe losing today was for the best," Drake said.

The mechanic frowned. "How do you figure?"

"They already beat us once. We come back, this time betting higher stakes, they'll be confident, cocky. We win, we get back all we lost and then some."

The older man thought it over for a long while; to Drake's eyes, Amos didn't seem completely convinced. Surprisingly, in the end, he agreed.

"I still don't wanna stay here too long," Amos said. "But I suppose another couple days ain't gonna hurt. Maybe you're right. Maybe that dumb hick will give us 'nother race. And this time," he added with a grin, "you'll be the winner."

But Drake wasn't thinking about a rematch.

He was thinking only about Clara.

Last night, he'd made a mistake, pushed things between them too far, too fast, and he had been unable to think of much else since. Drake wanted to know her, to understand her better, but until this moment, he had thought he would never get the opportunity. Now, fate had seen fit to grant him another chance.

He was determined to use it.

Chapter Eleven

I THINK YOU SHORTED me one of my relatives."

Clara looked down at the coins spread out before her, then up at Ben Franklin. The pig farmer grinned broadly, his ample belly pressed up tight against her teller window, his clothes smelling particularly foul. Slowly, it dawned on her that he was right; not only did she have no idea what number she was at, she couldn't even remember what amount she was trying to reach.

"I'm sorry," she apologized, feeling more than a little embarrassed. "I'm afraid I lost count... What were we..."

"That's all right, darlin'. I come in to cash that check," Ben explained, pointing a meaty finger at the slip of paper next to Clara's elbow. "Pete Dixon paid me twenty-eight dollars and ninety-nine cents for a couple of piglets—stubborn old goat wouldn't part with that extra penny—and I was plannin' to turn it into fifty-seven of my namesake and a handful of those other fellas."

"That's right," Clara answered. Everything was laid out like it should've been, with stacks of shiny silver half-dollars arranged like soldiers. Regardless, she scooped up the coins and started over.

It had been that way all morning, one small mistake after another. No matter how hard she tried to pay attention, Clara couldn't think about anything other than her evening with Drake McCoy. All night and into the next day, she had replayed it in her mind: her surprise at finding him at her door, their conversation as they walked beneath the stars, the comfortable way she felt in his presence, how he'd made her laugh. But she particularly remembered that moment, standing in front of her house, when he was about to kiss her...

But that was when it had gone sour.

Now she would never see him again. He had come into her life by chance, had helped her in her time of need and then surprised her by lingering longer than expected; he was like a match burning brightly before being blown out, the smoke he left behind slowly drifting away.

But Clara couldn't stop thinking about him. She wondered what direction Drake and his mechanic friend had gone when they'd left Sunset, what sights he'd seen, and if he was thinking about her as much as she was about him.

"...fifty-five, fifty-six, and one more makes fifty-seven," she said, finishing with the right amount.

"On the button," Ben replied before he began scooping up the silver coins and shoving them into the pockets of his overalls.

Clara was just about to start counting the remaining coins when the pig farmer slapped one onto the counter. It was a shiny penny; she often wondered how a man so filthy had coins so clean.

"Why don't we just make it fifty-eight," he said with a chuckle. "I expect that will be easier on the both of us."

Ben was halfway to the door, the two of them having said their good-byes, when he stopped and turned back. "You want some advice?" he asked.

She nodded. "Sure."

"A long time ago, back when I was a boy, I learned that when somethin' was weighin' on my mind, gnawin' like a hungry dog with a soup bone, it didn't do no good to ignore it. I needed to get the better of my problems 'fore they bested me." He paused. "Whatever's on your mind, makin' your head all fuzzy, grab it by the back of the neck and wrestle it to the ground."

"That sounds like good advice," Clara answered.

"Well, it works pretty well with pigs too stupid and stubborn to get outta their pens," the farmer said with a loud chuckle.

Clara knew that Ben meant well, but hers was a problem that she could no longer confront. It was too late for that.

Drake was already gone.

Last night, even as she'd hurried away from him, Clara could already feel his absence. But no sooner had the door shut behind her, leaving Drake out on the sidewalk, than her mother had begun to barrage her with questions, one coming after the other so fast that she had trouble keeping them straight.

"Who was that man?"

"Where did the two of you go at such a late hour?"

"It looked like he was going to kiss you. *Was* he going to?"

"So why didn't you do it?"

That last question had thrown Clara for a loop, largely because she had no answer. Earlier that night, her mother had asked why she never went on any dates. Minutes later, a man had come calling, someone whose company she enjoyed, but also a man she'd ultimately rejected.

"His name is Drake," she explained. "Drake McCoy. This afternoon the truck broke down on my way back to the bank and he helped me get it running. He came by tonight to see if I'd had any more trouble," she added, using the first, not-quite-correct reason Drake had given.

"He's handsome, don't you think?" Before her daughter could answer, Christine went over to the window and peeled back the curtain.

"Don't do that!" she hissed.

"Whyever not? I've been doing it since you left."

"Please, Mom," Clara nearly begged. On the one hand, she hoped that Drake might still be outside, watching, waiting in case she reappeared, but on the other, she hated the thought of leaving him in such a state.

"Oh, all right," Christine answered, letting the curtain fall back into place. "Though you're ruining all my fun."

Clara sighed. She felt like a teenager again. When she and Joe started dating, her mother had done the same things, peppering them with questions before they left, pacing for hours, then pouncing on her daughter as soon as she got home, trying to wrangle every last detail of their night out.

"So what does Jake do for a living?" her mother asked.

"Drake," Clara corrected. "He races cars."

Christine's eyebrows raised. "That sounds more exciting than selling encyclopedias door-to-door. More dangerous, too. Why is he in Sunset?"

"He's just passing through. Another man was with him, an older fellow, the mechanic for his car. They're leaving in the morning."

"Was the older one as handsome?" her mother asked with a mischievous glint in her eyes.

Clara laughed. "I'm afraid not."

"That's too bad, for me, at least. But you seem to have hit the jackpot. It's not every day that a man knocks on your door."

Her mother was right. Someone like Drake, charming, interesting, and handsome, didn't come along often. Still, she'd turned him away. Clara thought about all the things that weighed her down, yet she wondered if she hadn't made a terrible mistake. By rejecting his kiss, had she turned her back on happiness?

"I'm going to get some sleep," Clara said, her thoughts churning. "Can you shut the house up?"

"Of course," her mother answered.

Clara was on the second step of the staircase when her mother called to her. "He was going to kiss you, wasn't he?"

She turned but didn't speak, still thinking about that lost moment...

"Why didn't you let him?"

Clara considered it. "I don't know," she answered softly.

Christine nodded. "Someday, I hope you find the answer."

So do I...

Clara watched the clock's hand slowly spin, second by agonizing second, crawling toward four o'clock. Most afternoons, the Sunset Bank and Trust saw a flurry of activity around closing time, people needing money or wanting to make one last transaction, but it had been almost an hour since the last customer walked through the door.

With so much idle time on her hands, Clara found it almost impossible not to think about Drake. She tried everything: she hummed a song, read the newspaper, and even counted the money in her drawer again and again, but nothing worked. She looked forward to going home, having a nice meal, hopefully with Tommy sitting at the table, all while trying to quiet her turbulent thoughts.

Three more minutes...

But then Eddie came out of his office and started walking straight for her teller window.

Clara's stomach sank. Ever since he'd called her into his office and professed his feelings for her, she'd been afraid of what would happen next. Every time she saw Eddie, his words were there, echoing in the back of her mind. Someday soon, he was going to repeat them and she was going to be forced to make a decision: her happiness or the well-being of those she loved.

Is this when I have to choose?

"Jane Russell," Eddie said once he'd reached her window.

"Excuse me?" Clara replied.

Pointing at her outfit, he answered, "Wasn't that the same dress Jane Russell wore in *Gentlemen Prefer Blondes*?"

"I...I haven't seen it..."

"The spitting image," Eddie declared. He leaned forward, giving Clara a whiff of his aftershave, a smell she found more repulsive than Ben Franklin's manure-covered overalls. With a wink, he added, "I think you wear it better."

Clara tried not to frown. After Eddie's outburst in his office, it was hard to take his lame attempt at a compliment lightly.

To do so risked everything.

"Thank you," she mumbled, unable to look him in the eyes.

More than ever, Clara was aware of how much Eddie repulsed her. The grating, whiny sound of his voice. The disgusting ring of sweat at the collar of his shirt. His smell. How he licked his dry lips.

But even with all that, he held her future in his hands.

"Do you have plans for tonight?" Eddie asked.

"I . . . I'm having dinner with my family."

"So nothing you couldn't miss."

After a moment, Clara slowly nodded. She knew *exactly* what he was implying; he wanted her to be with him. She felt ill.

Smiling his goofy grin, Eddie turned and loudly clapped his hands. "All right, everyone!" he nearly shouted. "Time to close up shop for the day."

Besides Clara and Eddie, there were two other people still in the bank. David Bookings had been half dozing at his desk, while Shirley Hoskins, whose teller window was next to Clara's, was inside the vault, locking away drawers and counting rolls of coins. When they heard Eddie's voice, they began to gather their things, just as they did every day at four o'clock.

Clara desperately wanted to go with them. The thought of staying behind with Eddie, of being alone with him, unnerved her. But there would be consequences if she rejected him so brazenly, so she didn't move.

Eddie held the door open, sharing a few meaningless words with Shirley and David, smiling all the while. As she stepped outside, Shirley noticed Clara's absence.

"Aren't you coming?" she called out.

But before Clara could answer, Eddie spoke. "She'll be staying awhile longer," he explained, shutting the door in the other woman's face.

When he turned his key in the lock, the loud click echoed through the bank; to Clara, it sounded like a prison cell's door being shut.

*　*　*

Drake leaned against the Plymouth's side panel, his feet crossed at the ankles and his arms folded across his chest, while the late afternoon sun warmed him. People occasionally walked past, some giving him a curious glance, but he paid them no mind. His eyes never left the Sunset Bank and Trust.

After he and Amos had returned to town, they'd checked back into the hotel, getting the same room as the night before. Amos had flopped onto his bed, still grumbling about losing the race and having to spend more time in Sunset. He went on and on, being a royal pain in the ass.

Drake did his best to ignore him.

All he wanted was to see Clara again.

Standing at the window, looking down at the street, he considered what he should do. His first thought was to wait until evening and then go back to Clara's house, but with every passing minute, he grew more impatient. Without another word to Amos, he went down to the lobby and struck up a conversation with the woman working behind the front desk. Casually, he mentioned Clara's name.

"Ain't she just the best?" the woman exclaimed. "Every time I go to the bank, she's as friendly as can be."

And just like that, he knew where to find her.

But now, standing outside the bank, Drake wasn't quite so sure of himself. After what had happened the night before, he wondered what he was going to say to her. While he hoped Clara would be surprised, even happy to see him, he didn't know with any certainty. Absently, he chewed at a fingernail. He considered entering the bank, then thought better of it; he didn't want to put her in an awkward spot. So instead, he waited outside, trying to remain patient, biding his time until the bank closed.

Finally, the clock above the movie theater chimed four times. Drake stood up, watching as the bank's door opened. Two people left, a man struggling to stifle a yawn, and then a woman. But no Clara.

Drake frowned. He wondered if there had been a mistake. Was there a second bank in town? Had Clara taken the day off?

He decided to find out.

The man had walked in the opposite direction, but the woman was headed right toward him. He stepped in front of her.

"Excuse me, ma'am," Drake said with a pleasant smile. "I'm sorry to bother you, but I'm looking for Clara Sinclair."

Immediately, the woman looked back over her shoulder. "She's still at the bank," she said, her expression showing a measure of concern.

"Is everything all right?" he asked.

"I . . . I think so," she answered. "It's just a little unusual, that's all. Usually we leave together, but . . ."

"Thanks for the help," Drake offered, then headed straight for the bank.

*   *   *

"I could hardly wait to lock that door."

And I can hardly wait to be as far away from you as possible.

But Clara didn't say that. She didn't dare. She'd come out from behind her teller window, drawn to the open door, wanting nothing more than to go home like everyone else. So when Eddie locked it, despair grabbed hold of her, squeezing tighter by the second.

"It's funny, don't you think?"

"What is?" Clara asked, confused by his words, as usual.

"The two of us. Alone. Here of all places," Eddie exclaimed, throwing his arms wide to indicate the otherwise empty bank, "right where my late father ordered me to stay away from you." He gave a short, humorless laugh. "Like most everything Theodore believed, he was wrong about us, too."

"Eddie, I think we should—"

But Clara's words fell on deaf ears; the banker was lost in thought, rambling out loud. "Everyone in this town thought my father was a saint," he grumbled. "But that couldn't be further from the truth. He was an overbearing tyrant who didn't want his own son to share in his success!"

Listening to Eddie rant as he grew more and more agitated, Clara took a small, scarcely noticeable step toward the door. Outside, the sun was slowly descending, though darkness was still hours away. She silently prayed that someone might walk past, notice them, understand the situation, and offer her a chance at salvation. Because if he took her to his office, far from prying eyes . . .

Eddie had started to pace back and forth, still carrying on. "I've often imagined how different things would be with my own son, how I would respect and encourage him at every turn instead of tearing him down!"

Abruptly, Eddie stopped, turned, and rushed over to Clara, grabbing her by the arms. "You want to have more children, don't you?" he blurted, squeezing her hard enough to make her wince in pain.

Clara was too shocked to answer.

"Don't worry," Eddie added. "I promise that I'll treat Tommy as if he was my very own! With a bassinet full of babies, we'll make one big, happy family!" With every word he squeezed tighter, until Clara cried out in agony, shrugging her shoulders to escape his grip. That seemed to break the spell Eddie was under; he blinked rapidly, as if coming out of a trance. Sweat beaded his brow.

"I'm . . . I'm sorry, Clara," he offered. Tentatively, he again reached out to touch her, his fingers brushing against her cheek; she trembled in response, realizing that there was no contact with Eddie that wouldn't repulse her. "Thinking about our future excites me so."

Clara fought back tears, fearful that Eddie would mistake them for romantic inclination; he did, smiling at the sight of them.

"Why don't we go to my office?" he asked. "We can have a drink, relax. There's plenty for us to talk about."

Once again, he grabbed her, holding her wrist; his grip wasn't as strong as before, but it was hard enough to make it clear she had little choice in the matter.

Clara didn't know what to do.

Should she scream?

Should she fight, clawing and scratching to get away?

Or should she give in and stop risking what little her family had left?

Suddenly, there was a loud knock on the bank's door.

Startled, both Clara and Eddie jumped at the sound. Clara's eyes grew wide in amazement and disbelief. There, peering through the glass, his fist poised to strike the door again, was Drake McCoy.

How...how could it be...?

"We're closed," Eddie said in a loud voice.

But Drake didn't move. His eyes remained locked on Clara. Once again, he pounded the door, the sound sharp and loud.

"Come back tomorrow!" the banker shouted.

In answer, Drake hit the glass, harder than before. With his other hand, he pulled at the door, rattling it in its frame.

Realizing that the stranger wasn't going to leave, Eddie let go of Clara's wrist and went to the door. Fumbling with the key, he finally managed to yank it open. Clara assumed that the banker would act all important, but Drake never gave him the chance; he pushed his way inside, barging past Eddie and walking straight toward her.

"Wh-what do you think you're doing?" Eddie demanded.

But Drake still wasn't listening. When he reached Clara, he took her by the hands; this time, she welcomed being touched.

"Are you all right?" he asked.

She nodded, a tear sliding down her cheek. "I am now."

"Let's get out of here," Drake said.

Hand in hand, they headed for the door. For a moment, Eddie looked as if he intended to step in front of them, to keep Clara from leaving, but then he appeared to notice how much bigger Drake was and decided to back down. Unfortunately, his mouth kept protesting.

"Clara? Clara, where do you think you're going?" he asked.

"Away from here," Drake snarled, making the banker take a quick step back.

Without another word, they were out the door.

Drake had saved her.

Chapter Twelve

WHAT WAS ALL that about?"

Clara walked beside Drake as they made their way from the bank. Her heart raced. She couldn't believe what had just happened, that she was no longer with Eddie, trapped behind a locked door. For an instant, she wondered what the consequences might be, worrying that she could even be fired, but Clara quickly put that out of her mind. All that mattered was that she was safe.

"It was nothing," she fibbed.

"That didn't look like nothing to me."

"What are you doing here?" Clara said, desperate to change the topic. "I thought you were leaving town."

"I was supposed to," Drake admitted. "But things changed a bit unexpectedly. I can't say for certain how much longer I'll be here, likely no more than another day or two, but as soon as I knew I was staying, I came looking for you. All day, you were all I could think about."

He looked at her intently, his eyes searching for her re-action.

"I know what you mean," she said. "I feel the same way..."

Drake stopped walking; when Clara did the same, he stepped closer. Out on Sunset's streets, she knew people would be watching, wondering who this stranger was and what she was doing with him, but she didn't care. Right now, nothing else mattered but what he had to say.

"Ever since you ran away, all I've wanted to do was apologize," Drake explained. "I was having such a good time with you that I let myself get carried away. By being so forward, I put you in a tough spot. It was all my fault."

Clara shook her head. "You don't have anything to apologize for."

"I'm sorry all the same."

They stood in silence for a while. Slowly, a smile spread across Drake's face.

"I have an idea," he said.

"What is it?"

His expression grew mischievous. "Do you trust me?"

After everything that he'd done for her, from helping her fix her truck, to coming to her aid with Eddie, and even to trying to take the responsibility for what had happened the night before, she knew that she did.

Clara nodded.

"Then let me make it up to you." Drake pointed farther down the street to a car parked against the curb. It was black, sleek, and powerful-looking, even though it was coated with dust. "Let me take you for a ride," he said. "You can show me around Sunset, and we can talk. What do you say?"

She looked from him to the car and then back again. His eyes searched her face; she could see how badly he wanted her to agree. Slowly, like a door opening on rusty hinges, Clara decided to take a chance. She thought of her mother's words the night before, about how she might as well reach for happiness, even when it came from somewhere completely unexpected.

"Are you planning on driving really fast?" Clara asked.

Drake grinned. "Only if you want me to."

And so she agreed.

Drake followed Clara's directions and drove down Main Street. Businesses soon gave way to rows of houses, but within minutes those too began to dwindle. The Plymouth bumped over railroad tracks, then sped away from Sunset and into the countryside. There, things moved at a different pace than in town, slower yet pleasant. The growl of the car's engine echoed off the thick trunks and broad boughs of the trees lining the road. A flock of birds, startled by their passing, furiously flapped their wings as they rose into the light of the setting sun; Clara had to shield her eyes to watch their flight. Drake honked at a farmer out in his field preparing that season's crops; the man waved from his tractor.

"That's a hard life," Drake said, nodding at the man and his farm. "At least it was back when I was the one living it."

"Do you ever miss it?"

"Not once since the day I left."

The wind teased at Clara's hair, forcing her to keep pulling it from her face, but she had no desire to roll up her window. The air was crisp and full of the smells of spring, from the sweet aroma of the wildflowers that filled the ditches to the pungent stink of manure. Above the whistling wind, she could hear the radio, the faint voice of a woman singing about heartbreak.

They drove over rickety bridges, around sharp corners, and up and down hills; on one steep incline, Drake worked the gears so smoothly that Clara could hardly feel them shift.

"You do that well," she observed, nodding at his hand.

"Lots of practice," he replied. "I've spent so much time behind the wheel of a car, I reckon I could do this in my sleep. Heck, most nights I probably do, pressing down on the clutch with my foot, one hand turning the steering wheel while the other works the shift, all of it under the covers."

His joke made them fill the car with laughter.

Clara couldn't help but notice how at ease Drake made her feel. Listening to him talk, no matter whether he was making fun of himself, offering her his heartfelt apologies, or even snarling protectively the way he had at Eddie, she found herself captivated. She wanted to know everything about him.

But if Clara was being honest with herself, it didn't hurt that she found him so handsome. Bouncing in the passenger's seat, she watched as sunlight streamed through the windshield and lit up his face. She noticed the small lines around his mouth and eyes, made all the more pronounced because he was squinting into the setting sun, and understood that Drake was getting older. But then again, so was she . . .

"What is it?" Drake asked; he had caught her looking at him.

"Nothing," she answered, looking away. Clara knew she was blushing; all she could hope was that with the sun in his eyes, he didn't notice.

Eventually, Clara directed him around a short bend, up a small rise, and then to stop next to a withered old tree, its empty branches so broad they spread out and over the road. Drake did as she asked, looked all around them, narrowed his eyes in curiosity, and then said, "So what now?"

She pointed out the window. The road stretched before them. From where they sat with the Plymouth's engine idling rhythmically, it slowly descended, running between fields of wild grass, looking endless. Far ahead, several miles at least, it curved out of sight.

"I want to know what it's like to ride in a race car," she said.

Drake turned to look at her, one forearm draped over the steering wheel, the other rising to lay across the top of their seat; his fingertips brushed against Clara's shoulder; the slight touch made her skin tingle.

"I thought you were joking," he said.

"What you do for a living sounds exciting to me."

"It's also dangerous."

"Then I suppose it's a good thing for me that you'll be doing the driving," Clara responded with a sly smile.

"All right," Drake said, grabbing the stick shift and putting the Plymouth into gear. "Just remember, you asked for this."

From the instant Drake pressed down on the gas pedal, Clara's excitement rose as steadily as their speed. In a matter of seconds, the Plymouth was rushing down the hill, gravel crunching loudly beneath its tires. Deftly, Drake shifted from first to second gear, the engine growing louder as its pistons pounded, its belts turned, and its fuel burned. Outside her open window, the countryside started to race by, the purples, yellows, and reds of the wildflowers spotting the ditches beginning to blur together.

"You sure you want to do this?" Drake asked with a grin.

Clara nodded, her heart pounding.

Before she knew it, they had moved all the way to fourth gear. Clara gasped as the Plymouth began to shudder. One hand dug into the seat beside her leg, while the other gripped the door frame; she squeezed them both so hard that her knuckles turned white.

By now, they had reached the bottom of the hill and were moving faster than Clara had ever gone in all her life. The wind whipped violently through their windows, causing her hair to fly in every direction; it was so strong that it even tugged at her clothing. She looked behind them and saw that they were kicking up an enormous cloud of dust. It was so exciting that she grinned from ear to ear.

The Plymouth hurtled forward, its engine roaring. Drake's hands held the steering wheel tight; thick cords of muscle stood out on his forearms. Clara was amazed at how effortlessly he kept the car steady, mastering the terrific speed at which they moved. She wondered what it was like for him to race other cars, against other drivers willing to drive just as dangerously as he did now. As she watched him, he glanced over at her.

"Are you having fun yet?" He shouted in order to be heard.

She nodded, her eyes a bit wide, the sight of which made him laugh.

Suddenly, Clara felt as if all her troubles had fallen away. Feeling bold, she leaned out the window; the full force of the wind struck her face and sent her hair sailing out behind her. Clara closed her eyes and felt the warmth of the setting sun on her skin. Somehow, even though the Plymouth was speeding forward, everything in motion, it felt as if this moment would forever be frozen in time, like a picture to be framed and cherished. Drake had already done so much for her, but this was yet another gift, a memory she knew she would never forget.

And so, even as Drake took his foot off the gas, the car imperceptibly beginning to slow as the sharp curve approached ahead, Clara tipped back her head and began to shout with joy as loudly as she could.

"I don't know when I last saw something so beautiful."

Clara nodded in agreement.

Once they had finished racing down the long stretch of road, Clara's pulse still beating fast, she had directed Drake back the way they had come; they drove down dirt roads, crossed bridges, passed through thick woods, and climbed up into the hills southeast of Sunset. Finally, with the sun still a good hour from the horizon, they entered a clearing that looked over the town, the river, and miles of country-side.

They got out of the car, climbed the front bumper, and sat on the Plymouth's warm hood. For ten minutes, nei-ther of them had said a word; instead they watched as a gentle breeze stirred the tall grass all around them. Bril-liant sunlight reflected off the slowly moving river. A boat chugged against the current, dark smoke puffing from its stack. A flock of geese winged their way north, passing close enough for their honking to reach Clara and Drake. It was as if they were looking at a work of art, priceless be-cause it was so very real.

"I don't know what could be better than this," Drake said.

"You should see it in the fall. When the leaves change color and the sun is on the water, everything as far as you can see is bright orange and gold."

"Is this how the town got its name?"

Clara shook her head. "I'm not sure. My husband used to say that..." she started, but then stopped.

This was the second time she had mentioned Joe to Drake, and it felt uncomfortable, even a little unfair. After everything he'd done for her, she was certain that the last thing Drake wanted was to hear about a man who had been dead for more than nine years.

But then Drake surprised her. "What was his name?" he asked.

Clara's heart again started to pound, although this time it wasn't because of excitement. "Joe," she answered softly.

"What was he like?"

She turned to face him; just like before in the Plymouth, the bright sun illuminated his face, which did nothing to slow her pulse. She offered him a faint smile. "You don't want to know any of that."

"Sure I do," Drake answered. He stared back at her, his dark eyes unwavering, his expression compassionate yet strong. "It's clear that he meant a lot to you, that he still does. If I'm going to get to know you better, then I want to hear all about him." He paused. "Please. Tell me."

And so, a bit reluctantly, Clara took a deep breath and began to speak of her life with Joe Sinclair. She told him how they'd met, how their first date had been at the movies, to see a comedy whose name she could never re-member, and about how she had known, even then, that he was special. Soon, she'd warmed up and the mem-ories came quickly: their wedding; building their home; Tommy's birth; and even the day, just after the Japanese had bombed Pearl Harbor, when Joe had enlisted in the army. She found herself talking about things she hadn't for a very long time, not even to her mother. When she told him a funny story, Drake laughed right along with her.

"Sounds like your husband was a great guy," Drake said,

his words completely genuine. "It's easy to see why you miss him."

Clara felt tears well up in her eyes, but she didn't want to cry, not here, not now. "How about you?" she asked. "Has there ever been someone special in your life?"

Drake chuckled, but it sounded forced. "Not anyone that mattered, and certainly not like what you had with Joe."

"Surely there was somebody..."

"When I was younger, sure, there were a few women who were with me for a while, but the life of a race car driver, going from town to town, never really knowing where you'll be from one day to the next, it's not a life worth sharing. Traveling with Amos is one thing," he explained with a smile, "but there aren't many ladies who are keen on bouncing around in the backseat while speeding down roads you can't find on any map."

Drake paused, his eyes staring far away. "Can I confess something to you?" he asked. "A thought that's been on my mind lately?"

"You can tell me anything," Clara replied.

He smiled, clearly pleased by her answer. "I don't know how much longer I want to do this," he explained. "Nowadays, it seems like whenever I run a race, I look over and the other driver is some pimply-faced kid who was probably in diapers the first time I got behind the wheel. Hell, it happened just this morning."

Clara's eyes widened. "You had a race today?"

He nodded.

"Did you win?"

Drake chuckled loudly. "Nope," he said. "Amos thought it'd be easy, but it sure didn't work out that way. Not by a mile."

"Why not? Your car seems awfully fast to me."

"Speed is a part of racing, but a car is only as good as the man driving it, and today I wasn't worth squat. I reckon I had too much on my mind."

He means me...and what happened between us last night...

Clara's mind raced to grasp all the implications of what Drake had just said. Her heart pounded and her skin flushed, making her somehow feel both flattered and embarrassed at the same time. There was a small part of her that wanted to press him about it, to know that she wasn't mistaken, that he'd been so lost in thought about *her* that he'd lost his race, but she just couldn't. Not yet...

"If you didn't race anymore, what would you do?" she asked instead.

"I always figured I'd open a garage. I might not be as good at fixing engines and the like as Amos, but I can more than hold my own. What with all the new models coming out—Fords, DeSotos, Studebakers—and folks buying them like they're going out of style, I figure there will always be a demand for a guy who doesn't mind getting his hands dirty." Drake paused. "Actually, that reminds me. I have a favor to ask."

"What is it?"

"I wanted to know if I could use your garage to work on

the Plymouth," he explained. "After every race, it pays to make sure that everything's running properly. I'd do it out in front of the hotel, but I don't think it'd go over well."

Clara nodded. "After everything you've done for me, how could I say no? Though I should warn you, the garage door is broken. I've asked Tommy to fix it, but he—well, he has other things on his mind these days."

"I'll take care of it," Drake said. "I won't need it for long. A couple of hours, maybe less."

"You don't have to hurry," she told him. She paused, then added, "You can stay as long as you'd like."

Silence stretched between them. Clara went back and forth between being angry at herself for being so forward and the next second wanting to say more; unable to choose, she did neither. It was uncomfortable, this dance between them; she was woefully out of practice. Down on the river, where the sun was starting to melt into the trees on the far bank, the boat blew its horn; the sound rolled across the water and up the hill. It was then that Drake unexpectedly slid off the Plymouth's hood to stand right in front of her. He placed a hand beside her and leaned forward slightly, staring into her eyes as she unflinchingly looked back.

"Last night," he began, "I moved too fast. I assumed things that I shouldn't have and ended up putting you in an uncomfortable spot."

"Drake, I told you that—" Clara began, but he cut her off.

"Listen to me," he said. "The reason I'm telling you this

is so that before I come closer, before I kiss you, there won't be any surprises."

"All right..." she murmured, suddenly breathless.

"This way, if you didn't want me to do it, you could stop me before I made a fool out of myself."

Clara's heart raced; she wondered if even the Plymouth's engine worked as hard. Drake's boldness was shocking yet refreshing. She was amazed at how easily he could tell her what he wanted without seeming embarrassed. She wondered how she should reply and then, like a bolt of lightning, she knew that the answer was as brazen as the man standing before her.

So Clara didn't move, didn't say a word, and she most definitely didn't try to dissuade Drake from what he intended to do. In the end, she knew without a shadow of a doubt that she wanted the exact same thing, wanted it so badly that it surprised her.

A thin smile spread across Drake's face. His hand found hers as he leaned closer, pausing for only a moment, surely wondering if she was going to once again change her mind. But when she didn't, he committed to kissing her. He tenderly placed his lips against hers. At first, their touch was tentative and their eyes remained open, watching each other as if neither of them could believe what was happening. But it didn't take long for Clara to give in to her feelings. It had been almost ten years since she'd last kissed a man, since well before Joe's death. She closed her eyes, wondering how she'd found herself here, with this man, but she was happy about it all the same. She didn't think about her mother's memory loss, her son's problems, their financial difficulties, or Eddie's unwanted advances. She didn't even think about her deceased husband, up till then the last man she had touched.

All she could think about was Drake McCoy, the way he kissed her, and all the wonderful ways he made her feel.

Chapter Thirteen

I CAN'T BELIEVE the nerve of that old goat! Why, it took all the restraint I had to keep from knockin' that grin off his damn face!"

Drake fought back a grin of his own. Amos paced quickly across their small hotel room, his eyes narrow and angry as his hands waved wildly, punctuating the air after every word he spat. Just minutes earlier, he'd whipped open the door and begun ranting, complaining that his efforts to convince the old man and his son to give them a rematch had met with unexpected resistance.

"So there I go, walkin' into that dump of a diner, swallowin' my pride, and headin' over to where he's sittin'. 'Fore I know it, he's offerin' to buy me breakfast," Amos said with a sneer. "Like I'm some charity case! Like he took the last dime I owned when that hillbilly son of his crossed the bridge first!"

"But he pretty much did, didn't he?" Drake asked, unable to resist the urge to give his friend a little ribbing.

"He don't know that!" Amos barked. "So I wave him off, take a seat, order a cup a coffee, and start layin' it all out. I done just like we agreed. I complimented his boy's drivin', the car, everythin' I could think of. He's just soakin' it all in, noddin' like a sunflower in a stiff breeze, but then when I suggest we do it again, that we raise the stakes a bit, suddenly he ain't so sure. He's hemmin' and hawin', makin' one excuse after another. I walked outta there madder than a hornet. Dumb, stubborn bastard!"

There was a part of Drake that understood the mechanic's frustration. Deep down, he was angry that he had allowed himself to be distracted enough to lose the race. He wanted another chance to win. But there was also a part of him that was thrilled by the other man's reluctance to give them an opportunity to win back their money. If he was dragging things out, it meant more time that he could spend with Clara.

"We should just give up and hit the road," Amos argued.

Drake shook his head. "Not yet. Be patient. He's just making you sweat it a little. He'll eventually come around. Tempt him with a high enough wager, he won't be able to turn it down forever."

The mechanic frowned. "You got the money to stake on it?"

"I told you not to worry. It'll be taken care of."

Drake grabbed the Plymouth's keys and headed for the door. "You sure you don't want to come along?" he asked; last night, he had told Amos about Clara's agreeing to let them use her garage.

"Naw," he answered. "As riled up as I am, I'm likely to do more harm than good. I'm just gonna stay here and wear a hole in the floor. Who knows, maybe I'll calm down enough to have another go at that old fart . . ."

"Don't get too worked up. Your ticker might not be able to take it."

When Drake shut the door behind him, Amos was already back to complaining.

Drake drove toward Clara's house. He had hitched up the small trailer that held his tools; it bounced along behind. Above, clouds blotted out the sun, growing darker to the north, threatening rain. But even with a gloomier day, he found himself smiling at familiar sights, as if the small town was growing on him.

His only regret was that he wouldn't see Clara. Last night, when he'd dropped her off, she had explained that she would have to return to the bank in the morning. Drake had frowned. He remembered the strange scene he had stumbled across: the pudgy man in his poorly fitting suit, how relieved Clara had been to see him, the fact that the banker had continued to protest about her leaving all the way up until Drake had snarled threateningly, and the way Clara avoided his questions about what had happened after they left. Last night, he had pressed her for more details, but she insisted that nothing was wrong and he'd let the matter drop.

Instead, he dwelled on their kiss...

From the moment he had watched Clara stick her head out the Plymouth's window as they sped along and shout with joy, Drake had known that he would again try to hold her in his arms, to place his lips against hers. Still, he wasn't about to make the same mistake twice. Asking for her permission had been necessary. Fortunately, Clara hadn't objected and so they'd kissed.

And what a kiss it had been!

Even if he'd been dreaming about it ever since he'd met her, their kiss had still been greater than his wildest expectations. The warmth of her skin. The smell of her hair. The taste of her lips. The way her hand squeezed his arm. How he'd held her in his arms as they watched the sun disappear out of sight. All of it had left Drake lying awake in his bed far into the night, wondering if he'd ever truly known happiness before Clara.

Drake turned down Clara's street and pulled into her driveway. No sooner had he shut off the Plymouth's engine and gotten out than the side door of the house opened and a woman came outside. She was older, her hair a silvery white with only a few darker streaks, but there was something about her that was immediately familiar to him; the soft curve of her mouth and the shape of her eyes. A damp apron was tied around her waist and she held a knife in one hand.

"Who are you?" she asked, her expression a potent mix

of confusion and anger. "What do you think you're doing parking here?"

Clara had warned him about the sort of reception he might receive from her mother. Delicately, and without much detail, she'd told him that Christine's memory wasn't what it used to be, and that even if she explained that he would be coming over, her mother might not remember it by the time he arrived. Clearly, her worries had been well-founded.

"Good afternoon, ma'am," he said, putting on his friendliest smile, glancing at the knife. "My name is Drake McCoy. I'm an acquaintance of Clara, your daughter. She might have mentioned me..."

Faster than he could have snapped his fingers, Christine's expression changed. "Oh, that's right!" she exclaimed, a hand rising to her cheek; Drake was relieved that it wasn't the one holding the knife. "Clara told me all about it, but I plumb forgot. I'm terribly sorry."

"There's no need to be. I'm the one intruding." He motioned toward the Plymouth. "I hope I won't be putting you out any."

"Not at all. Quite frankly, it'll be nice to have someone else around. Most days I'm the only one here."

"I shouldn't be long. A couple of hours at the most."

"Take your time." Suddenly, Christine frowned. "I suppose you'd like to use the garage."

"I would," Drake replied.

Christine pointed toward the rear of the drive. Drake's gaze followed and he saw a building in dire need of repair.

Its white paint was chipped and weathered, and there was a broken pane of glass in the side door. Worst of all, the two swinging doors of the main entrance had come loose from their hinges, awkwardly tipping inward like a pair of warped teeth.

"I'm afraid it isn't in the best of shape," Clara's mother commented. "Tommy's tried to put the doors back up but he's never managed."

"I'll see what I can do."

"All right, then. I suppose I'll go finish my dishes and let you get to work."

"It was nice to meet you," he offered.

"Likewise."

But then, just as Christine reached the house, her hand on the door, she stopped, turned, and walked back to where Drake stood; he had been lost in thought, staring at the garage, wondering where to start. For a moment, there was an awkward silence between them. Drake began to question whether the older woman had had an episode, if she wasn't sure who he was or what they had just talked about. There was a sudden break in the clouds and sunlight streamed down, glinting brightly off the knife's blade.

"I have a question for you," she finally said. "Maybe it isn't my place to ask, but I'm having a hard time holding my tongue."

"Go ahead," he told her.

"What are your intentions toward my daughter?"

Somewhere down in Drake's gut, he'd had a suspicion

that this was what Clara's mother would ask, though answering wasn't going to be easy. "I've enjoyed getting to know her," he began. "I can honestly tell you that I've never met a woman quite like Clara."

Christine took a small step closer. "The reason I'm asking is because she's been through an awful lot," she explained. "Her husband died in the war. Tommy, though I love him dearly, is going over Fool's Hill. Now, on top of everything else, she's saddled with a mother who struggles to remember what day it is," she added with a short, sad laugh. "When someone's got so many things working against her, the slightest glimmer of hope becomes a precious jewel, something to hold on to tightly, like a life preserver in a raging sea. With the way Clara's been acting these last couple of days, I can't help but think that she sees you as her knight in shining armor come along to rescue her. The last thing I'd want would be for her to end up disappointed." Christine paused. "Or hurt, intentionally or otherwise."

Drake could see how much Christine loved her daughter. She was doing what any good parent would; she was protecting her child. In many ways, he wanted the same thing for Clara, to see her smile and be happy. But he also didn't want to make any promises he couldn't keep, to lead her on in any way.

When he'd met Clara, Drake had felt something between them. Other than that first night when she'd run from him, those sparks had grown, bursting into flames when they had kissed. Drake couldn't have said for certain how high their passion might go, where it might take them, but he wanted to find out.

"I give you my word," he finally said. "I won't do her wrong."

A smile brightened Christine's face. "See that you don't," she answered, giving the knife one last shake for good measure.

Drake watched as Clara's mother walked back to the house; this time she entered, leaving him alone with his thoughts. He couldn't help but wonder if, given Christine's memory troubles, she might soon forget what they had talked about.

He knew that he wouldn't.

Once Drake had pulled the Plymouth closer to the garage, he decided to do something about the broken doors. Examining them closer, he saw that some screws had come free from the framing, many of which were missing altogether. He grabbed some replacements and tools and set about trying to drive them back into place, but soon found that the doors were too heavy to hold while he worked.

Instead, he popped the Plymouth's hood, occasionally glancing up at the darkening sky, wondering just how long it would be before the rain began to fall. He began by checking the fluid levels; satisfied, he moved on to the engine's belts, looking for any signs of wear.

He whistled while he worked.

Drake had always found comfort working with machines, especially engines. Under a car's hood, everything had a purpose, somewhere it was supposed to be and something it was supposed to do. If even one bolt or lug nut was out of place, broken, or unable to do its intended job, then the whole car suffered. Any good mechanic knew that he had to take good care of his vehicle and do whatever work was needed to keep it running smooth and strong. Work like this had other benefits, too, such as letting him forget about all the things on his mind, allowing his hands to make the hard choices instead of his head.

He was just about to inspect the Plymouth's hoses when he heard footsteps behind him. He figured it was Christine, but when he ducked out from under the hood, wiping his grease-stained hands on a rag, he found that he was wrong.

A teenage boy watched him warily. His hair was dark and worn longer than Drake's had been at the same age, which he guessed to be somewhere around sixteen. He was tall and a little on the thin side, which made his clothes hang a bit loosely on his frame. Drake might've wondered who his visitor was if it hadn't been for the boy's eyes: green with flecks of gold, the spitting image of his mother's.

"Howdy," Drake said with a nod.

The boy didn't answer; he just kept staring, his arms folded defiantly across his chest.

"You must be Tommy," Drake continued, stuffing the dirty rag into his back pocket and sticking out his hand. "I've heard a lot about you."

Clara's son's stubbornness showed no signs of letting up. Drake let his extended hand linger in the air for a few seconds before dropping it.

"I'm Drake," he said, straining to tamp down his growing irritation, reminding himself that he wanted to make a good impression.

"I know," the boy said petulantly. "My grandmother told me."

Tommy's words removed Drake's concern, that Christine wouldn't remember who he was or why he was there.

"How do you know my mother?" Tommy blurted.

"I helped her out when her truck broke down," Drake explained.

"That thing's a hunk of junk."

Drake chuckled. "It's seen better days," he agreed. "In return, your mother was kind enough to let me come over so I could work on my car. I'd planned on driving it into the garage..."

"But the doors are broken," Tommy finished.

Drake had an idea. "They don't have to be," he said. "Not if you help me."

The boy kept on frowning. Drake wondered if he wasn't about to make up an excuse to walk away, but Tommy surprised him by shrugging his shoulders and asking, "What do you need me to do?"

Once he'd gathered his tools, Drake showed Tommy where to stand and had him lift one of the garage doors by its bottom edge; the boy's knees wavered, but to protect Tommy's pride, Drake decided not to ask if he needed any help. Instead, he aligned the holes at the hinge and began to drive the metal back into the wooden frame, one twist of the screwdriver at a time.

"So this is your car?" Tommy asked, looking at the Plymouth.

"It is," Drake answered.

"Is it fast?"

"It better be or I won't make any money." Noticing the boy's confusion, Drake explained, "I race it for a living."

Tommy's eyes widened a bit. "Around a track?"

"There or down a long stretch of road, the straighter the better. Anywhere someone wants to challenge me."

"And you win?"

"Most of the time," he answered, still feeling the sting of his loss the day before. "It wouldn't be worth it if I didn't." Noticing the way Clara's son was still staring at the car, he added, "Do you like to drive?"

"Sure, although my mom's truck is usually more work than fun." Drake noticed that Tommy's arms shook slightly from the strain of holding the door steady and that he was starting to sweat. "Naomi's dad just bought a brand-new Studebaker and she's gonna try to talk him into letting us take it for a spin."

"Is Naomi your gal?"

To Drake, the question was as innocent as a newborn babe; he vaguely remembered Clara mentioning the name and figured that asking about her might be a way to extend their conversation, for them to bond a bit. Tommy's reaction said otherwise; it was as harsh as it was swift.

"Like you don't know," the boy snapped, his voice trembling more than his arms. "I can only imagine what my mother's told you about her."

"Tommy, listen, I don't—"

"She's just jealous! She doesn't care if I'm happy! I don't want to hear it from her, and I sure as hell ain't gonna take it from you!"

Without warning, Tommy let go of the garage door; unfortunately for Drake, he hadn't yet replaced enough of the screws and the weight of the door yanked them all out again. Everything crashed to the ground with a jarring bang. Before Drake could say anything, Tommy was already stalking off; when he reached the house, he slammed the door shut behind him. Drake was still watching, feeling a little stunned, when the first drops of rain began to fall.

"Stupid," he muttered to himself. Unknowingly, he had lit the boy's fuse, and like a firecracker, Tommy had exploded.

Nice first impression...

Chapter Fourteen

Amos Barstow was conflicted.

He paced. He mumbled angrily. He sat down on the edge of his bed and ran a hand through his thinning hair. He went to stand at the window, nervously looking up and down the street, wondering when he would see Drake returning, worrying that he might find Sweet and his boys, frightened that the drug dealer had finally tracked him down. He paced some more.

"How in the hell did I end up in this mess?" he asked himself.

But Amos already knew the answer.

He was an addict. He was a thief.

And now, as he stared longingly at Drake's duffel bag, leaned in the corner, he wondered how much longer he could call himself a friend.

Yesterday, after Drake's unexpected defeat, Amos had tried to lose his mounting worries in what remained of his morphine. No sooner had Drake left, no doubt to visit that widow who'd caught his eye, than Amos had escaped to a better place. For hours, he had rested peacefully, turning events over and over again in his head. But in the end, he hadn't been able to stop thinking about one thing in particular.

The money for the bet Drake was proposing.

Amos was broke; all his cash, what was left of his winnings along with what he'd stolen from Sweet, had been lost in Drake's disastrous defeat. Amos had considered it a safe wager; unfortunately, it had been anything but. Still, the solution Drake had offered to their troubles sounded good, but only if they actually had the money to throw into the pot. Drake claimed to have it, which left Amos with one very important question in need of an answer.

Where is he hiding it?

Rising groggily, trying to shake off the effects of the morphine, Amos had searched the hotel room. He pulled open drawers, pawed through the closet, dropped to the floor to peer under each bed, and had even lifted the mattresses, desperate to find Drake's hidden money. Once he was certain it wasn't to be found inside, he'd gone out to rummage inside the Plymouth's trailer.

But still, he'd found nothing.

Back in the room, sweaty and growing frustrated, the answer had suddenly struck Amos like a ton of bricks: it was in Drake's duffel bag. Unfortunately, the bag was nowhere to be seen; it must still be in the Plymouth. He'd waited and waited until finally, later that night, Drake returned with it slung over his shoulder. Every moment since, Amos had struggled not to stare at it.

Now Drake was gone and the bag was right there...

Still, Amos hesitated. Even though he'd done his share of despicable things lately, he knew that rooting around in Drake's belongings would be crossing a line. Drake was like family. They'd been through thick and thin, racing together more times than Amos could count. Drake trusted him. Amos knew that the racer would give him the shirt off his back if asked. But the longer the mechanic stared at the bag, the more he tried to justify taking a look.

You aren't going to take the money. All you're gonna do is see if it's there, nothin' more. This way, you'll know for certain.

He locked the door and closed the curtains; the idea of someone witnessing his betrayal made him nauseous. Grabbing the duffel bag, he put it on his bed. Seconds later, he dug in, working his way down past Drake's clothes and the paperback books he was always reading until he was nearly to the bottom. And then, just like that, there it was...

Money. Lots of it. Wads of cash rubber-banded together.

Amos didn't remove any of the bills; he wondered if it was because he didn't want to disturb them too much and make Drake suspect his things had been ransacked, or because he feared he would take off with it right then and there. Instead, he rubbed the bills between his thumb and forefinger, counting them; he soon arrived at a number that sent chills racing across his skin.

He couldn't believe Drake had so much. Amos knew

that if he took it, he could run for months, go somewhere far to the west, escape his pursuers, and buy whatever drugs he wanted. Most if not all of his worries would be gone.

Slowly, Amos put back the money, straightened Drake's things, and then placed the duffel bag back in the corner. No matter how badly he needed the money, regardless of how frightened he was that Sweet Woods would catch up to him, and ignoring the fact that he was running low on morphine, he just couldn't do it to Drake. He wouldn't steal from his friend.

At least not yet...

Eddie Fuller was drunk.

He swirled the scotch in his glass, spinning it faster and faster until a tiny wave sloshed over the lip, wet his thumb, and then fell to the floor, where it stained an antique rug his father had imported from Egypt.

"What a waste," he muttered.

The grandfather clock in his study chimed three times. Outside, the afternoon was overcast, with occasional fits of rain. Most days, at that hour, he would've been sitting behind his desk at the bank, going over reports, making telephone calls, doing all the things that were his responsibility as the man in charge.

But not today. Not after what had happened...

Frustration, anger, and even, if he was being completely honest with himself, a little fear coursed through him. It wasn't supposed to be this way.

How had everything gone so wrong?

He'd given Clara some time to think about the pampered future he was proposing to her. While he was disappointed she hadn't immediately accepted, later, he understood that she had others to think about besides herself. Still, he'd felt certain that with some space and a few days to work it out, she'd see that becoming Mrs. Edward Fuller was the only logical choice she could make.

Besides, she knew what would happen if she decided otherwise...

With that in mind, Eddie had begun making plans for his courtship. They were every bit as romantic as they were meticulous. When it came time to close the bank for the day, he would send the other employees home, ensuring that he and Clara could be alone. Stashed in his office were candles, a bouquet of red roses, an extremely expensive bottle of wine, and even a radio to provide just the right ambiance. Everything had been in place. It was perfect.

But then, unexpectedly, it had all gone terribly wrong.

Eddie drained the last inch of alcohol, barely noticing it burn its way down his throat. Before the booze had time to settle in his stomach, he was already pouring himself more. He was growing pleasantly used to the way alcohol clouded his thoughts. Now he understood why his father had kept so much of it around. But on this night, no matter how hard he tried to drown his troubles, they kept bubbling back to the surface. Over and over, the same question rose in Eddie's mind, teasing him, tormenting him.

Who was that man?

At first, he had assumed that the stranger's interruption was an accident, that he'd wanted to use the bank but had shown up too late. But as the man continued to pound on the door, ignoring Eddie's shouts that they were closed, his eyes never left Clara; it soon became obvious that his arrival wasn't mere happenstance. The stranger's growing insistence to get inside was because of *her*. Clara had been relieved to see *him*.

The most humiliating thing was that Eddie had been frightened; when the stranger barged inside the bank, Eddie had wanted to stop them from leaving, but when the man spoke, his voice a threatening growl, Eddie had backed down. Even though he was rich, one of the most important and powerful men in Sunset, at that moment he'd been a coward. A mixture of shame and fear had kept him holed up in his house ever since, alone, drinking the hours away, far from Clara Sinclair.

But he couldn't stay hidden forever.

No matter what it took, he would learn the identity of the stranger, where he came from, and how he and Clara knew each other. Yesterday, Eddie had assumed that it would only be a matter of time before he and Clara were happily married. But now, things had changed. Doubt had crept into his thoughts. His heart overflowed with love for her, but now he wondered if she would ever give him the chance to show it to her, at least voluntarily. Something had to be done.

He had to make the stranger go away, and soon.

Eddie tossed back his drink, winced as he swallowed hard, and banged the empty glass down on his desk. He took a deep breath.

It was time to get to work.

Naomi Marsh was bored.

All afternoon, she'd sat at the window of her father's bar, absently watching the sky turn gray and then finally let loose, rain drumming against the glass. The Marshland was almost empty; other than Wilbur, drying glasses with a dirty rag while taking nips from a bottle of whiskey, there were only a handful of Sunset's most depressing and desperate, the sort of drunks who had nowhere else to be on a weekday afternoon, the kind of people on the road to ruin.

So what does that say about me? If I'm sitting here with them, doesn't that make me every bit as pathetic?

Naomi shook her head. She was nothing like those people. She had prospects, a future far away from this place. Someday soon she would leave and never return.

To further distract herself, Naomi thought of Tommy. She'd even begun to entertain the thought that she was being too harsh with the boy, that instead of teasing him, making promises of her flesh that never seemed to come true, she should just give him a taste. After all, the only reason she hadn't slept with him yet was because of the thrill of power it gave her, like having a dog on a leash. But sex could be plenty thrilling, too. If she gave in, they could both have a little fun.

But then Tommy had shown up madder than a hornet.

"Who the hell does he think he is, anyway?"

He paced back and forth, frowning as the floorboards creaked loudly beneath his feet. They had left the bar in favor of the apartment Naomi shared with her father, directly across the street from the bar; with her old man tending to his customers, they wouldn't be bothered for hours. Naomi had brought Tommy there before but had never let him into her room, and had certainly never let him see her sprawled out on her bed, inviting, willing...

Not that he seemed to care...

"What are you talking about?" she asked, growing annoyed.

"The guy who knows my mom. The one with the car," he snapped, showing some annoyance of his own, angry that she hadn't been listening.

"Which car?"

Faintly, Naomi remembered Tommy mentioning this already, but she couldn't recall any of the details. While he rambled on, she'd been busy running her fingers along the inside of his leg, tracing the seam of his jeans; she'd been stunned when he took her hand away so he could get up and pace.

"I don't know what make it is," he answered. "An Oldsmobile, maybe. He races it for a living. Goes around making bets."

Naomi sat up on the edge of the bed and made a show of slowly rebuttoning the front of her blouse, which she'd unbuttoned soon after they arrived.

"Why was he at your house?" she asked.

"Because my mother told him that he could use our garage."

"But your garage is broken."

"He wanted me to help him fix it," Tommy said.

"So did you?"

He nodded. "He was fine for a while. We talked about his car, how fast it went, but then he started in about you..."

Naomi stopped what she was doing; what he'd said had finally grabbed her attention. "What did he say?"

"I don't remember...not exactly," Tommy answered, pacing faster, growing more worked up by the second.

"How would he know anything about me?"

"From my mom, no doubt, so you know that what he heard wasn't good."

"So then what did you do?"

"I took off," Tommy told her. "I'd been holding the garage door so I let it go. Probably broke it worse than it already was, but I couldn't care less."

But once again, Naomi wasn't paying attention. Her mind churned as she considered the opportunity that had unexpectedly presented itself. This was a chance to have some *real* fun, one that might prove more entertaining than messing around with a boy pretending to be a man.

"What did you say this guy's name was?" she asked.

"Drake McCoy," he answered.

As Tommy went back to ranting, Naomi couldn't help but smile. In a town as small as Sunset, it wouldn't be hard for her to learn more about the driver, particularly where he was staying. All she needed was for them to have an "accidental" meeting, for him to get a good look at a young, beautiful woman like her, and then Drake McCoy would be hers. The thought of sticking it to Clara Sinclair, and even to her son, just because she could, was too enticing to ignore.

Maybe she would have some fun after all...

Ronald "Sweet" Woods was tired.

For days, they had driven up and down dirt roads, passed through sleepy towns, pushed open the doors of roadside markets and seedy taverns, rousted drunks and regular folks who weren't looking for any trouble, all in the increasingly futile hope of finding some sign of Amos Barstow or the money and drugs he'd stolen. So far, they'd come up empty.

"How much further do you intend to take this?"

Sweet glanced up. Jesse Church yawned into the back of his hand. Malcolm Child stood a ways off, lighting a cigarette; the match illuminated the night for a second before he shook it out. High above, a thin moon shone dully.

"As long as it takes," Sweet answered.

"This keeps up, we might still be lookin' come Christmas."

Sweet unwrapped a candy and popped it into his mouth, as much to keep himself from losing his temper as to satisfy a desire for sugar.

The Cadillac was parked at a crossroads smack dab in the middle of nowhere. Many long miles had passed since they'd last seen a house. Crickets sang their unending melody in the tall grass. Sweet had spread their well-worn map across the car's hood as he tried to figure out where they were, as well as where they might go next. After that first successful sighting, they had branched out in different directions, like the spokes of a bicycle wheel, looking to stay on Barstow's trail. Unfortunately, every path had so far ended in failure. Now only a couple of options remained. They were close, Sweet was sure of it. It was no time to quit.

"You wantin' to pack it in?" he asked, rolling the hard candy around in his mouth, knocking it against his teeth.

"I'm not saying that, boss," Jesse replied, aware that he was treading on dangerous ground.

"Go on, then. Explain it to me so I understand."

"It's just that we've been at this for more than a week now," the thug explained. "We're tired. None of us has gotten more than a couple of hours of sleep at a time, usually when we're parked on the side of the road. It's been so long since I slept in a bed that I've darn near forgotten what it feels like." Jesse laughed nervously. "Hell, I wish I had, that way I wouldn't miss it so much."

Sweet didn't disagree. All of them looked like hell, their clothes rumpled and stained from their time on the road, their eyes bloodshot from another night of fitful sleep. He missed St. Louis and its never-ending hustle, so completely different from the slow boredom of the country. He wanted nothing more than to sit down for a nice meal, soak in a hot tub of water, sleep with one of his favorite whores, and then doze for days. But that wasn't in the cards, not until that bastard Barstow was dead and Sweet's wounded pride restored.

So in answer to Jesse's complaints, he drew his gun.

"You want to rest so bad," Sweet said, cocking the pistol's hammer and leveling the barrel at the middle of Jesse's chest, "I might be able to help."

"Now...now, wait a second, boss..." the henchman stammered, all the bravado falling from his face, his hands raised in submission.

Without hesitation, Sweet tugged on the trigger and fired a bullet into the ground just to the side of where Jesse stood, kicking up a cloud of dirt. In the otherwise quiet night, the gunshot was deafeningly loud.

Jesse had been too frightened to make a sound.

"You still want to quit lookin'?" Sweet asked.

Jesse panted, his eyes wider than the moon. "No... no...let's go..."

For a few seconds longer, Sweet kept the gun right where it was, as if he was still weighing whether or not to kill Jesse where he stood. It was more than just a desire not to show weakness to someone beneath him; he *needed* to catch Amos Barstow, to make him pay for what he'd done. Finally, he uncocked the gun and put it back in his waistband. Jesse's chest continued to heave, his heart struggling to slow. Sweet noticed that through it all, Malcolm had never moved or said a word, but only watched as he smoked his cigarette.

"We'll go toward Clarion and then on to Sunset," Sweet

explained. "From either one of those places, they might've crossed over the river, so we'll have to expand our search if we don't find their trail."

Malcolm got behind the wheel, flicking his cigarette butt into the dark. Though he'd yet to get his legs underneath him, Jesse managed to stumble into the passenger's seat. Sweet let them wait.

He looked all around them, at the woods, the sky, down the road in the direction they'd come and then the other way, where they were headed. Somewhere out there, Barstow, McCoy, and his revenge waited.

And I'm going to find them . . . no matter what . . .

Chapter Fifteen

CLARA WALKED DOWN Main Street with a spring in her step. She reveled in the warmth of the early-evening sun against her skin. Greetings were given from shopkeepers shutting up their businesses for the night, hailed down sidewalks and across the street. She marveled at how different one day could be from the next, how something as simple as a kiss could change the way everything looked.

When her day began it had been filled with nervous apprehension. After her run-in with Eddie at the bank, his plans thwarted by Drake's unexpected arrival, she had dreaded the thought of seeing him again. All the way to work, she wondered what he would say, imagined the withering looks he might give. But then, miraculously, Eddie hadn't come to the bank; his office door had remained shut, his grating voice unheard. And so, Clara's fears had lifted like a fog. She laughed with the people who came to her teller window. She went outside to enjoy lunch. She thought about Drake, the ride they'd shared, and how his lips felt against hers.

After the bank closed, Clara wasn't ready to go home; since it was such a beautiful day, she'd started walking. She hadn't had a destination in mind, but wasn't the least bit surprised when she found herself standing across the street from the Sunset Hotel.

So now what?

This was the question Clara had struggled to answer all night and throughout the day. Drake McCoy had enchanted her. Being with him had stoked a fire in her she'd long thought extinguished. He was charming, easy to talk to, and handsome. But despite all of those things, there was a part of Clara that still felt as if she had cheated on Joe, or at the least, his memory. She was full of contradictions: happy yet sad, excited yet nervous, flattered yet ashamed. But as conflicted as Clara was, she still stood outside Drake's hotel completely unsure of what to do with her hands, taking one step forward, then another back; it was as if he was a magnet and she was made out of metal, unable to resist his pull.

Clara knew that to go inside, to be the one who came looking for him, was bold, almost inappropriate. But she was impatient, unable and unwilling to wait for him to make the next move. She *wanted* to see him again, as soon as possible, to find out where their relationship would go next.

She took a deep breath and crossed the street.

*   *   *

"Now ain't this a strange turn of events! Usually, I'm the one standin' on that side of the counter! Almost didn't recognize you this way!"

Edna Gilbert laughed loudly from behind the front desk. In her middle sixties now, she had founded the hotel with her husband, Leonard, back when Clara had been a little girl. Though Edna had been a widow for going on two decades, she refused to believe that there was a job she couldn't do; she hauled heavy bags without complaint, fixed broken toilets, washed an endless amount of bedding, and even painted the hotel's exterior when it needed a new coat. Though Clara had always thought that the way Edna dyed her hair dark black made her look older than she really was, the woman's personality was undoubtedly young.

"I bet I know why you're here," the hotel owner declared.

"You do?" Clara asked with a slight frown.

Edna nodded. "I'd be willin' to bet every dollar I got deposited in that bank of yours that you're here to see the fella up in number six," she explained. "The younger one, of course."

Clara was taken aback. She'd told no one about Drake except her mother, and even with Christine she had left out most of the important details. As far as she knew, with the notable exception of Eddie, no one in Sunset had seen them together.

Her confusion must have shown. "It ain't like he's been gossipin' or nothin'," Edna said. "He come down the other day and asked 'bout you. Real innocent and the like. Havin' stood behind this desk for more years than I care to count, I know how to put two and two together. You showin' up like this proves that I ain't barkin' up the wrong tree."

Now Clara was definitely embarrassed. Blushing, she looked away.

"If you don't mind my sayin'," Edna continued, leaning heavily on the counter, her voice dropping conspiratorially, "that Drake fella is mighty easy on the eyes. Why, I think he looks an awful lot like that Hollywood actor, the one who was in—" But before Edna could say more, the hotel's phone began to ring. Clearly annoyed, she said, "I'll be right back," and went to answer it.

Clara exhaled; she was happy to be alone. She considered using Edna's preoccupation to go up to Drake's room, but when she turned around, she discovered Amos coming down the stairs into the small lobby.

The mechanic looked rougher around the edges than when they'd first met; his clothes were a wrinkled mess and several days' worth of white whiskers covered his cheeks. Clara wondered if he might be sick. When he noticed her, his eyes narrowed a bit, as if he was suspicious of her.

"Evenin'," Amos said; his voice sounded friendlier than he looked. "I suppose you're here to see Drake. He's up in the room."

"What makes you think I'm here for him?"

"'Cause I can't think of any other reason you'd be in a dump like this," Amos replied with a short chuckle. He hazarded a quick glance at Edna, who was still talking animatedly on the phone. Lowering his voice, he added, "This ain't the sort of place respectable folk visit. Even a crumb bum like me knows that much."

"It's not *that* bad," Clara disagreed.

"Take it from someone who spends plenty of time checkin' in and outta hotels," Amos said. "This one ain't that good."

Clara couldn't imagine the life that Amos, as well as Drake, lived. Traveling up and down country roads. Countless miles in their car. Sleeping in whatever moth-infested place had an empty bed for the night. Eating in greasy diners. Everything unfamiliar but strangely the same. It seemed like a hard life, one with few friends and, like Drake had told her, even fewer chances at love.

"I never had a chance to thank you for helping me with my truck the other day," Clara said, wanting to change the subject.

Amos shrugged. "Weren't nothin' to it," he said. Then his expression soured. "Damn shame to lose that hose, but I suppose it shouldn't surprise me none, what with the way Drake got all moony-eyed."

"Excuse me?" Clara blurted, caught off guard.

"Now, don't go gettin' all offended," the mechanic replied. "It ain't personal. It's just the way it is. Here the two of you are, actin' like a couple teenagers, when you both oughta know there ain't no future in it. In a few days, me and Drake are gonna get back in the Plymouth and head down the road, and 'fore long, ain't neither one of you is gonna remember the other's name. That hose I put in your truck is gonna last longer'n your memory a these few days."

"It's more than that," she insisted, her voice trembling.

Amos's eyes held a hint of pity. "It's a darn shame you feel that way."

Clara felt sick. Even as her feelings for Drake McCoy grew, especially after they'd kissed, she'd worried that maybe she was making a mountain out of a molehill. Still, she had clung to hope, believing what her heart was telling her. But hearing Amos speak so dismissively, so bluntly, calling what she had with Drake a meaningless fling, wounded her deeply. She could see that the mechanic was well aware that he'd hurt her; she wondered if he cared. Maybe he was jealous of all the time she was spending with Drake, or annoyed that his friend was distracted by her instead of focused on his racing, or mad about losing the hose. Clara suspected that it was all three.

Amos nodded toward the stairs. "You might as well go on up and enjoy what little time you got left," he said. "I'm gonna go get some grub."

With that, he left, letting the hotel door swing shut with a bang.

"What's bothering you?"

Clara had been waiting for Drake to ask that very question ever since she had knocked on his door. When he'd opened it, a smile had lit up his face; she'd tried to match it, but hers had quickly faltered. He had invited her in, but she had shaken her head and asked if they might take a walk instead. Drake had readily agreed. Taking the stairs, he'd made small talk, but she couldn't bring herself to answer. When they passed the front desk, Edna had wished them a good night, giving Clara a wink when Drake wasn't looking. Outside on the sidewalk, when she was still quiet, he'd asked his question.

"Nothing," she lied, thinking herself a coward. "I'm fine."

"You could've fooled me," he said. "It doesn't have anything to do with that fella at the bank, does it?"

"Eddie never showed up. I actually had a nice day."

"So what changed? Why the long face?"

Your friend just told me that we're having a fling, something that both of us will forget soon after you leave Sunset forever...

Clara knew she couldn't say *that*, but she also couldn't keep what Amos had said locked away. She had to say *something*. She needed answers.

"What... what do I mean to you?" she asked.

"You want to know what my intentions toward you are."

She nodded.

Drake chuckled. "Your mother asked me the same thing this afternoon."

Taken aback, Clara managed to say, "You're kidding..."

"Cross my heart, it's the truth."

"I didn't say a word to her about what happened between us," she told him, her voice rising, her tone defensive.

"I wasn't implying otherwise," Drake said, "but when two people meet, when they start spending time together, doing all the things we have, it's to be expected that the folks around them, family, friends, and the like, are going to wonder where it's headed. They're curious, that's all."

"What about you? Don't you want to know?"

Drake stopped walking and turned to face her. "Of course I do. Neither one of us is a kid anymore. I don't want to waste time playing games."

Clara's heart raced. "We've only known each other a couple of days..."

"That's plenty long to believe that how I feel is real," Drake said, his tone as strong as his words. "Don't you agree?"

She nodded. "But you're leaving soon..."

He held her eyes, his jaw tight, and then looked away. "Thing is, I'm not so sure about that anymore."

"What do you mean?" she asked, reaching out to grab his forearm, imploring him to tell her the truth.

Drake took a deep breath. "Remember what I told you? That in all the years I've spent driving around, running races, I've never found someone who was willing to share that life with me?"

Clara nodded; she remembered every word.

"I've always expected the women I met to change their lives to match mine, for them to give up what they wanted to be with me out on the road," Drake explained. "But over the last couple of days, I've started to wonder if I haven't spent years looking at it the wrong way. Maybe the problem is me."

She remained silent, letting him talk.

He took her hand. "All I've ever done is move," he told her. "Ever since I left my father's farm, I haven't stayed in one place for long. Racing in some lonely little town one day, another the next. I've never put down roots. Instead, I've wandered, trying to convince myself that the grass is always greener somewhere else. I just kept driving, the faster the better.

"But then I came here. I met you and everything I thought I knew was turned upside down. I finally found someone who was funny, smart, and beautiful, all the things I've spent my whole life looking for. But for us to be together, something is going to have to change." Drake paused, the silence lingering. "So what if I gave up racing, settled down, and opened that garage I've always dreamed about? Ten years ago, I would never have considered it, but now..."

Clara couldn't believe what he was saying. For Drake to express his feelings for her, to say words she hadn't heard a man utter for almost a decade, was strange, unfamiliar, yet welcome. That he was echoing some of the same thoughts she wrestled with, acknowledging that something special was growing between them, and that he, too, wanted to find out where it all led, was comforting. She knew things between them were moving fast, but she didn't want to stop. Still, what he was suggesting also made her feel guilty.

"I could never ask you to give up racing," she said.

"You're not," he replied. "I'm making this choice on my own. All that matters is that when I walk away, you'll be there."

She searched his eyes, looking for some sign that he wasn't serious, that this was a joke or some game he was playing, but his gaze never wavered. "I can't believe I've made you feel this way."

Drake smiled. "Your son helped, too."

"Tommy? What does he have to do with this?"

"I met him this afternoon, and to say that things didn't go the way I'd hoped would be one heck of an under-statement." Drake told her about what had happened, how he'd finally gotten Tommy to open up a little, had even talked him into helping fix the garage door, but then things had quickly soured, all because he'd asked about a certain young woman.

Clara frowned. "Naomi."

"The way he reacted, seems like that girl has dug her claws in awful deep."

"To the bone, it seems," she said, shaking her head. "But I still don't understand what Tommy has to do with you wanting to give up racing."

"There I was at your house," he explained. "Your mother introduced herself with a knife in her hand. Your son stomped away from me as mad as a hornet. Crazy as it might seem, it made me realize all that I've been missing."

"My mother had a knife?" Clara asked, dazed.

Drake laughed. "It doesn't matter. What's important is

that at that moment I saw things clearly. I've never known what it's like to have a family, to come home to the same house every day, to try to build something that matters." He gave her hand a gentle squeeze. "And before you start thinking that this is because I'm lonely or that I'm afraid I won't find someone, nothing could be further from the truth." He leaned closer. "The reason is that I finally met someone worth stopping for. Somehow, when I least expected it, I found you."

"What about Amos?" she asked. "What will he think?"

"He won't like it," Drake answered, with a heavy sigh. "Amos is the closest thing I've got to family—hell, he's been more of a father to me than my own managed to be—but I have to do this. It's the right choice at the right time. I'll do my damnedest to make him see it my way, but if he can't or won't, then after we run one last race to try to win back what we lost, I reckon we'll go our separate ways."

Clara remembered what Amos had said back at the hotel. She had no doubt that the mechanic would be furious about Drake's decision; he would blame her, understandably, and he would be right, in a way.

"I'm ready for a new day to come," Drake said.

Gently yet insistently, he pulled her toward him until their bodies touched. Clara knew he wanted to kiss her again; even though they were on the sidewalk where anyone could see them, she had no desire to stop him.

But then, just as Clara closed her eyes, their lips about to touch, a car horn honked down the street. It wasn't directed at them, someone being smart, but a coincidence; still, it ruined the moment and they both stepped back.

Drake ran a hand through his dark hair. Clara walked over to look in the window of the bakery, empty except for a wedding cake.

"That looks good enough to eat," Drake said as he joined her.

"It's probably hard as a rock. It's been in there for more than a week."

"Hungry as I am, I doubt it would matter much."

Clara suddenly had an idea. "How would you like to have dinner at my house tonight?"

He laughed. "I wasn't dropping a hint."

"I'm serious."

"I don't want to impose."

"You wouldn't be. My mother has a roast in the oven. There'll be plenty."

"In that case, sure, I'd love to." His eyes narrowed and he gave her a little smile. "Your mother won't pull another knife on me, will she?"

"No promises," she answered, and they both laughed, but Drake's laughter soon faded.

He reached for her and Clara again placed her hand in his.

"I meant what I told you," Drake said. "I mean to give up racing, to settle down here in Sunset, to start a new life with you. But I want you to believe in me. I *need* you to believe in *us*."

Clara's eyes searched his. "I do."

His easy smile bloomed. "I'm glad," he said. "With you by my side, I'm headed for a bunch of bright tomorrows."

She nodded. Drake's life wasn't the only one that was changing.

Chapter Sixteen

How in the heck do you drive this thing?"

Clara laughed loudly in the passenger seat. After they'd walked back to the bank, Drake had asked if he could drive them to her house, expressing an interest in seeing how the old truck handled. She'd happily given him the keys and then watched as he struggled to get it started. Once he finally managed to get them going, it hadn't gotten much better; at the first stop sign, the truck had sputtered hard enough to shake, nearly stalling out.

"I thought you were some sort of fancy race car driver," she said, teasing him. "Shouldn't this be easy for you?"

"No car I've *ever* driven has been as bad as this!"

Accelerating, he tried to shift into a higher gear, but the stick fought him, grinding loudly until he jammed it into place.

"You do this every day?" Drake asked with a laugh.

"It's not any nicer to me, you know."

"I tell you one thing, if I manage to open a garage in this town, I know who my first customer is going to be!"

Listening to him, Clara couldn't believe how quickly her life had changed. Whereas a week ago she had been plagued with worry and apprehension, now, suddenly and unexpectedly, things were looking better.

And it was all because of Drake McCoy.

When they turned onto the street where she lived, he was still talking about the truck. "With a clunker like this, the only question is whether repairs are worth it. In the end, it might be cheaper to buy something else," he explained. "The way I figure it, we could look around at—"

But before Drake could finish, Clara let out a short scream, a reaction to what she'd seen: black smoke billowing from her house and into the sky.

When Drake saw what had alarmed her, his reaction was swift; he made the truck go faster, working the gearshift forcefully, ignoring its protests. Within seconds, he braked hard in front of the house, skidding a few feet before bringing them to a sudden, jarring stop. The next thing Clara knew, she was standing on the sidewalk, staring as if in a trance.

My house...It's on fire...

Though she couldn't see any flames, smoke leaked skyward from the rear of the house. Clara could only imagine what was happening inside—the flames devouring everything in sight, burning up her belongings, taking away her memories until nothing was left.

Instead of being frozen with shock and surprise, Drake

acted. He grabbed her hand and pulled her toward the house. "Come on!"

Together, they raced onto the porch. Drake whipped open the front door and plunged inside, with Clara right behind. The smoke made her eyes water, but it wasn't as thick as she'd expected. Wherever the fire was, it hadn't yet reached the front of the house.

"Tommy...my mother..." Clara managed, frightened out of her wits.

Drake pointed at the stairs. "Go see if anyone is up there! I'll check down here!" When Clara still hadn't moved, he shouted, "Get going!" before disappearing into the smoke toward the rear of the house.

Clara didn't hesitate long before doing as he said.

Something about this doesn't add up...

When Drake had yanked open Clara's front door, he'd expected to be assaulted by a wave of heat hot enough to burn exposed skin. He had assumed that the smoke would be chokingly thick and dense. But neither had been true.

Even now, as he pushed through the living room and toward an open doorway at the back of the house, he only needed to keep his face pressed against his sleeve, his eyes squinted, and his breathing shallow.

Don't relax, not for a minute!

His hope was that they'd arrived before the fire grew out of control. If he could reach it in time, stop it before any real damage was done...

Drake stepped into the kitchen and finally got some answers.

Bright orange and yellow flames leaped from a cast-iron skillet on the stove where something crackled and burned. Smoke billowed from the conflagration. Fortunately, the door just off the kitchen was open; it allowed smoke to pass through the screen of the inner door and up into the sky; that was what Clara had seen when they drove up.

Drake stepped to the sink, filled a glass with water, and was just about to throw it on the fire when he suddenly stopped; he had no way of knowing what was burning. If it was grease, then tossing water on it would send it splattering in every direction and make the situation worse than it already was.

Instead, he rummaged through Clara's cabinets, searching for something he could use. Finally, down among the pots and pans, he found a dented metal tray. Carefully, his arm extended far from his body, he dropped it onto the skillet with a bang, covering it completely and choking out the fire's air; without any fuel, the blaze was spent in seconds. Once he'd shut off the burner, the danger was no more. But even as he threw open windows to hasten the smoke's departure, Drake kept asking himself the same question, over and over.

What happened here?

With a sickening feeling in his stomach, he wondered if he didn't already know the answer.

* * *

Clara raced up the staircase as fast as her feet could take her, rising through the smoke, causing it to swirl around her. On the landing, she turned left and pushed open the door to Tommy's room. Shouting his name, she frantically searched for some sign of her son, fear and desperation gripping her tight, but he wasn't there. She hurried back in the opposite direction, past the bathroom and her own bedroom, both of them empty, before reaching her mother's door. Clara stepped inside and gasped at what she saw.

Christine lay sprawled across her bed. She was on her side, completely still, her hair covering her face. At first glance, she looked peaceful; Clara's thoughts were anything but. Fearing that her mother had been overcome by the smoke, terrified that Christine could be dead, Clara rushed over and began roughly shaking the older woman's shoulder.

"Mom!" she shouted, her voice panicked. "Wake up!"

At first, there was no response, so Clara shouted louder and shook harder. But then Christine sputtered awake, her eyes narrow slits, unfocused and disoriented.

"What . . . what's going on?" she mumbled.

"There's a fire!" Clara yelled. "We have to get out of here! Quick!"

"Fire? What fire? What are you talking about?"

Before Clara could respond, Christine became aware of the haze of smoke filling her room. Her eyes went wide as she turned to her daughter, then away, raising a trembling hand to cover her mouth.

"Oh, no," she moaned. "Oh, God, please no..."

"What is it?" Clara asked, her stomach twisting into knots.

"I...I didn't mean to...I just came up here and..."

"Mom," Clara said softly, almost pleading. "What happened?"

When Christine looked at her, her eyes were wet. "I...I started cooking dinner..." she explained. "I put a pan on the stove...I was going to fry some onions to go with the roast..." But it was there that her story ended.

She didn't have to say more. Clara knew what had happened next: her mother had forgotten about the stove, come upstairs, lain down, and fallen asleep while what was in the pan burned to a crisp, filling the house with smoke.

"Oh, Clara," Christine cried, punctuating her words with a sob.

An awkward silence stretched between them, broken when Drake shouted from downstairs. "Fire's out!" he shouted. "I'm going to open up the windows!"

"All right," Clara answered; her voice sounded as out of sorts as she felt, as shaken by what had happened as her mother.

The worst part was the way Christine looked at her; her gaze was pleading, as if she was a child, helpless to deal with the circumstances in which she unexpectedly found herself.

"It was an accident," Clara offered, wiping away a tear.

Her mother shook her head. "I could've burned the house down!"

"But you didn't."

"But I *could have!*" her mother insisted. "What if you hadn't come home when you did? What if Tommy had been hurt? What if I got up in the middle of the night, put a pot on the stove, and killed us all in our sleep?"

Clara didn't answer. *What can I possibly say?*

Suddenly, the sound of a fire engine's siren rose in the distance; no doubt it was headed for their house. More than likely, a neighbor had called in because of the smoke. With every fevered beat of Clara's heart, the noise grew louder.

Christine started to cry. If the fire truck was coming, that meant there would be questions; if they answered truthfully, Clara's mother would be humiliated. For those who knew about Christine's troubles, it wouldn't be just a simple accident, but rather another indication that she was losing her marbles.

"I'll take care of it," Clara said, putting a comforting hand on her mother's shoulder. "Don't worry."

But by now, Christine wasn't listening. Her body shook as she sobbed into the mattress, overcome by shame, fear, and sadness.

Clara stepped out of the room, shutting the door behind her. The siren drew closer; within seconds, the truck would be parked right outside. Even with the slowly dissipating smoke, she took a deep breath.

She had a lie to tell.

* * *

For the next hour, Clara weaved an explanation for what had happened that didn't place the blame on her mother, but on herself. She spoke with the firemen, wearing a sheepish smile, and told them she'd put a skillet on the stove but forgot about it when she and Drake went for a drive. When they came home, they'd found the house filled with smoke. Clara tried to look embarrassed, but worried that all it did was make her appear guilty. When Sheriff Oglesby arrived, the lights on his police car flashing, she repeated her story. The lawman took it all in, then started asking questions; when he inquired about whether Tommy or her mother had been home, Clara dug her hole a little deeper, admitting that she wasn't sure where Tommy was, but then claiming that her mother had gone to the library. Guilt ate at her, but she managed to convince herself that her lie hurt no one; in fact, it went a long way toward protecting what little was left of her mother's pride. She saw her neighbors watching from across the street and up on their porches, but no one came over to talk, for which Clara was thankful; she didn't want anyone to contradict her.

Drake went along with her story, even trying to claim responsibility by saying that he had asked Clara to show him more of town. At first, she thought that Sheriff Oglesby was eyeing Drake suspiciously on account of his being a newcomer to Sunset, but the more they talked, the more it seemed as if the driver's charm put the lawman at ease.

For her part, Christine remained hidden in her room.

"Let's make sure this here's the only accident we have," the sheriff said with a wink as he got in his car and drove off.

Once everyone had left, Clara and Drake exchanged looks of relief.

Back inside, Clara went up to her mother's room to tell her that everything was fine, but the door was locked. When she knocked, there was no answer.

Clara walked onto the porch. Night had fallen, wrapping the neighborhood in darkness; a few lights shone inside houses and from the streetlamp on the far corner, but they couldn't hold a candle to the brilliance of the countless stars that filled the sky. Crickets chirped. Weary, she lowered herself into the porch swing and absently began to push herself back and forth, causing the hinges to squeak.

She and Drake had eaten a hasty dinner; he had gone to the grocery store and bought the fixings for sandwiches and a six-pack of beer. Together in the still smoky kitchen, they said little. Christine had yet to leave her room, so Clara had taken her a plate, setting it on the floor outside the door. Tommy still hadn't come home. Once their meal was finished, and as Drake began to clear the table, Clara had wandered from the room and soon found herself outside. It wasn't because she was trying to get away from Drake, or even that she wanted to be alone, but only that she had drifted, drawn by the dark and silence.

The porch swing was a familiar place for Clara to seek refuge. In the months and years after Joe's death, after Tommy had been put in bed, after she had managed to survive another day, she would often come outside and sit. She would cry. She would remember better times. She would even talk to Joe, hoping he could still hear her, just like when she visited his grave. But of course, she'd never gotten a reply, though it was comforting all the same.

"You mind a little company?"

Clara looked up and found Drake. He held a beer bottle in his hand. When she nodded, he sat down on the railing opposite her.

"Nice night," he commented, taking a swig.

"It is," she answered.

After that, neither of them spoke for a while. Across the street, a couple walked by hand in hand, too far away for Clara to hear what they were saying; whatever it was, it must have been funny, since the man burst out laughing.

"When I was little," Clara finally said, breaking their silence, giving voice to a memory that she couldn't keep inside, "there was a girl in my class at school named Evelyn Price. Every day, she waited for me on my walk home, and no matter how fast I ran, no matter how hard I tried to get away, she always caught me. She would push me down, pull my hair, throw my books into a mud puddle, that sort of thing. I'd come home bruised and crying my eyes out, complaining about Evelyn to my mother, begging her to do something."

"Did she?" Drake asked, taking another drink.

Clara shook her head. "Not the way I wanted her to," she answered. "Instead of talking with my teacher or with the Prices about what their daughter was doing, she told me that I had to stand up for myself, that she wouldn't always be there for me and that if there wasn't another choice, I had to fight."

"So what happened?"

"The next time Evelyn came after me, I stood my ground. She grabbed my hair and I socked her in the nose."

Drake chuckled. "Sounds like you were a regular Joe Louis."

"It's the only time I've ever thrown a punch. It made me sick to my stomach, but it was worse for Evelyn. She took off running as fast as she could. It was the last time she ever bothered me.

"So why is it that now, when my mother needs my help, when her problems are getting worse, I don't know what to do?" She paused, hugging herself tightly, wrestling with the day's terrifying events. "She almost burned the house down. What do I do when she can't take care of herself anymore? What if there's another accident? What happens when her memory gets so bad that she doesn't recognize me?"

For a while, Drake didn't answer; when he did, his tone was serious. "Back on the farm," he began, "my father thought I was one hell of a disappointment. Most days, he'd shout or shove me out of the way, complaining about some chore I hadn't done to his liking. The only time he gave a damn about me was when we brought in the harvest. From morning to nights far darker than this, my brothers and I were like slaves to him. Sure, we had a responsibility to help our family, but whenever we complained about being hungry, cold, or tired, my father had no compassion. All he had was his belt.

"The difference between our folks," he explained, finishing his beer and setting it on the railing, "is that yours tried and mine didn't. So when it comes to now, to having to care for your mother, all you can do is listen to your heart and let it tell you what's right. Even if you fail, you'll always know that you did your best. That's the same as your mother did by you all those years ago."

Drake came to sit beside Clara on the swing. At first, she thought he wanted to comfort her, to pull her into his arms. But all he did was put his hand over hers; she quickly accepted his touch, entwining their fingers.

Sitting quietly beside him, Clara was nearly overcome with emotion. Tremors raced across her heart, her eyes misted, her skin grew warm. Because of Drake, she hadn't had to face this terrible, trying day alone. He had rushed into the smoke-filled house without a thought for his own safety, remaining calm in the face of crisis. When the fire truck and the sheriff had arrived, he'd followed her lead without hesitation, helping to create a story in which the blame wouldn't fall on her mother. And now, by telling her about the troubles he'd had with his father, he was trying to ease her burden. What she felt just then was greater than any kiss or embrace, no matter how tender. It was special. Magical. Unbelievable, even.

Sitting there, her hand in his, neither of them feeling the need to say a word, Clara suddenly realized something she wouldn't have ever thought possible.

I'm falling in love with Drake McCoy . . .

Chapter Seventeen

EDDIE WALKED QUICKLY down the streets of Sunset. The early-morning sun shone brightly. He had a touch of headache and his stomach felt queasy, undoubtedly due to all the alcohol he'd drunk the day before, but he refused to let it keep him from the task at hand. While downing scotch, he'd formulated a plan: he would learn the identity of the stranger who had interrupted him and Clara.

He began by making phone calls. His newfound focus had cleared his head, although he suspected that some of his words must have been slurred. Asking around Sunset, he'd wanted to know of any recent arrivals. It didn't take long for his efforts to bear fruit. He discovered where the man was staying: the Sunset Hotel. From there it was easy. Eddie had telephoned Edna Gilbert and learned every detail he could, beginning with the stranger's name.

Drake McCoy . . .

With that nugget of information, he had made more

phone calls, up and down the highways, across the country-side, all the way to St. Louis. What Eddie learned was interesting. McCoy was a race car driver, a man who pitted his skills against others' for money; from what he gathered, McCoy won more often than he lost. How the man had met Clara was still something of a mystery. Surely it was happenstance; McCoy had stumbled across the widow, be-come smitten, and thought he had some sort of claim to her. And that was why Eddie was headed to what passed for a hotel in these parts.

He was going to dissuade the man.

The truth was that Eddie wanted Clara Sinclair for his wife, which meant he was insanely jealous of McCoy. What could she possibly see in such a ruffian? How could a race car driver who probably didn't have two nickels to rub together hold a candle to someone like himself, a man who was both important and incredibly rich? The answers eluded him.

Eddie opened the front door of the hotel and stepped inside. The place was just as dingy as he remembered; the tabletops were covered in dust, the pictures on the walls had been bleached almost white by the sun, and a few windowpanes were cracked. When Eddie had been much younger, his father had gone out of his way to help Edna and her husband get the hotel off the ground and regularly brought his son with him to see how the Gilberts' business was doing; to Eddie's eyes, it had looked run-down even when it was new.

"Mornin', Eddie," Edna welcomed him from behind the

front desk. The hotel's owner looked rough, her eyes red and her hair a rat's nest of tangles. Clearly, she'd just woken up.

"Is he here?" Eddie asked.

"Who do you mean?" the older woman answered, stifling a yawn.

"The driver! McCoy! Who else would I be talking about?" he snapped, the words coming out in a rush, startling even him with their intensity.

The banker's anger cleared the fog in Edna's head. She stood a bit straighter and pushed some wayward hair back behind her ear. "He and that fella with him is roomin' up on the second floor," she said. "I ain't seen neither one of 'em this mornin', so I reckon they're still there."

"Then call him down here," Eddie told her.

The older woman nodded, sending her hair flying every which way, undoing the work she'd done. She reached for the phone.

Eddie folded his arms across his chest, satisfied. The last thing he wanted was to knock on McCoy's door. He wanted their meeting to be on *his* terms.

It's time the two of us had a talk . . .

"You don't look so good."

Drake put it as politely as he could. Amos sat on his bed, leaning forward with his elbows on his knees and his head in his hands. He'd been asleep while Drake got dressed, snoring loudly, and had only just woken. Amos wore a stained undershirt and a pair of boxer shorts, with plenty of wrinkled and sagging skin exposed. He slowly looked up to reveal a face that seemed as if it'd been in an accident. His eyes were narrow, watery, and bloodshot; they peeked out over the top of dark bags. He hadn't shaved in days; a patchy beard was coming in, making him look ten years older. His mouth hung open and his lips were red and chapped. As pale as he was, if Amos had been lying back on the bed, staring up at the ceiling, Drake might have wondered if he was dead.

"Thanks for noticin'," the mechanic snarled without much humor.

"You want me to fetch a doctor?"

Amos shook his head, an act that looked to have hurt. "I ain't got the time or the money. 'Sides, we gotta get the car ready to race tomorrow."

Drake's eyes narrowed. "You got them to agree to it?"

"Weren't easy," the older man explained. "By the time he accepted, I felt like I was beggin'." He winced, closing his eyes. "That hillbilly was actin' like he was doin' us a favor."

"He can think whatever he wants, just so long as we got a race."

Amos scratched his cheek. "There's one hang-up, though."

"What is it?" Drake asked.

"He wants to see the cash up front 'fore we race. Probably thinks we're tryin' to bet with money we ain't got."

"No problem. Was he fine with the wager?"

The mechanic coughed and nodded at the same time. "If I hadn't proposed it, I suspect he was gonna try to raise it himself. He thinks his boy could beat Zeus racin' his damn chariot. He don't believe it's possible they could lose."

"Then he's in for a heap of disappointment."

"That's what I thought the first time we raced 'em," Amos spat angrily. "We wouldn't be in this pickle if you'da kept your damn head on what you was supposed to be doin' 'stead of lettin' it daydream 'bout some broad you just met."

Drake struggled to hold his tongue as his temper rose; he knew that if he spoke now, nothing good would come of it.

But that didn't stop Amos from stirring the hornet's nest further. "I suppose you come back late last night 'cause you were with her."

"That's right," Drake answered.

"I figured as much. I was hopin' to have a word with you 'bout our upcomin' race, but seems like you have different priorities. With the way you're carryin' on, maybe I oughta be worried 'bout you showin' up."

"Now, just hold on a second! You know damn well that—"

Amos interrupted with a wet cough that wheezed its way out of his lungs. "Damn it all," the mechanic groaned. "You got no idea how happy I'm gonna be when we finally leave this two-bit town."

Drake frowned. He'd been hoping for a better time to talk to Amos about his decision to give up racing and settle down in Sunset with Clara. He knew that his friend would disagree, that he would try to talk him out of it, but Drake was committed. The events of the day before, walking the streets with Clara, the scare of her mother's accident, and then sharing a seat with her on the porch, the two of them holding hands, had convinced Drake that she was the woman he'd been waiting for his whole life. To leave now would be shutting the door on his one chance at love, and that was something he would not do. So while he feared breaking off his friendship with Amos, worried that the man he cared for like a father wouldn't understand, he knew he didn't have any other choice.

"About that," he began. "We need to talk."

"Oh, yeah?" Amos asked. "'Bout what?"

But before Drake could say another word, the phone rang; the way Amos reacted, wincing in agony, the sound was worse than being punched. At first, Drake considered ignoring it, but then he wondered if it might be Clara and answered. Instead, it was the hotel's owner.

"Mr. McCoy?" she began. "Sorry to bother you, but there's a fella down here who wants a word with you."

"Who is it?" Drake asked.

The woman paused. "You should just come hear what he has to say," she said. "I reckon that if he bothered to come, it's bound to be important."

With that, she hung up.

For a moment, Drake stood with the silent receiver in his hand. Eventually, he put it back on its cradle, his thoughts churning.

"What was that about?" Amos asked.

"I've got to take care of something real quick," he answered, too curious to ignore the summons. Drake had the doorknob in his hand when he stopped, turning back to his friend and partner. "We've still got things we need to talk about."

"Whenever you can find the time," Amos replied dismissively. With a groan, he lay back on his bed, rolled away from Drake, and pulled the blanket over his head. "You know where I'll be."

When he reached the bottom of the stairs, Drake saw who was calling on him; it was the banker, the same man who had upset Clara a couple of days before. He stood near the front door, facing away from the staircase, one foot nervously tapping the floor. He wore an expensive suit, the fabric too tight around his waist. A gold watch chain hung from his pocket. Drake glanced at the woman who ran the hotel. She kept looking back and forth between the two men, her face sour, as if she'd just bitten into a lemon. Abruptly, she turned and disappeared through a curtain hung behind the front desk.

What in the hell's going on here?

Drake cleared his throat.

The man spun around, looking surprised. "Ah, Mr. McCoy!" he said cheerfully, although there was an obvious fakeness to his voice, a nervous tremor. "I didn't hear you come down. I hope you don't mind my dropping by like this, but I thought we should meet under better circumstances." He walked over and stuck out his hand. "I'm Eddie Fuller. I own the bank."

Drake took the offered greeting, giving the man's hand one firm pump before letting go; Eddie's grip was cold and clammy.

"What can I do for you?" he asked flatly.

"Well," the banker began, fishing in his pocket for a silk handkerchief, which he used to wipe the rapidly accumulating sweat from his brow, "I was hoping we might discuss what we can do for each other."

Eddie smiled strangely as he talked, flashing plenty of teeth; he acted as if they were old friends. But Drake saw right through the banker's fake cheer. Over the years, he'd met plenty of con artists, liars, and thieves: grizzled men in raggedy old suits who sold bottled tap water out of the backs of their trucks, talking as fast and slick as a carnival barker, claiming that it would cure any ailment under the sun; trashy young women who hopped from one rich man to the next, sucking their wallets drier than a creek bed in summer, getting by on their looks for as long as Father Time allowed; and so-called men of the cloth, going around the countryside preaching in God's name, but always with their hands out and most donations finding a way into their pockets. Eddie might not be so blatantly rotten, but like those others he was out for only himself, no matter who he had to trample to get what he wanted.

"So say your bit," Drake replied.

Eddie looked toward the hotel desk; it was currently unoccupied, but Edna couldn't have gone far. "Let's step into the parlor," he suggested. Drake gave a curt nod and followed him into the hotel's front room.

The parlor was small, but felt even tinier for being crammed with too many tables and chairs; however, with its fancy wallpaper and huge glass chandelier, it was surely the ritziest room the Sunset Hotel had to offer. Eddie took a seat near the window and beckoned for Drake to join him.

"I'll stand," he answered.

"Please," the banker replied. "We don't have to be enemies. We're both businessmen, unless I'm mistaken and you race cars just for sport."

Drake's eyes narrowed.

Eddie again flashed his goofy smile. "Are you surprised that I'd try to learn something about you?"

"I shouldn't be. I just don't know why you'd go to the trouble."

The rich man's cheeks flushed. "I would have thought that to be obvious."

Drake's jaw tightened. "Clara..."

Eddie nodded, still unable to meet the other man's gaze. "That's right. I can only assume from your arrival at the bank that you're interested in her as well. Unfortunately, that's a problem," he said, finally turning to face Drake.

"Is it now?"

"I'm in love with her."

Looking at the banker, it was obvious to Drake that, from the outside, Eddie Fuller wasn't much of a rival; his looks weren't the sort that attracted much attention. But the fact that he was probably the richest man in town meant that dismissing Eddie out of hand would be a mistake. Drake had to tread carefully, as if driving on a wet track.

"You're not her type," he replied.

"Of course I am," the banker disagreed defiantly. "She *deserves* a man like me, someone successful enough to give her whatever she desires."

"And what is it that you think Clara wants?"

"Why, the same as every woman. A big home, a new car, jewels, fur coats, and parties at which to show it all off."

Even though he'd known Clara for only a short time, Drake was convinced that she longed for none of those things; it was good for him that she didn't, because he couldn't have afforded any of them. But what he *could* give her was the thing she wanted most, even needed, and something Eddie had neglected to mention.

Love.

"When I saw the two of you inside the bank," Drake said, "she didn't seem all that interested in you or any of what you're offering."

Eddie's ridiculous grin faltered, revealing the ugliness underneath. "She will be," the banker insisted. "The more time we spend together, the more she will understand that there's no better husband for her than me. What I had planned that day would've gone a long way toward that if you hadn't interrupted and ruined everything."

Eddie Fuller didn't strike Drake as the sort of man who handled rejection well. Rich men were used to getting what they wanted. Drake was convinced that if Clara was left alone with Eddie, no matter how much she rejected his advances, the banker would pressure her relentlessly until she gave in.

"Clara would tell you otherwise," Drake said.

Eddie shook his head. "Though it pains me to say it, right now Clara isn't smart enough to know what's in her own best interest." One eyebrow rose quizzically. "I wonder if *you're* any better."

"What the hell are you talking about?"

Slowly, Eddie reached into his suit coat and pulled out a folded slip of paper. "I have something for you." He put it on the table and slid it across to Drake, who, with no small amount of trepidation, picked it up. When he unfolded it, his eyes grew wide and his breath caught in his throat.

It was a check. It was made out in his name for two thousand dollars.

"Why...why would..." he stammered.

"This is business," Eddie explained. "That money is yours, no strings attached, so long as you do one thing."

Drake's pulse hammered in his ears.

Eddie leaned forward. "All you have to do is pack your things, throw them in that fancy car of yours, and drive away. And then, once you've left Sunset, you don't ever come back. As a matter of fact, you never so much as think about Clara Sinclair again."

He looked into the banker's eyes, sure that this was some sort of joke, but even though Eddie couldn't meet the intensity of his gaze for long, the businessman was serious. He wondered if the man had done this before: buying someone off, making them give up something they cared about in exchange for money.

Drake wasn't a rich man, never had been.

There were times in his life when he'd struggled with money, wondering where his next meal might come from, how he was going to pay for a hotel room on a rainy night, or how he might afford enough gas to race. Somehow, through hard work and the strength of his convictions, he'd always managed to come up with what he needed. But Clara wasn't for sale. Love wasn't something that could be bought at a roadside stand. It was a priceless jewel. For Drake to surrender Clara and walk away from something he'd spent his whole life searching for would have been ridiculous. It was too great a cost, one he would never pay.

"You're insane," Drake spat as he began ripping the check into little pieces.

For a split second, Eddie looked stunned, wide-eyed at the turn of events. But then his face hardened. He reached inside his suit and pulled out his checkbook.

"All right, then. You want more, is it?" he asked. "Name your price."

"You don't have enough to make me leave Clara."

"Come on, now. What if I double it?" Eddie prodded, raising his pen, poising it above another check.

"Go to hell," Drake snarled.

"You would walk away from *four thousand dollars*?"

"You're damn right I would," he replied, and made to do exactly that.

But then Eddie said something that made Drake stop in

his tracks. "Do you know what will happen to Clara if you refuse this money?"

Drake turned back.

"You see, my bank owns the note on Clara's house," Eddie explained. "With some creative accounting, by changing a number here and there, I can make it appear that Clara's behind in her payments. Her loan would be in arrears." He paused, his tongue darting out to lick his dry lips. "If she couldn't come up with the money, the bank would own the house and she'd be out on the street."

Drake fumed, his thoughts churning. It was obvious that this was the leverage Eddie was using against Clara; it explained why she'd been so reluctant to talk about what had happened at the bank. If she didn't give in to Eddie, he would take her house and ruin her life, along with those of her mother and son.

"You'd never get away with it."

"Oh, I most certainly would. If I were you, it's a risk I wouldn't be willing to take," the banker said, flashing a smug, irritating smile.

"You son of a bitch," Drake growled.

Eddie held up his hands, as if he was afraid that Drake was about to tear him limb from limb. "I don't want to do it that way," he said. "I want her love unconditionally, but to have her, I *will* use force if I have to."

Unfortunately, Drake believed every word the bastard said.

So what was he going to do about it?

But then, surprisingly, Eddie gave him a sliver of hope.

"I know this is a lot to think about," the banker said, nervously drumming his fingers on the table. "How about you take a day or two to think it over, to fantasize about what all this money might buy you? With some time, I'm sure you'll see it my way. If you actually have feelings for Clara, you'll agree that the best thing you can do is get as far away from her as possible. Because if you don't..."

Drake understood all too clearly.

Without a word, he turned and left. The clock was ticking...

Chapter Eighteen

OPEN UP, MOM," Clara said as she leaned against the closed bedroom door, her ear pressed against the wood, straining for a sound. "Please..."

She held another plate of food in her hands, the third she had brought for Christine to eat: a couple of eggs, some sausage, and two pieces of toast. Clara hoped this one would have a different fate than the others; each had remained untouched, reluctantly taken away after they'd turned cold as stone.

After Drake had left the night before, Clara had gone to bed but once again hadn't been able to sleep. She had stared at the ceiling, listening for any sound her mother might make: the creak of a floorboard, the rustling of bedsheets, even a cough or a snore. But all she heard was the beating of her own heart. Eventually, it had calmed her to sleep.

But once morning had come, still without a sound, a

touched plate, or an opened door, Clara had started to grow concerned.

"Mom! Can you hear me?" She knocked hard, insistently, her fist pounding against the wood, but there was still no answer.

Suddenly, panic flared in Clara's heart. What if something had happened to her mother? What if she was hurt, in need of help?

"Mom! Open up! Open your door!"

Even as Clara yelled, her imagination began to run wild, creating one horrible scenario after another, terrifying her. She grabbed the doorknob, turned it while pulling at the same time, rattling the door in its frame in a desperate attempt to make it open. Shame filled her for not doing it sooner, for letting her mother wallow in her pain, for not trying to help. She was only vaguely aware of the plate shattering on the floor, food spilling at her feet. She pounded and yanked and shouted, all at the same time.

But then, just as she was about to ram the door with her shoulder, hoping she might be able to force it open, Clara heard something.

"Leave me alone..." Christine said from inside, her voice faint.

Clara gasped with a mixture of relief and sadness. Tears filled her eyes. "Mom...Oh, Mom..." she answered, her face again pressed against the door. "Please...open the door..."

Once more, there was silence.

Slowly, Clara straightened, wiping away her tears as she

tried to compose herself. Her mother had given her what she wanted, the acknowledgment that she was alive. But she would grant nothing more.

Reluctantly, and with a heavy heart, Clara walked away.

Clara absently pushed herself on the porch swing. Lazy clouds drifted by on the afternoon breeze. On the opposite side of the street, George Atkinson, Sunset's mailman, went about his appointed rounds. Somewhere nearby, a car honked its horn; two short beeps followed by one long note, its own Morse code.

How different everything looked last night…

Hours earlier, she had sat in the swing beside Drake, their fingers entwined, the warmth of his skin enough to ward off the evening's chill. After the day's excitement, his presence had been a comfort. She wanted him beside her, and was thankful that that was right where he wished to be. So much had changed in such a short time; she could only imagine how different it would become now that Drake had expressed a desire to remain in Sunset, to stay by her side.

Drake's declaration had surprised her. That he was willing to give up a part of his life *for her* was amazing. When she listened to him talk, about their relationship, opening a garage, a future in Sunset, it gave her hope. Her life since Joe's death had been so gloomy, it was hard to believe that sunnier days were on the horizon. She was scared that she could be wrong, that she was misunderstanding something about the situation, but she refused to surrender to her fears that she couldn't find happiness, that she didn't deserve love. She most certainly did.

Still, there were problems.

Foremost on Clara's mind was Tommy. Her son still hadn't come home since his grandmother had nearly lit the house on fire. He was surely with Naomi, unaware of the calamity that had struck his family. But what alarmed Clara most was her reaction to his absence; she'd started to get used to it. She knew that it was wrong of her, that Tommy was in a precarious spot in his life where one mistake could ruin him. So right then and there, Clara decided that regardless of her mother's deteriorating health, her troubles with Eddie, and even her relationship with Drake, her son had to come first. Nothing else was more important.

It was then that Clara heard a sound that stunned her.

Piano music.

Without hesitation, Clara was out of the porch swing and hurrying for the front door. Inside, she froze, dumbfounded by what she saw.

Her mother was playing the piano.

Christine sat on the small bench, her hands moving quickly, dancing from one note to another. Bright sunlight streamed through the windows to fall across the wooden floor, wash over the black instrument, its heavy lid closed, and finally reach the edges of the ivory keys. Music echoed around the room. The melody was familiar, a song that Clara had listened to often when she'd been a little girl: "Song of the Lark," by Tchaikovsky. Christine's hands worked up and down the keys, her face a mask of concentration, while her foot gently pumped the pedals.

Tears filled Clara's eyes. Happiness and relief flooded her heart. It had been many long years since her mother had last played. For as long as Clara could remember, music had been Christine's greatest passion. She plunked children's tunes, contorted her fingers through the complexities of Mozart, somberly played during funerals, reveled at weddings, and had even composed a few songs of her own. But then her memory had begun to fade...

One day, years ago, Clara had suddenly realized that her mother hadn't played for a long time; it was easy to understand why. For Christine, the frustration of tripping over a note she'd struck thousands of times before had become unbearable. Rather than embarrass herself, it was easier to shut the lid over the keys. That was the end of it.

Until today.

Once she finished Tchaikovsky, Christine moved on to a church processional, then a show tune that Clara recognized but couldn't name, and finally a lively Duke Ellington number. Sweat beaded on her brow, but Christine never slowed. Occasionally, she would stumble over a note, making the slightest of errors, but Clara didn't know if it was because of a deficiency in her memory or simply the rust from not having played for so long. Listening to the music, Clara was reminded of happier times, back when Tommy used to stand next to his grandmother and sing with the enthusiasm of a child, not the least bit self-conscious of his voice; reminiscing made her happy and sad at the same time.

Clara wondered if her mother knew she was there, listening, but when Christine finished playing with a flourish, she looked up and right into her daughter's eyes; a small, satisfied smiled lit up her face.

"That was incredible," Clara said.

Her mother didn't answer, but a bit of color rose in her cheeks. For a moment, neither of them spoke; after so much music, the silence felt heavy, ominous.

"I'm sorry I didn't answer the door," Christine finally said. "I...I'm just so ashamed of what happened. I could have killed us all."

"But you *didn't*," Clara insisted; it was the same conversation they'd had yesterday, which made her wonder if her mother had forgotten.

"What if you hadn't come home when you did? What then?"

"I didn't call the fire department, so that means one of our neighbors did. They would have put it out instead of Drake."

Clara's reassurance seemed to have no effect on her mother; Christine shook her head as her eyes grew wet. "I can't stop thinking about it," she explained. "Every time I try to recall what I was doing, so much of it stays hidden away, like it's wrapped in fog. I remember wanting to start dinner. I got out the skillet, put in some lard, turned on the stove, but then a curtain comes down and the next thing

I know, you're shaking me awake and telling me that the house is on fire."

"Everyone has moments like that," Clara argued. "There are lots of times when I can't remember doing something. Why, just last week, I—"

"Stop it," her mother interrupted.

"But it's not as bad as—"

"Clara Elizabeth, you just hush up right now!" Christine snapped, using her daughter's middle name to silence her. "Don't you lie to make me feel better. We both know I'm getting worse. There's no use in acting any different."

Slowly, reluctantly, Clara nodded.

"Can you imagine what this is like for me?" Christine asked, her lip trembling. "To know that the day might come when I don't recognize you? That I might do something that gets Tommy hurt? It's unbearable."

Though she wanted to say something, anything that might alleviate her mother's suffering and worries, Clara couldn't. The truth was, she had the same concerns and had yet to come up with any answers.

"I know you won't want to hear this," her mother continued, tears flowing down her cheeks, "but some nights, just before I fall asleep, I think it would be better for you and Tommy if I didn't wake up..."

Clara rushed to her mother's side, sitting beside her on the piano bench. She pulled Christine close, wrapping her arms around the older woman's shoulders as the two of them sobbed. It devastated Clara to hear her mother say such things, to admit that she would rather die than live with the fear of her deteriorating memory. She was angry, at both the unfairness of what was happening and her inability to do anything about it. Whenever Clara had needed her mother, especially in the years after Joe's death, Christine had always been there, providing support, care for Tommy, anything that might be needed. But now that their situation was reversed, the mother needing her child, Clara was helpless.

Once their tears had subsided, Clara tried to come up with a solution. "Maybe we could hire a nurse, someone who can be with you all day."

Christine shook her head. "You know we can't afford that."

"How about one of your friends? Ruth Mitchell is retired now. She might be willing to come over while I'm at work."

Her mother didn't respond; Clara suspected that the idea was too embarrassing to consider.

"Then I'll stay home with you."

"And what will we do for money? We can barely make ends meet now, especially since I'm not at the library anymore."

"We'll find a way," Clara declared, though she had no idea how.

Her mother was right; they were scraping by as it was. The house was slowly falling apart, one broken thing after another, to say nothing of the problems with the pickup truck. On top of everything, there was Eddie's threat to take away the house. If that happened, they would lose everything. But then, Clara thought about what Drake had said the night before.

"Do you remember Evelyn Price?" she asked.

Her mother smiled. "That's a name I haven't heard for a very long time. Her family moved away ten years ago or so, didn't they?"

Clara nodded. "She used to bully me on the way home from school when we were little. I asked you to make her stop, but you wouldn't do it."

"I made you stick up for yourself," Christine said. "It was one of the hardest lessons I ever had to learn as a mother, to let you fight your own battles. All I wanted was to march over to the Prices' and give her parents a piece of my mind, but I couldn't. You needed to learn how to stand up for yourself."

"And I did. I fought back and she never bothered me again."

"Why are you telling me this?"

Clara took a deep breath. "Because you encouraged me. You gave me strength. Because of what you said, even if Evelyn had continued to bully me, I wouldn't have quit. So that's just what we're going to do now. We're going to fight this." As she spoke, Clara's voice, as well as her conviction, grew stronger. "You're not going to lock yourself in your room anymore, too frightened to do something because of what might happen. Each one of us, together as a family, Tommy included, we're going to get through this."

Her mother nodded, but she didn't seem very convinced, so Clara tried a different approach. "What made you decide to play the piano again?"

"I don't know...not exactly..." Christine answered. "Whenever I used to be out of sorts, sad or angry, I would sit at the piano and play until those bad feelings went away. After what happened yesterday...after the fire...I was drawn to it." Offering a weak smile, she added, "Maybe I forgot I *couldn't* play."

"But you still can."

"Today, at least. But what about tomorrow or the day after that?"

"There are no guarantees," Clara answered. "But you're never going to know what you can or can't do unless you try. It doesn't matter if you forget what you wanted for breakfast or if you already went to get the mail or even how to play the piano. You just find something else to eat, check the mailbox again, or sit back down and start plunking the keys. Mistakes and failures are only temporary." Nodding toward the piano, she added, "They clearly don't mean forever."

"I...I don't want to be a burden to you..." Christine said.

"You couldn't ever be," Clara told her, smiling through tears. "But there is something you could do that would make me plenty angry."

"What's that?"

"You could give up," Clara replied. "Now is the time to fight, not surrender. Isn't that what you taught me?"

Christine smiled, more genuinely than before. "And you actually listened. If that isn't a miracle, I don't know what is."

This time, instead of music or sobs, laughter filled the room.

Clara put the last of the dishes from lunch into the sink. Her mother had gone upstairs to lie down, promising that she wouldn't so much as shut her door, let alone lock it. After their conversation at the piano, things between them felt easier. Trying to keep things positive, Clara told Christine that this was a new beginning for all of them, a chance to start fresh. But then, just as she started to hum one of the melodies her mother had played, there was a knock at the front door. She slipped off her apron, dried her hands, and went to answer.

She opened the door to find Drake standing there, running a hand through his dark hair. But unlike the night after they first met, this time he seemed distracted, and the smile he gave her looked forced.

"What's the matter?" Clara asked, frowning.

But instead of answering her question, Drake asked one of his own. "How are things with your mother?"

Clara told him what had happened, from trying in vain to get Christine to open her door to her shock at hearing the piano, and then about their conversation.

Drake occasionally nodded during her story, a bit absently, she thought. He wasn't even looking at her when he said, "That's great."

"Why don't you come in," Clara told him, stepping aside. "I can fix you something to eat."

Drake shook his head. "If you don't mind, I'd like to stay out here. I'm so worked up right now that I can hardly stay still."

Once again, she asked, "What's wrong?"

He took a deep breath. "You might want to sit down..."

Clara sat on the porch swing. Unlike the night before, Drake didn't join her; instead he paced back and forth in front of the railing. She began to feel uneasy.

"Drake..." Clara said.

He stopped and looked at her. "When I came to get you at the bank, what was happening between you and your boss?"

"Eddie...had asked me to stay after work..." Clara answered, uncomfortable with the question but unwilling to lie. "He was upset about something I hadn't done..."

"Something that had to wait until after the bank was closed?"

Clara froze. This question was more direct, one she couldn't deflect so easily; in the end, she chose not to say anything.

Drake came over and leaned against the porch railing opposite her. "Clara," he said softly, insistently. "Tell me."

She looked up at him, the sun shining off the side of her face, uncertain about what she should do. Hesitantly, she said, "Eddie...is infatuated with me. He...wanted me to stay after work so that we could talk...He said that if I didn't...I could lose...my job..."

"That's all?" Drake pressed. "Your position at the bank?"

Clara knew that this was her moment of truth. All she had to do was tell Drake that Eddie threatened to take away her home in order to force her to marry him. But she couldn't do it. It was too embarrassing, a blow to her pride not all that different from what her mother suffered because of her memory loss. Besides, what good would come of her telling Drake? How could he possibly help? Somehow, some way, she would find a solution on her own.

"That's all," she lied.

Drake was silent for a long while, watching her closely. Finally, he nodded his head, got up from the railing, and headed for the stairs. He was halfway down the walk before Clara, confused by what was happening, shouted to him.

"Where are you going?" she asked.

He stopped, his shoulders slumped, then turned back; his expression was one of disappointment. "You're lying to me."

Clara's heart raced. Shame forced her to look away. Somehow, he knew.

"Drake, I...I..." she stammered.

"I already know everything," Drake told her. "I know *exactly* what that bastard is holding over you."

Chapter Nineteen

WALKING AWAY FROM Clara was one of the hardest things Drake had ever done. But she'd left him little choice. He knew everything about her and Eddie, that the banker was blackmailing her into becoming his wife. Drake had even been offered thousands of dollars to step aside and let it happen. But when he'd given the woman he was falling in love with a chance to be honest with him, Clara had lied to his face. This wasn't a time for secrets. All of their cards needed to be laid on the table.

"How...how do you know?" Clara asked, astonished.

"Eddie came to see me at the hotel this morning. He was upset that I'd interrupted the two of you and wanted to make sure it wouldn't happen again. He offered me money to leave town."

"He tried to bribe you?"

Drake nodded. "He wasn't playing around. It was an awful lot."

"And... and you...?" She didn't finish her question, but Drake could see the hope in her eyes as plainly as if she had, wishing for the right answer.

"I tore up the check," he said. "But that didn't bother Eddie for long. He pulled out his checkbook and offered to double it." Drake paused, letting the words linger. "I told him there was no amount he could pay to make me leave you."

Relief washed over Clara's face, but Drake quickly wiped it away.

"But that's not all," he explained. "Eddie said that if I didn't do as he asked, if I refused to take the money, he'd take your home." He looked up at the porch. "He said that he'd doctor the books to make it look like you were behind on the payments. If you didn't agree to marry him, he'd throw you out on the street."

Drake watched Clara crumble. Tears flowed down her cheeks. She hugged herself tightly, as if she was trying to keep from shaking. But her gaze never wavered, holding his, though her lip trembled.

"Why didn't you tell me?" Drake demanded. "Why did you lie?"

His questions were enough to make her look away. "Because I was embarrassed," she answered. "Because I'm ashamed to be in this position. Because I've spent the last nine years struggling, doing most everything on my own, and I'm sick of asking for help." Her eyes once again found his; they were narrow, smoldering. "I still have some pride left. It might not be much, beaten down and tired as it is, but it's enough so that I don't want to bare every problem I have. Not to you. Not to anyone."

Drake's respect for Clara grew. Inside her, no matter how deep it was buried, remained a spark of strength that neither Eddie nor any of her other troubles could extinguish. He had noticed it the day they met; it was one of the many things that had attracted him to her.

"How much do you still owe on the house?" he asked.

"It doesn't matter."

"Yes, it does," Drake insisted.

"Lots. More than I could ever hope to raise if Eddie actually went through with his threat. I'd lose everything, and he knows it."

Drake had a thought. There was the money he'd been squirreling away, both the little amount in the bank in Illinois and what was buried in the bottom of his duffel bag back at the hotel. It likely wouldn't be enough to pay off the loan, but it wasn't chicken feed, either; it might buy them time, a chance to find another bank without such an unscrupulous owner or to expose Eddie's lies. Slowly, a plan began to take form in his mind. The thought struck Drake that maybe all those years of diligently socking away cash had been so that right here, right now, he could save Clara. So that they could start a life together.

"Maybe there's another way . . ."

Clara's eyes narrowed. "What do you mean?"

"Even if Eddie called in your loan," he said, "nothing would happen right away. You'd have some time."

"Enough to pack my things and get out," Clara added.

He shook his head. "That's not what I mean. You might be able to get another bank to cover you."

"Why would they do that?"

"Why not?"

"If Eddie has gone through with his threat, it's because I turned down his proposal," she explained. "If I don't agree to marry him, he'll fire me for sure. That means I won't have any income. Without that, no one, certainly no other bank, would be willing to take a risk on me."

"Unless you could give them some money up front. A down payment."

"Which I don't have," Clara said, frustrated.

"You might not," he answered. "But *I* do."

"What are you talking about?"

Once again, Drake began to pace, growing more energized with every step. "Ever since I started racing, I've put away some of my winnings," he began. "It was never a lot of money at once, a hundred dollars here, twenty there, whatever I could spare. But if you do that for a decade or more, it adds up. I've been hauling it around with me, waiting for the rainy day when I might need it. Looks to me like that day has finally arrived."

"No," Clara answered emphatically, shaking her head. "I can't let you do that. I won't take your money."

"Why not?" he asked.

"Your garage," she said, coming down the stairs to stand before him. "You were planning to open it with your savings, weren't you?"

"But that was before I knew—"

"If you give me that money," Clara interrupted him, "will you have enough left over to get started?"

Drake took a deep breath. "I won't," he admitted.

"And that's why I can't let you do it."

"It isn't your choice to make. Besides, what if we said that I'm not giving it to you, but that it's a loan?"

"We'd be old and wrinkled before I could pay you back."

Drake smiled. "I wouldn't mind, as long as we're still together."

His words stunned Clara. He'd said it lightly, yet when she searched his face, there was no humor in his eyes. It was no joke. What Drake was suggesting was life-changing for both of them. He was offering commitment, stability, and hope, things that she hadn't had in so long they felt unfamiliar. He was proposing a plan to keep Eddie from taking her home, but also something grander, the idea that they could build a life together. And while she was surprised, Clara found herself wanting to take him up on his offer, to believe it was possible. In a way, Drake was asking her to take a leap of faith.

But Clara was having trouble taking that first step...

"Let me help you," Drake said again.

"I...I...can't..." she said. "You're offering too much..."

"No, I'm not," he insisted. "Ever since we met, you've talked about all the troubles weighing you down. But here I am, trying to make things better, and you won't let me."

Clara didn't know how to answer.

Drake stepped closer, reached out, and took her hand. "In a way," he began, "I understand why you don't want my help."

"You do?"

He nodded. "For years, you've had to do it on your own. But it doesn't have to be that way anymore. You're not alone. I'm here now."

"I'm a widow. I have a son..."

Drake shook his head. "None of that changes a thing. I want to be there... for all of you."

Clara's heart knocked hard in her chest.

"I'm not your husband. I'm not Joe," Drake continued as he searched her eyes, looking into their depths. "I can't ever replace what you had with him. The truth is, I don't want to. All I want is a chance to create something special with you. Our *own* love. But that won't happen while you're living in the past. Yesterdays are fine and dandy, but if you aren't careful, you'll spend all your time looking backward and miss tomorrow."

Clara squeezed his hand tightly, clinging to him, her knees unsteady.

"I've spent my whole life going from one place to the next," Drake said. "It's time for me to stop running, to put down roots. This is my chance to build something, but I can't do it on my own. You need to meet me halfway."

I want to... I really do...

But Clara still couldn't bring herself to say the words. "You're right," she answered, wiping away a tear. "Things have been a mess for so long that I don't remember it being any different. Even now, with you a part of my life, I have to deal with Eddie, my mother almost burned the house down, and then there's Tommy...I...I don't know where he is..."

Drake frowned. "He still hasn't come back?"

Clara shook her head.

Drake looked past her and toward the street, as if he was searching for her son. "All right, then," he said. "Let's take care of one problem at a time. First, we find Tommy, and then we can talk about what to do with Eddie."

Clara glanced back at the house. "I can't leave my mother," she explained. "Not now. Not so soon after what happened."

"Then I'll go look for him."

"What will you do if you find him?" She recalled what Drake had said about his first encounter with Tommy, her son storming off at the mention of Naomi.

"Nothing. Anything I say will likely go in one ear and out the other anyway. Right now, the most important thing is to find out if he's all right."

"The first place I'd look is the Marshland Tavern. Naomi's father owns it."

"Then that's where I'll start."

For a short while, neither of them spoke. Then, gently yet insistently, Drake pulled her to him. Clara felt as if she floated into his arms, her feet never touching the ground. She raised her chin and closed her eyes, her breath catching in her throat. When he kissed her, it was tender, as soft

Inside was livelier, too. People milled about after work, most everyone drinking. A couple kissed beside the juke-box, the man's hand roaming across his gal's rear end, oblivious to or uncaring about the scene they were making. Over the din of voices and music came a hoot of triumph. In a small back room, two men were playing pool; one pumped his cue in the air, his laugh a sharp cackle, while the other reluctantly held out a couple of crumpled dollars. Leaning against the bar, customers held up empty glasses, placing orders just as fast as the bartender could fill them; a younger woman stood with him behind the bar, though she seemed unwilling to help. The same drunk who had been there during his first visit was still slumped in his chair, although this time, he appeared to be awake.

Drake walked the bar looking for Tommy, but he wasn't there. Tired, as well as a little thirsty, he decided to wait and see if Clara's son would show up; after all, he'd already searched the whole town.

As he neared the bar, a seat suddenly emptied, and Drake slid into it. Minutes passed before the bartender could work his way to him, but soon enough the man asked, "What can I get for ya?"

Drake ordered a beer. When the man returned with his drink, Drake plunked a few coins on the bar and asked, "Do you know Tommy Sinclair?"

The bartender's eyes narrowed a bit. "Sure," he said.

"Has he been around lately?"

"Been a while. Couple a days, I reckon."

Drake nodded. "Thanks anyway."

He took a draw from his beer and then turned around to face the door. From here, he could see the whole bar and out the window to the sidewalk. If Tommy came in or happened to walk by, Drake would see him. He could afford to be patient. He didn't want to return to Clara empty-handed, but if he did, he'd know it wasn't for lack of trying.

"You're in my seat," a deep voice grumbled.

Drake turned to find a mountain of a man standing beside him. He was broad-shouldered, with muscles that strained against the fabric of his shirt. His expression was ugly, his frown so deep that Drake expected it would have taken him an hour to turn it into a smile. He wasn't the man who'd left the seat.

"Nobody laid claim to it before I sat down," he answered warily.

"Don't matter none. I done told you it's mine."

There was a time, not all that long ago, when Drake would have taken the man's threatening words as a challenge. He would've told the brute to get lost and then, when things inevitably went downhill from there, bunched up his fists and tried to give as good as he got. But he was a different man now. A new life with Clara beckoned to him, so close he could almost reach out and touch it. A barroom brawl wasn't worth the hassle. It was easier to walk away.

"All right," Drake said as he started to get out of the chair. "Let me grab my beer and then you can—"

But before he could finish, the man punched him in the face.

Chapter Twenty

WHY IN HEAVEN'S NAME are you still *here*?"

Clara thought of her mother's words as she turned her truck onto Main Street, struggling to shift gears. Up ahead, the setting sun was still high enough to shine in her eyes, forcing her to raise her hand for shade. Another day in Sunset was ending; families would soon sit together to eat dinner, to talk about work and school, to share a laugh.

But not Clara's. Hers was as troubled as always.

Once Drake left to look for Tommy, Clara had gone back inside to wait for her mother to wake. She'd expected Christine to agree with her, to understand her reasons for staying behind, especially after the accidental fire.

She'd been dead wrong.

"Stop worrying about me," Christine had scolded her. "All you should be concerned with is Tommy."

"Drake is out looking for him."

"Then get in your truck and do the same! Two sets of eyes are twice as good as one! Get going!"

And so Clara had been shooed out of the house. While Tommy had been absent longer than this before, even angrier from time to time, something about this felt different to her, more foreboding. Her heart raced faster, sweat slicked her palms, and her nerves felt frayed. She couldn't have said exactly why, but she desperately needed to know that her son was safe.

Because she had sent Drake to look at Wilbur Marsh's tavern, the most likely place to find her son, Clara checked elsewhere. She drove past his school, wondering when Tommy had last attended. She checked at Dowager's Pond, a watering hole on Millicent Granger's property where Tommy and his friends used to swim when they were younger. Clara passed the post office, the bakery, the movie theater, everywhere she could think he might be.

But so far, she hadn't found him.

In the end, it was as if Tommy had vanished.

So here she was, making her third trip down Main Street, still looking, refusing to give up. But this time, something was different. Nearing the tavern, she noticed Drake's car parked in the lot. Clara considered stopping, her foot hovering over the brake. She imagined that Drake was inside, talking with Tommy; the thought made her heart pound. But just as quickly as the impulse arrived, it passed; if her son *was* there, the last thing he'd want would be for his mother to come walking through the front door.

She drove on. She would leave this to Drake.

Besides, as the day had gone on, Clara had felt, more and more clearly, that there was one more place she had to go, one more person she had to talk to.

And it couldn't wait any longer...

For a moment, Drake saw stars.

The first punch had clipped his chin; at the last possible instant, he'd turned his head, keeping the damage from being much worse. But the blow had still been enough to knock him down. His glass flew from his hand; it fell onto the floor and shattered into pieces. Stunned and disoriented, Drake tried to shake the cobwebs loose.

Get it together! Quick!

No sooner had Drake looked up than the other man was back on the attack. The brute raised a booted foot, determined to bring it crashing down on his head and end the fight before it had even really begun. Drake rose quickly to one knee, closing the distance between them while twisting to one side. The kick whizzed past his head, an inch from its intended target, and slammed hard onto the floor. Without hesitation, Drake threw a short punch into the soft flesh at the small of the man's back. The goon let out a sharp bark of pain and moved away, angry and surprised that his seemingly bested victim had managed to fight back.

Drake rose to his feet, his head slowly clearing. "We don't have to do this," he said, wondering if he still had a chance to talk the other man down.

He didn't. "Go to hell!" his attacker snarled, then charged.

Snapping out a sharp jab, Drake punched his opponent's nose, feeling it crunch and sending blood spurting, but it wasn't enough to keep the other man at bay. The brute slammed into him, driving him into the bar and forcing the air from his lungs. Chairs and patrons scattered.

One punch struck his ribs, then another. An elbow cut his cheekbone; the blood left a hot, wet trail down his face to go along with the pain.

But Drake wasn't about to fall. Not again. He hadn't started this fight, but he would damn well finish it.

Drake gave the thug a hard shove in the middle of his chest, forcing the man back and giving himself some room. He took a small step forward, put his weight on his front foot, and with all the strength he could muster, smashed his fist into his opponent's jaw. Sharp pain shot from his hand down his arm, but he ignored it, hitting the man again and again, on his jaw, deep into his stomach, and once again in the nose. The man wobbled like a chair missing a leg.

"Summabitch..." the goon mumbled through busted lips, bloody saliva leaking down the front of his shirt.

But the brute wasn't finished yet. He reared back, nearly toppling over, and threw a haymaker that Drake easily dodged.

With his opponent completely off balance, it was a simple matter for Drake to grab the man's shoulder and spin him around. He cocked his hand and threw a hard, heavy punch that landed flush with the side of the brute's face. The man fell, not slowly like a tree, but more like a load of bricks, quickly and with a lot of clatter. One second he was upright, the next he was flat on his back. His eyes fluttered once, twice, then fell shut and still.

Drake didn't let his guard down.

Even though his body ached, he looked quickly around the bar, expecting another attack from some tough or drunk who wanted to keep the brawl going. But no one moved. Every face in the place was turned toward him: he noticed expressions of disbelief, most likely those who couldn't believe he'd won; some were entertained, their mouths curled in devilish grins; there were even a few who looked embarrassed by their own curiosity, turning away quickly when they caught Drake's eye. Even the couple at the jukebox had stopped kissing to watch, still wrapped in each other's arms, the music playing beneath them the only sound in the bar besides his own fevered breaths.

But it was the bartender's reaction that surprised Drake the most.

While everyone else in the bar was dumbfounded, the man who ran it calmly grabbed another glass, filled it with beer, and sat it on the counter.

"I reckon you could use this," he said. When Drake reached into his pocket to fish out a few more coins, the bartender waved him off. "No charge."

"Much obliged," Drake answered. He grabbed the beer and took a deep draw, wincing because of his split lip, but the drink was worth the discomfort.

When he finished, Drake took another look around the bar; nothing had changed. Standing there, every eye in the place still on him, he understood he couldn't wait for Tommy here. Though the bartender had extended a favor, a compassionate act for the victor, he was a stranger in Sunset. Even if there weren't splatters of blood down the front of his shirt, he stood out like a sore thumb. To stay would be risky. He had to return to Clara without her son.

When he left, the sound of voices returned.

The silence went with him.

Clara drove into the cemetery. The sun hung just below the treetops, painting the clouds a deep, dark orange, a color like rust. A pair of crows was startled by her sudden arrival, flapping their wings as they leaped from tombstones, cawing loudly to voice their displeasure at being interrupted.

For hours, she had been looking for Tommy. From one side of town to the other, out into the countryside, at every place she thought her son might go, returning to some in order to check again, but there had been no sign.

Through it all, Clara had felt the pull of the cemetery.

She had ignored it for as long as she could, so when she'd finally surrendered and decided to go, she'd told herself that she was just being thorough; after all, Tommy had been there recently, getting arrested for allegedly breaking a tombstone. But deep down, Clara knew there was another reason.

One that has everything to do with Drake McCoy...

Lost in thought, she drove down the same path she

always took, meandering along the creek, shadowed by trees. At the next intersection, she braked to look toward where, the last time she was there, workmen had been loading the broken stone; the space remained empty, the identity of the deceased known only to the family he or she had left behind.

Clara moved on.

Up another short hill, she pulled over and shut off the engine. She stared out the dirty windshield at Joe's grave. Her heart raced.

It was hard to believe she had been here only a few days earlier to mark the anniversary of Joe's death. So much had changed in that short time. Since Drake had come into her life, she wasn't the same person. With his decision to stay in Sunset, to remain by her side, things would undoubtedly change even more. Because of that, in her heart, Clara had known she had to come here to try to explain it all to Joe, her dead husband, the first man she'd given her heart.

She had to tell him that she was falling in love with another man.

For more than nine years now, Clara had been alone. Suddenly, unexpectedly, a man had come along. But to accept Drake into her life, she knew that she needed to make peace with her past. She would never forget Joe, or even stop loving him, but she had to stop mourning. Holding their memories too close wouldn't allow her to make new ones. Just thinking about what she had to do, what she had to say now, brought tears to her eyes.

She opened the truck door and got out. When she

reached Joe's plot, she got down on one knee and placed a hand on the stone.

"Joe," Clara said, her voice cracking. "We need to talk..."

Drake crossed the parking lot and headed for the Plymouth, gravel crunching beneath his feet. Absently, he ran a hand across his already bruising chin, tender from the punches he'd taken. Reaching inside his mouth, he wiggled an aching tooth, wondering if it didn't feel loose. He wasn't a vain man, would've had a hard time calling himself handsome, but after what had just happened, he could only imagine what he'd look like in the morning. Hopefully, Clara wouldn't find it *too* hard to look at him.

Try as he might, Drake couldn't figure out why the brute had attacked him. He hadn't seemed drunk. Drake hadn't been flirting with his lady. Out of the blue, the man had demanded the seat, but then, when Drake agreed to surrender it, he'd thrown a punch. It didn't make any damn sense. He had seen plenty of brawls before, some born out of family feuds, others from some version of love gone wrong or another, plenty on account of too much drink. However, most of them had had a reason, no matter how misguided. Drake shook his head; there wasn't much point in thinking about something he wasn't ever going to understand.

But then, just as he was fishing his keys from his pocket, he saw something that made him pause.

Another row of cars past the Plymouth, the bar's parking lot ended up against an empty lot. On the far side, a dirt road fronted a row of run-down houses, one with an upstairs window busted out and dark; it looked like the building was winking. But what had caught Drake's attention was a person walking quickly down the road, a man with his hands stuffed into his pockets. As Drake watched, the figure stepped out of the growing shadows, lengthening by the second as the sun slowly but steadily descended, his face turned up to the weak light for only an instant. Drake hadn't gotten a long look, but it had been enough.

It was Tommy. Drake was sure of it.

He hurried after him, determined not to let Clara's son out of his sight.

"Tommy!" he shouted, but the kid didn't stop; was it Drake's imagination or had he quickened his step?

Still aching from the bar brawl, Drake moved as quickly as he could, ignoring the pain, but before he could catch up, the figure turned down a narrow alleyway between two buildings. Moments later, Drake did the same, but he immediately had to stop to keep from running into someone.

"Watch it, fella!" a surprised voice yelled.

In the murky gloom, Drake couldn't make out the man's features; he helped Drake out by striking a match, cupping his hands, and lighting a cigarette. Before he shook out the flame, Drake got a good look; beady little eyes that made him resemble a rat, along with a crooked nose, probably broken a time or two.

He wasn't Tommy.

But was he the man Drake had been following? His clothes looked about right, but that didn't mean much; the same was true for his size. Maybe Drake had imagined the resemblance to Tommy; he had wanted to find Clara's son so badly that his mind convinced him that the man was someone he was not. Maybe the punches he had taken during the fight were worse than he thought.

Then again, maybe he *had* seen Tommy . . .

Drake peered down the alley. With the disappearing light, it was like looking into a deep well. He couldn't see clearly more than twenty feet in front of his face.

"Did someone just come past here?" Drake asked.

The man took a deep drag on his cigarette, his eyes narrowing. "You lookin' for trouble?" he growled.

Drake thought about pressing the issue, but instead mumbled an apology and walked away. He'd already been in one fight; he didn't need another. Besides, even if it *had* been Tommy, the boy was long gone by now.

Retracing his steps, Drake found he had another surprise waiting for him. A young woman was leaning against his car. Surprisingly, he recognized her; she'd been standing behind the bar when he arrived. She grinned, the look meant to be seductive, as if she was sizing him up. Her arms were folded across her chest beneath her breasts, purposefully pushing them up and out.

"Decide to go for a walk?" she asked.

"I thought I'd get a breath of fresh air," Drake answered.

"Good," the woman replied as she pushed off the Plymouth and closed the short distance between them. "You're going to need it."

And then she kissed him.

* * *

Damn... this is gonna be fun...

Naomi lounged against the car and watched the man make his way across Lou Torkelson's empty lot. She hadn't paid him much attention when he'd entered the bar, but when her father said that he was asking about Tommy, everything changed. This was the man Tommy had told her about, the one spending time with his mother, the race car driver. Drake McCoy.

It had been simple for Naomi to proposition Chet Miller, a roughneck farmer who spent so much time in the bar that it sometimes felt as if he lived there. He wanted her, just like half the other men in the bar, so he was keen to do whatever she asked; having a go at McCoy was the same as buying her a drink. Naomi wanted to be entertained. So when Chet walked over and began causing a ruckus, she leaned back against the bar, smiled, and waited for the fun to begin.

But then, shockingly, the race car driver had come out on top and, for the second time in a matter of minutes, everything changed.

When McCoy left the bar, Naomi had slipped out the side door and followed. She stayed a safe distance behind him, trying to keep from being noticed, at least until she wanted to be seen. She licked her lips, adjusted her bra, and wished that she'd squirted herself with perfume. But then, just as she was about to reveal herself, McCoy had hurried across the empty lot. He'd shouted something, but Naomi hadn't been able to make it out. Unexpectedly alone, she decided to lean against his car and wait for him to return.

While she waited, Naomi thought about what she'd do with the race car driver. Since beast had failed, it was time for beauty. She wondered how long it had been since McCoy had touched a young woman like her; probably longer than he wanted. No man resisted her for long. Eventually, he would break, bending over backward to please her. Then, once she was finished having her fun, she'd spread every last salacious detail around town. She'd already ensnared Clara Sinclair's son; she wondered how the old widow would feel if she claimed her new man, too. The possibility of such chaos was too delicious for her to ignore.

Just then, she noticed McCoy walking back toward her. She smiled, flashing him a look that had won her plenty of men.

"Decide to go for a walk?" she asked with a voice like spun honey.

Chapter Twenty-One

I'VE MET SOMEONE..."

Clara knelt on the grass that grew above her husband's body, resting a hand on his tombstone. The sun fell steadily, causing shadows to reach across the ground toward her. A breeze rustled the trees. But as idyllic as it was, Clara's thoughts were in turmoil. Her mouth had gone dry and her heart raced. She felt like she was speaking to Joe face-to-face, revealing something shameful, as if she had done something wrong.

"His name is Drake McCoy...and he...he..."

She sputtered to a stop, not because she was embarrassed, but rather because she didn't know where to start. How could she possibly describe Drake, what he meant to her, or how he made her feel? Should she talk about how they'd met? What words would explain the indescribable feeling of racing down the hill in the Plymouth, her head sticking out the window? What about when she'd kissed Drake for the first time? Then there was the way he'd rushed into the house they both feared was on fire, willing to risk his life to protect her family.

Could she say these things to Joe?

In the end, Clara knew she had to. So she took a deep breath and began. "I was driving back to the bank one afternoon when the truck broke down..."

The more she talked, always being honest, choosing not to leave anything out, the easier it became. Clara felt no shame for the things she'd done with Drake. The opposite was true; speaking of him, of their time together, talking about the qualities that attracted her to him, made her happy.

"Ever since you died, my life has been so hard," she continued. "The house...my mother's health, the bank... and especially Tommy...Nothing has gone the way I hoped it would. Every year I come here to remember the anniversary of your death so that I can unburden myself. But no matter what I say, nothing ever gets any better.

"For nine years, I've been so utterly alone. When those men came to the house and told me that you'd been killed, right then and there, I gave up. I swore to myself that there would never be another man, that I would be a widow and that would be that. But I was a fool. I had no idea what lay ahead of me. But then, Drake came along and everything I thought I knew got turned upside down."

Clara told Joe about how the race car driver made her feel, about his smile, the sound of his laugh, even the strong, confident way he drove his car. The more she thought about it, the more Clara realized that the two men had much in common; both were strong, proud, and willing to put a stranger's needs ahead of their own. She imagined that had all of their lives been different, Drake and Joe might very well have been friends.

"Drake makes me happy. You don't need to worry about me..."

With those words, Clara began to cry. She supposed that, in a way, one door was opening, while another was being shut.

"I will *never* forget you," Clara said tearfully. "All I ever wanted was your love, to raise a family, to spend the rest of our lives together. But we can't." She paused, marshalling herself for the words that still needed to be said. "When we got married, I promised to love you until death did us part, a vow I've continued to keep for nine years. Part of me will keep it forever. But things need to change. My memories won't ever go away, but it's time for me to make new ones. I can't keep living in the past. I know you wouldn't want me to."

Clara believed it. If anything, Joe would have been annoyed that she'd waited so long. He would've wanted her to be happy.

"I don't know how it happened," she said, smiling through tears, "but I've found love twice in a lifetime."

Suddenly, a loud caw startled her. Clara looked up to see two crows circling above her, gliding effortlessly through the darkening sky. She watched, spellbound, as they landed on a tombstone two rows from where she knelt. She couldn't have known for certain whether they were the same birds she had spooked when she entered the cemetery, but she suspected they were.

She watched them intently as they stared back at her. Then both birds cawed noisily before one flew off, its wings flapping furiously as it soared across the river before disappearing into the thick woods beyond. The other remained where it was; its beady eyes never left her.

Clara trembled. This was a sign, she was sure of it. In her heart, she believed that Joe was looking down on her. He was giving her his approval for what she had told him, for her feelings for Drake.

The lone crow cawed, but it didn't fly away.

She smiled, crying tears of joy, and said the only thing that felt right.

"Thank you."

What in the hell?!

Drake couldn't move. The last thing he'd expected was for the young woman to kiss him, yet that was just what she'd done. Her boldness stunned him. So here he was in the tavern's parking lot, the Plymouth a car's length away, its keys dangling from his hand, with the arms of someone he didn't know wrapped around his neck, her lips pressed against his.

"Mmmmmm," she purred into his mouth.

Drake finally shook off his surprise. He grabbed the woman by the arms and pried her loose. He pushed her away a little harder than he'd intended, causing her feet to skid in the gravel. Strangely, she didn't seem bothered. In fact, his rejection appeared to excite her all the more; her eyes narrowed and she smiled mischievously, with only a hint of teeth showing.

"Don't do that," Drake warned; he fought down the urge to wipe his lips with the back of his hand.

"Come on, now," she replied. "You enjoyed it while it lasted. Just think of all the things we can do if we get in the backseat of your fancy car..."

"No, thanks."

"Don't you find me pretty?"

If Drake were to give an honest answer, it would be yes. She was at an age where she was just beginning to understand how seductive her looks could be. Everything about her would catch a man's eye: the curve of her hips; the color and curl of her hair; the way her blouse had been unbuttoned just far enough to reveal a hint of cleavage; even her voice, honeyed and deep at the same time, sort of like Greta Garbo's, tugged at that part of him that was still in his teens and twenties, back when he was a skirt chaser, his head on a swivel for the next pretty girl.

But he wasn't that boy anymore.

It wasn't hard for Drake to see past her beauty and into her darker depths, down to the person she was on the inside. This lady was poison. To become involved with her, even for a night, was a dangerous proposition.

"Still not interested," he replied coolly.

She licked her lips. "You would be if you gave me half a chance."

"You don't even know my name."

"Drake McCoy," she said with a smirk. "You're the race car driver."

Again, he was caught off guard; she seemed to have a knack for surprising him. "Well, then," he managed to recover, "I don't know yours."

Before she answered, she moved a step closer. "I'm Naomi. My father owns this place," she told him, nodding toward the bar, but her eyes never left him.

Her name made Drake pause; it was like inserting the right key into a stubborn lock, causing the door to creak open.

"Naomi..." he echoed. "Naomi Marsh..."

"That's right," she answered him with a smile, as if she was pleased at the recognition. She shouldn't have been.

"Tommy Sinclair's gal?"

Her expression soured. "I'm not anyone's gal," Naomi replied. "Not exclusively. Right now, I could be *yours*." She took another step closer.

Like a boulder building momentum as it began rolling down a hill, Drake steadily began to put it all together; suddenly, what had happened in the bar, especially the unprovoked brawl, made a lot more sense.

"It was because of you, wasn't it?" he asked.

"You'll have to be a bit more specific."

"That big lug started a fight with me because you told him to."

"Guilty as charged," Naomi answered, giving him a wink. "I thought for sure that Chet would make short work of you, but was I ever wrong. Watching you break him down like you did sure got my blood up. I figure that if you *fight* like a wildcat, imagine what you can do in bed..."

Drake couldn't believe what he was hearing. "You're nuts."

Naomi laughed like she was really having fun. "That right there is why you interest me so much. You're nothing like the men I usually meet. They're always after one thing," she explained, slowly running a hand across her body, starting at her hip and ending on one of her breasts. "They'll lie through their teeth trying to get it, but they don't fool me. Every last one is all dick and no brains."

"Even Tommy?" Drake asked.

She shrugged. "Yeah, even him. Tommy was fun for a while, but a girl like me has needs a boy can't fulfill. I want a man."

This time, when Naomi threw herself at him, Drake was ready. He grabbed her by the shoulders, stopping her in midair. Once again, he pushed her back, but this time, Naomi lost her balance; her eyes went wide before she landed hard on her backside in the loose stones.

"Stop it," he told her. "You're making a fool out of yourself."

"How dare you!" Naomi shouted.

Furious, she scrambled to her feet and stepped toward him, all her sexuality and looks of seduction gone. Rearing back, she slapped him hard across the face. Drake made no move to stop her, even though his cheek hurt like hell, more from the bar brawl than her slap. He'd allowed her to hit him in the hopes that it would get the anger out of her system, but it looked to have been in vain; when she reared back to strike him again, he snatched her by the wrist.

"Let me go!" she screeched.

"Settle down," he told her. "It's finished."

"Why?!" Naomi demanded through a storm of tears. Drake couldn't know if her show of emotion was on account of pain, shame, or the frustration of being rejected; it was probably a mix of all three. Yanking her hand free, she shouted, "Why don't you want to be with me?"

Drake didn't answer, but instead pushed past her and got in the Plymouth. He turned the key in the ignition and the engine roared to life.

"Tell me!" Naomi demanded, her hands balled into fists.

Slowly, Drake turned to look at her, his arm draped over the steering wheel. Even after everything he had been through, the beating he'd both given and received and his fruitless search for Tommy, he still felt pity for Naomi; he imagined that nothing in her future was going to go the way she expected it would.

"You've got a hell of a lot of growing up to do," he said before putting the Plymouth in gear and roaring away.

Naomi watched Drake McCoy race his fancy car out of the parking lot; his tires sprayed gravel before they reached the pavement. Within seconds, his taillights had disappeared into the night. But Naomi still stood there, stunned, staring in disbelief. Absently, she rubbed her wrist where he'd grabbed her; it would probably be bruised come morning, along with her rear end.

What... what in the hell just happened?

In the span of half an hour, she had gone from wanting the race car driver beaten to a pulp to hoping he would tear her clothes off and ravish her, but unbelievably she was now right back where she'd started.

She wanted him ruined, even dead.

The only silver lining to her rejection was that there wasn't anyone around to see it; if there had been, Naomi thought she would have died from the embarrassment. Never in her life had she been turned down like this. She hadn't thought it possible. No man had ever been able to resist her; she desperately wanted to believe that Drake McCoy's doing so wasn't a mark against her, but rather showed him for a fool. Either way, he had to pay.

The only question was how...

Suddenly, an idea occurred to her. It was devilish, even a bit dangerous, but that was part of its appeal. If she actually went through with it, a whole lot of people might end up ruined, especially Drake McCoy. With every passing second, Naomi began to believe it was the *only* choice she could make. When she was finished, the race car driver would regret turning her down.

Naomi smiled. This time, she showed plenty of teeth.

Before Clara got back in her truck, she wiped away a few tears. She stole one last glance at Joe's grave, smiling easily.

One story had ended while a new one began. It was time to look forward.

I'll never forget you...I promise.

Now that night had arrived, Clara turned on the truck's headlights, managed to start the engine, and followed the road back toward the cemetery's entrance. Above her, the moon had climbed high enough to reflect off the creek. Birds dipped and swooped, devouring bugs.

She drove past rows of tombstones before pausing at the cemetery's gates. But then, just as she began to pull out onto the main road, Clara pressed the brakes. To her left was a sharp bend, tight enough for the road to quickly disappear from sight; to make matters worse, a weeping willow's branches drooped low to the ground, further blocking her view. Suddenly, without any warning, a car roared around the bend, racing right toward her. Clara gasped. Even though it was almost pitch black out, the vehicle had its headlights turned off. In seconds, the car reached her; it honked as it went past, missing her by a foot, if that.

Clara gripped the steering wheel tightly, her heart pounding. If she hadn't already believed that Joe was watching over her, this would have convinced her.

"Goddamn it! Watch where the hell you're goin'!"

Sweet Woods swiveled in the back of the Cadillac to look out the rear window; the truck they'd just missed dwindled into the darkness. He had been half-asleep when Malcolm suddenly jerked the wheel to the side and he'd been pressed up against the door, forced awake and plenty angry.

"It's as much our fault as theirs," Jesse said, slumped in the passenger's seat. "Drivin' like we are with our lights off."

"I can see fine," Malcolm grunted from behind the wheel.

"Ain't a matter of *your* eyes, but theirs."

For a quarter of a mile farther, they rode in darkness, Sweet still swearing a blue streak from the backseat, but then Malcolm flipped on the Cadillac's headlights; he did so just in time to illuminate the sign that announced their arrival in Sunset.

"We headin' straight to the hotel?" Jesse asked hopefully.

Sweet shook his head. "I wanna check out this shithole town. Look for some sign of Barstow, McCoy, or that car a theirs. Might be easier than we expect."

"But if we don't see 'em, *then* we get a room, right?"

Sweet smirked. He knew that Jesse hated sleeping in the Cadillac. Though the man was a stone-cold killer, he was also a bit of a dandy; with his nice clothes and carefully coifed hair, he would prefer sleeping in a bed, even the kind found in some two-bit dive, to roughing it.

"We'll just pull off the road and catch a few hours," the drug dealer answered, only because he wanted to piss off the other man.

Jesse groaned. Malcolm didn't seem to care.

"Come mornin'," Sweet continued, "we'll ask around and see if anyone's seen 'em. They mighta passed through a week back."

"And if no one's seen 'em?" Jesse asked, clearly annoyed that he was going to spend another restless night sleeping in the cramped car.

"Then we keep lookin'," Sweet answered as he leaned back in his seat.

Ever since he'd left St. Louis, he'd had only one goal: to find that son of a bitch Barstow. Sweet wouldn't rest until he got back everything that had been stolen from him. The mechanic would pay.

And so would anyone stupid enough to be mixed up with him.

Chapter Twenty-Two

CLARA HAD JUST SHUT the pickup truck's door when the Plymouth pulled into the driveway behind her. She peered through the windshield at the passenger seat, hopeful that Drake would have Tommy with him, but he was alone. For a long while, he stayed behind the wheel, staring out at her, before finally shutting off the engine and getting out. It was then, just as Clara was about to ask him what he'd found, that Drake stepped into the meager light of the bulb above her side door.

She gasped at what she saw.

His face was covered in bruises, dark and mottled, the corner of his mouth and one eye badly swollen. His cheek had been cut; dried blood stained his skin. He smiled at her, trying to downplay his injuries, but doing so caused him to wince.

"What happened?" Clara asked, rushing to him, her

hand rising to his face, where it hovered; she was afraid to touch him.

Drake shrugged. "It's no big deal," he told her. "I just had a disagreement with some guy about which of the Andrews Sisters was the best singer. He swore by Patty, but I've always been partial to LaVerne."

Clara knew that his attempt at a joke was for her sake, to put her at ease, but the sight of his battered face made her feel sick to her stomach.

She grabbed his arm. "Come inside so I can clean you up."

Drake shook his head. "You don't have to. It's not that bad," he said. "Besides, you should see the other guy."

Without a word, she pulled at him; Drake offered only the slightest resistance before giving in and following. Clara sat him down at the kitchen table. Under the brighter light, his wounds looked even worse; if Drake was correct and he'd gotten the better of the fight, then Clara felt sorry for whoever was going to have to tend to his opponent. She wet a washcloth and gently wiped away the dried blood on his face and hands. Drake flinched the first couple of times she touched him, but he refused to turn away or complain.

"I'm going to go get some things," she told him. "Don't move."

"Hurts too much for that," he said with a weak smile.

In the upstairs bathroom, Clara gathered what she would need: some bandages, alcohol to disinfect his cuts, and a pair of scissors. The whole time, her mind raced, wondering what had actually happened. Who had Drake fought? Did it have anything to do with Tommy? All she wanted was to ask Drake questions until he told her the truth, but deep down, Clara knew she had to trust that he would tell her in due time.

Before she went back downstairs, Clara checked on her mother. Christine's door was open as they'd agreed, but she was sleeping, her nightstand light still on, a book lying across her stomach. Clara was glad; she wanted to be alone with Drake.

Back in the kitchen, Clara sat facing him. She poured alcohol onto a clean cloth and prepared to properly clean his wounds.

"This is going to sting," she told him.

Drake smirked. "Worse than what you were doing before?"

"Probably."

When she touched the cloth to the angry red cut on his cheek, his reaction, a quick spasm and tightening of his jaw, told Clara she had been right.

Once she finished putting the last bandage on the row of small cuts crisscrossing his bloodied knuckles, Clara sat back. "No more jokes," she said. "Tell me what happened."

He nodded and took a deep breath.

Drake told her about all the places he'd looked for her son, roaming across town, and about how he'd gone to the tavern as she had suggested. He recounted how he had gone inside, ordered a beer, and sat down at the bar to wait and see if Tommy showed up.

"The next thing I know, someone starts a fight with me."

"Who was it?" Clara asked.

"Some big lug, tall and wide as a mountain with hands the size of canned hams. Ornerier than a hound dog with a soup bone."

She thought for a moment. "That sounds like Chet Miller. He's there so much that I'm surprised they don't make him pay rent."

Drake rubbed his jaw. "He didn't seem interested in introductions."

"He just started a fight with you for no reason?"

"That's what I thought at the time, but later I found out otherwise."

"What do you mean?" Clara asked.

"I'll get to that."

He told her about winning the fight, not in a bragging way, but more matter-of-fact, admitting that he could have just as easily lost. Still unsteady on his feet, he'd left the bar, but then, when he was almost to the Plymouth, he thought he saw Tommy. When he ran after him, he hadn't been able to catch up.

"After that, I headed back to the car," he told her. "But when I got there, I found a young woman leaning against it."

Clara tensed. She wanted to ask who it was but couldn't find her voice; she had a sneaking suspicion that she already knew.

"It was Naomi," he confirmed, "the girl I've heard so much about."

"What...what did she want?"

"That's the same question I had," Drake answered. "But before I could ask it, she did something I hadn't figured on."

"What was that?"

Drake's eyes found hers. "She kissed me."

"You . . . you kissed her . . . ?"

Even as Drake had driven out of the tavern's parking lot, he'd known that what had happened with Naomi was going to hurt Clara. His fears had been proven to be well founded. But he wasn't going to lie. If the two of them were going to have a strong, secure relationship, it had to be built on honesty and trust. So while Drake knew that he'd done nothing wrong, that he had never been tempted by Naomi, convincing Clara otherwise wasn't going to be so easy.

"Not exactly," Drake corrected her. "It's more that *she* kissed *me*."

Carefully, painstakingly, he explained how Naomi had thrown herself at him, emphasizing that he had pushed her away, rejecting her advances. Drake told Clara how he had anticipated her trying to kiss him again, how he'd stopped her, and that Naomi had ended up on her backside in the gravel. Finally, he recounted how he'd been slapped for denying her. He finished by describing Naomi as he'd left her, furiously angry in the middle of the bar's parking lot.

"Naomi threw herself at you?" she asked, trying to piece it all together.

"She wasn't really interested in me," he answered.

"Then why did she do it?"

"Because all a gal like Naomi wants is a reaction, the stronger the better," Drake told her. "If she'd gotten her mitts on me, if I'd been willing, it would've hurt you and Tommy. She would have stirred up a hornet's nest, just to be entertained. Then, when the fire she lit burned down, she would've moved on to the next sucker willing to buy what she was selling."

Drake could see that while Clara was listening to him, she wasn't *hearing* what he said, struggling to get past the kiss. She searched his face for something, a sign to put her aching heart at ease; when she didn't find what she was looking for, she glanced away. "You...you weren't tempted?" she asked, her voice faint, almost a whisper. "She's a pretty girl..."

"Don't you believe me?" he asked.

Clara turned to look at him. She nodded. "It's just that..." she began, but her voice trailed off.

Drake took her hand. He rubbed his rough, calloused thumb over her palm, feeling her warmth, hoping that his touch was comforting. "I'm not a boy, interested in every skirt that comes along," he told her. "I haven't been one for a long time. Naomi never had a chance. What I want is something different, something real." He squeezed her hand hard enough to make Clara look him in the eyes. "I want *you*. Nothing will ever convince me otherwise."

Slowly, Drake leaned forward, lowering his face toward hers. The look in Clara's eyes clearly said that his words had moved her. She showed no hesitation in moving closer, inclining her head so that their lips would meet. At first, their kiss was tender, almost chaste, but it soon grew in intensity. Their mouths opened, their tongues touching, their passion potent enough for him to ignore the ache of the bruises marring his face. He considered being cautious and backing away, not giving in to his desire for fear that he was reading the situation wrong, that he was about to make another mistake; but instead, he decided to damn his caution, to live for the moment, to show Clara exactly how he felt.

"Drake..." she moaned into his mouth.

Growing bold, Drake grabbed her elbow and pulled her to him; Clara didn't resist, rising out of her seat. She sat on his knee, wrapping herself in his arms.

His hand rose to touch her cheek, tracing the curve of her jaw. Their kiss continued hungrily, as if each of them had been starved for the other's touch. Drake's fingers descended across her shoulder and onto her collarbone. When he traced the soft underside of her breast, Clara gasped but didn't move away. But when he lifted her blouse to feel the bare skin beneath, she abruptly broke their kiss and leaned back.

"Wait," Clara told him breathlessly.

"What's wrong?" he asked, worried that he'd gone too far, too fast.

"This...this is what you want?" she asked.

"Yes, I do," he insisted.

"You want to be with me...*this* way..."

Drake nodded. "More than I could ever tell you with words."

"Then we can't do this here. Someone could interrupt us," Clara explained.

She got out of his lap, took his hand, and led him to the door. Before Drake could ask where they were going, she stepped into the night, the darkness swallowing her as she hurried toward the garage.

Drake followed.

As Clara walked from the house to the garage, her heart raced. The night had grown cool, causing the gooseflesh on her arms to rise, but she hardly felt it. Drake's kisses and touches had ignited a desire in her that couldn't be extinguished, that she didn't want to put out. Years had passed since a man had touched her, but her yearning for such attention had never completely disappeared; rather it had hibernated, sleeping until the right man had come along to wake it. Drake McCoy was that man.

When he'd pulled her into his lap, Clara had decided that she would give herself to him, if that was what he wanted; clearly, he longed for the same. But making love to Drake in her home came with risks; her mother was sleeping upstairs, and while Tommy hadn't been around for days, the thought of him walking in on them was terrifying. Since they couldn't go back to Drake's hotel room because of Amos, that left only one place where they could be alone.

Clara opened the side entrance to the garage—the front

doors were still broken—and flipped on the bare bulb hanging from the ceiling.

"Where are we going?" Drake asked when he caught up.

"Come with me," she answered.

At the back of the garage, a drop cord hung between two beams. Clara pulled down hard, revealing a folding staircase. After a quick look back at Drake, she began to climb.

The room Joe had built above the garage was small and sparsely furnished; a chair and desk were on one side of the room, while a small bed and nightstand sat against the opposite wall beneath the only window. Because of the roof's slant, there wasn't much room to stand. In the summer it was as hot as an oven, and in the dead of winter it could feel like an icebox, but now, in the springtime, it was quite pleasant. A decade ago, Joe had used it after a long night of fine-tuning the truck or tinkering at his workbench; he would sleep here rather than risk waking Clara.

For what she planned to do with Drake, it wasn't ideal, but it was the only place they could go to ensure they would be alone.

Drake immediately understood.

He took her hand and led her to the bed. Little light shone through the window or up the stairs, but it was enough for them to see where they were going. Drake leaned down and began to kiss her, tender yet insistent, both of their passions still aroused, and it wasn't long before he began to undo the buttons of her blouse. He was halfway down, the tops of her breasts revealed, silver in the moonlight, when she stopped him.

Drake frowned with no anger or annoyance, but with concern. "Clara..."

She nodded but found that she couldn't speak. She didn't know how to tell him what she was feeling. There was no denying that she wanted him. Her body ached for his touch. But as much as she yearned for the physical, she was nearly overcome by emotion. What was about to happen was a turning point in her life; she'd had the same feeling when kneeling at Joe's grave, a sense that things were about to change forever. Making love to Drake would set them both on a new course, toward some unknown future. It was both exciting and frightening. She knew that she could still stop, even now.

But she didn't want to.

Every fiber of her body, of her heart wanted this, *needed* it. She had made her decision. There was no more looking back.

Clara rose on her tiptoes and kissed him. Drake was slow to react, but his hesitance didn't last long. He soon put his hand on her cheek, his fingers sliding back to disappear into her hair, then drew her closer, their tongues touching tenderly, his breath hot in her mouth. Clara was dimly aware that he'd resumed undoing her blouse; as if in a trance, she returned the favor, her fingers tugging at his shirt, stumbling over the buttons. What happened next was a blur. One by one, items of clothing were removed; her blouse, his boots, her skirt, his shirt, her bra, until both of them stood naked before each other.

"You're the most beautiful woman I've ever seen," he told her.

Clara couldn't contain her flush of embarrassment and turned away.

"Look at me," Drake said.

She did as he asked and saw that, while it was hard for her to accept such a compliment, he had given it honestly, believing every word.

Once again, they began to kiss. Drake's hand gently cupped one of her breasts, holding its weight for an instant before giving it a soft squeeze. Gasping with pleasure, Clara placed a hand on Drake's thigh, then ran her fingers across his skin, rising toward his hip before sliding over to brush against his penis, already stiff with desire and anticipation. Now it was his turn to gasp.

"Clara..." he moaned, breathing hard.

They sat on the bed together, still kissing. Clara lay on her back above the wool blanket, staring up into the face of the man she'd fallen in love with; a few twinkling stars were visible through the window over his shoulder. She felt as if she was adrift at sea, both unable and unwilling to stop the current from taking her. She closed her eyes and let pleasure wash over her.

Though it was obvious that Drake was almost bursting with desire to be inside her, he didn't hurry. Clara trembled as his hands roamed her body; his thumb traced a circle around her nipple, his fingers danced across her rib cage, the flat of his palm brushed her stomach. Finally, his hand slid down the inside of her thigh to touch between her legs, feeling her warmth and wetness; she wanted him as badly as he did her. But while Drake knew she wasn't inexperienced, he was still gentle, increasing in fervor only when she gave him a sign; a moan, the hiss of breath between clenched teeth, the arch of her back.

"Drake, I...I just..." But before Clara could say more, his mouth found hers, making words unnecessary.

Clara spread her legs and Drake moved between them, holding his body over hers, supporting his weight on strong, muscular arms. She was filled with nervous excitement. He positioned himself, moving until he could enter her, which he did slowly, gently; in seconds, he was all the way inside, filling her. Neither of them moved. She wrapped her arms around his broad back and held tight.

"I love you," he said softly.

Clara could only nod as tears of joy filled her eyes.

When she had fallen in love with Joe Sinclair, Clara had imagined that there would never be another man in her life. Then Joe had died. For many long years, she was alone, convinced that things would never change. But then Drake McCoy had come to Sunset and enchanted her. Now she had rediscovered intimacy, the touch of a man, and she was overjoyed. Clara had found love again.

This time, she hoped with all her heart that it would last forever.

Drake began to move, slowly at first. Clara was so excited that he slid effortlessly in and out of her. It didn't take long for him to start going faster, the small bed squeaking in rhythm with their bodies. Their breathing was shallow and came in pants. Sweat beaded on their skin, occasionally falling from Drake's brow to land on her chest. Huge waves of pleasure washed over her, every crest rising higher than the one before.

"Clara..." Drake managed.

"Drake, I...I...It feels so..." But she couldn't finish, the words lost as a spasm of pleasure ripped through her, causing her to grab his forearms tightly. Clara's breath was trapped in her throat. She closed her eyes to a feeling of beautiful agony, an ecstasy so powerful that it almost hurt.

Clara gasped as Drake kept going, his hips pumping furiously, their bodies coming together again and again, wetly, passionately. He moved in and out of her until finally shuddering to a stop, his body pressed against hers, his arms quaking as his seed spilled, filling her with warmth. Clara peppered his face with kisses. Slowly, he lowered himself to rest beside her. Both of them panted with exhaustion.

"That was...that was..." Drake began.

"Incredible..." Clara finished for the both of them.

"How was I ever lucky enough to find you?"

Clara laughed.

Drake's brow furrowed. "What's so funny?" he asked.

"I was just thinking about where the credit for our being together *really* belongs," she replied.

"Where's that?"

"My truck. If it drove like it was just off the assembly line, then we wouldn't be here right now, like this."

Now it was Drake's turn to laugh. "Crazy as it sounds, I reckon it's true."

Lying there, entwined with Drake, truly happy for the first time in longer than she could remember, Clara was finally grateful to that old hunk of junk sitting in her drive. It had been good for something after all...

Clara awoke slowly out of a forgettable dream, her eyes fluttering open. For a brief moment, she didn't know where she was, but her confusion was short-lived. A smile spread across her face. She rolled over on the narrow bed and reached to touch Drake, to feel his warmth, but no matter how much she groped around in the darkness, her hand kept coming up empty.

She sat up with a start, worry teasing at the edge of her thoughts. Just then, she heard a board creak on the other side of the room. Clara looked up to find Drake standing at the stairs, fully dressed, peering down into the garage.

"What is it?" she asked, whispering.

"I heard a car door shut," he answered. "I'm going to go take a look." With that, he descended the stairs, leaving her alone.

Clara got out of bed, hurriedly threw on her own clothes, and followed. Stepping out of the garage, the evening's chill making her shiver, she was surprised by what she saw. Frank Oglesby's car was parked behind the Plymouth. The sheriff stood in the bright glare of his headlights, talking with Drake; the driver looked upset.

Her heart pounded. Watching them, she was suddenly

fearful that the sheriff's unexpected arrival had something to do with Tommy. Maybe he'd been arrested again. What if there had been an accident? Walking toward the two men, she silently berated herself, furious that she'd chosen her own pleasure over continuing to look for Tommy.

"Did something happen?" Clara asked when she reached them; she glanced at Drake and realized that she had misread him. He was angry.

She feared the worst, and that was just what she got, although it came in a way she never would have anticipated.

"I'm sorry to have to come over like this," the lawman explained, "but it couldn't wait till morning."

"What is it? What's so urgent?"

Sheriff Oglesby took a deep breath. "Mr. McCoy here is under arrest."

Chapter Twenty-Three

CLARA WAS SO STUNNED by what the sheriff said that she had to put a hand on the back of the Plymouth to steady herself. She wondered if she hadn't misheard, if there was another, more believable explanation for the lawman's presence, but as she looked from one man to the other, both of their faces grim, she knew there was no misunderstanding.

"Let me make myself clear," Sheriff Oglesby explained. "I'm not looking to put you in handcuffs or make a big scene. That won't do any of us a lick of good. Until I can sort out what happened, you won't be charged."

"But until then, I'm going to be sitting in a jail cell," Drake replied.

The lawman nodded. "There's no other choice. I can't just let you walk free, not with what you've been accused of doing."

"And what is that?" Clara asked, as confused as she was frightened.

It was Drake who answered. "Naomi says that I attacked her," he explained, "and this two-bit tinhorn actually believes her story. Isn't that right?"

"Right now, it's too soon to say which version is the truth," Sheriff Oglesby answered, not acting the least bit put out by Drake's insult. "But Naomi claims you grabbed her wrist, hauled her into the parking lot, and tried to force her into your car. She says that when she wouldn't do what you wanted, you got angry and smacked her around a little."

Clara listened in disbelief. What Frank Oglesby was saying was completely different from what Drake had told her. It was impossible. It sounded nothing like the man she knew and loved.

"I grabbed her wrist when *she* came after *me*," Drake angrily defended himself. "The second time she did it, I pushed her and she fell. All Naomi has to complain about is a bruised ass."

"Her face says otherwise."

"What are you talking about?" Drake asked. "She was fine when I left the bar. Mad as hell, but she wasn't hurt."

"When she came to see me, she had a bruise the size of an apple at the corner of her mouth, a split lip, and she was crying so hard that it wasn't easy to make out what she was saying. How do you suppose she got that way?"

"Beats the hell out of me!"

The sheriff's eyes narrowed. "Interesting choice of words."

"Come on now, Frank," Clara interjected. "Drake didn't do anything wrong."

"You don't know that for certain," he answered. Turning back to Drake, he asked, "Did you do any drinking tonight?"

"I had one beer."

The sheriff pointed at Drake's face. "Way I heard it, you had plenty more than that. Enough to put you in a fightin' mood."

Drake's temper again flared. "I was just sitting there, minding my own business, when this big lug walked up and decked me!"

"Naomi said you came in and started poundin' down drinks as fast as her father could pour them, and then you started getting too friendly with some woman. She said that Chet Miller tried to get you to stop and that was when you attacked him. By the time the dust settled, you'd given him one hell of a beatin'. It was then that Naomi's old man managed to throw you out . . ."

"She's lying!" Drake snapped. "Go ask any of the other people who were there! They'll tell you!"

Clara stepped between the two men in the hopes she might defuse the rapidly growing tension. "Surely you don't believe her," she said to the sheriff.

"If you'd seen her face . . ."

"Everyone in town knows that Naomi is a liar," Clara continued, trying to convince him. "It isn't as if Pastor Hendrickson filed a complaint."

"I can't dismiss her claim out of hand."

"Maybe there's another explanation."

"Like what?"

"If things happened the way Drake says they did, then it would stand to reason that Naomi would be angry enough to try to get revenge," Clara suggested. "Or maybe someone else hurt her."

"Someone like Tommy?" the sheriff asked.

Clara was taken aback. She thought back to when she'd sat across the desk from the sheriff after Tommy had been picked up in the cemetery. That morning, she had begged and pleaded, doing everything she could to convince him that her son was innocent; but now Clara understood that she'd failed. To Sheriff Oglesby, Tommy was always going to be under suspicion; that the lawman could even suggest that her son was capable of hurting someone, especially a woman, hurt deeply.

"That's enough," Drake growled, putting his arm around Clara's shoulder, protecting her. "Her son no more hurt that girl than I did. Naomi's lying."

"She might be," the sheriff agreed, "but the only way to find out for certain is if you come with me and we sort it all out."

"I'm not going anywhere," Drake replied defiantly.

With that, what little remained of the lawman's patience vanished. Making a show of it, Sheriff Oglesby snatched the handcuffs off his belt and held them up for both Drake and Clara to see. "There's two ways we can do this," he explained. "Either you get in my car, right now, without any trouble, or you can keep arguin' with me and I force you in there. I don't want this to get rough, but..."

He didn't finish, but they knew what he was implying.

"I'm not sitting in a jail cell for something I didn't do," Drake repeated.

"Please, Frank," Clara pleaded. "There has to be another way."

The sheriff shook his head. "I have to do this. I know it's nothing more than her word against his, but my hands are tied. There isn't anyone else who has stepped forward to say they saw what happened."

"There is now," a voice spoke from the shadows near the garage. All three of them watched as a figure stepped into the bright glow of the sheriff's headlights.

Clara gasped.

It was Tommy.

Drake was angry. Talking with the sheriff had been a lesson in frustration. No matter what he said, the lawman wasn't listening. Early on, Drake had decided that he would never allow himself to be taken to the jail. He didn't give a damn about tomorrow's race, the money that was on the line, or even standing before some small-town judge; all that mattered was what it would look like to Clara. He wouldn't go, not now, not after what they had just done.

Mostly, he was furious at himself. He should have known better. He should've expected Naomi to try to get back at him. And she'd almost succeeded.

But then Tommy had shown up. Clara rushed over to her son and threw her arms around him, hugging him close, thankful that he was home and safe; she started to ask questions, wanting to know where he had been, not accusingly but out of justified concern, but the sheriff's deep voice spoke over hers.

"What are you talking about, son?" the lawman asked.

Tommy shrugged. "*I saw what happened,*" he answered. "I was there watching." He paused and looked right at Drake. "I saw everything."

Drake wondered if the boy was telling the truth. He was dressed in a simple white T-shirt and a pair of jeans; Drake tried to remember what the person he'd chased had been wearing, but the memories were too distant now, fuzzy, made up more of generalities than specifics. He couldn't say it had been Tommy; he couldn't say it *hadn't* been.

"You were there? At the bar?" Clara asked her son.

Tommy nodded. "Outside."

"Then you can clear this whole mess up," she said hopefully. "Tell the sheriff that Drake didn't do what Naomi is accusing him of. Tell him!"

"Stop that, Clara," the lawman chided her. "All we want is the truth, not how we want things to be." He turned toward Tommy. "All right then, son," he said. "Why don't you start at the beginning, and don't leave anything out."

Once again, Tommy glanced at Drake, his eyes flat; the race car driver suddenly understood how precarious, how dangerous of a situation he was in. He thought back to how badly the boy had reacted when they'd tried to repair the garage door, flying off the handle at the mention of Naomi's name. For the bar owner's daughter, he had practically abandoned his own family. Even if Tommy hadn't seen a thing, had instead been miles from the seedy bar, all he had to do was agree with whatever story Naomi had cooked up and Drake would be spending a long time behind bars, no matter how loudly he proclaimed his innocence. His fate rested in Tommy's hands.

"Well," the boy began, "it happened like this..."

Tommy stood down the street from Sheriff Oglesby's office, smoking a cigarette as he watched the front door. Darkness had fallen; other than the occasional car, no one was out. Almost two hours had passed since he had watched Naomi's run-in with Drake McCoy; it had been half that since he'd followed her here, staying out of sight. For reasons he didn't completely understand, he hadn't revealed himself to her. All that time, one question kept racing around in his head.

What the heck is she up to?

He had a few guesses, none of them good. To Naomi, everything was a game. He saw it in the way she argued with her father, brutally, as if she was trying to draw blood. It was there in how she manipulated him into doing what she wanted. And it was painfully obvious in the way she strung him along, offering up a kiss here, a touch there, but always stopping him just before things went too far. Deep down, Tommy had begun to suspect that she was playing him for a fool.

Lately, he had started to notice the way other men looked at him in the tavern and around town, as if they were holding back laughter; if the rumors about Naomi were true, then a good number of them had likely shared her bed. Tommy often thought about what his mother had said, her many warnings about the bartender's daughter, about how she would lead him down the road to ruin. Not that he wanted to admit it, but Tommy had wondered if she was right. It bothered him enough that he had been pacing, trying to sort through his tempestuous thoughts, considering whether to go into the bar, when Drake had spotted him and given chase. It had been easy to ditch the race car driver, but when he hung around, Tommy had gotten more of a show than he'd expected.

Suddenly, the sheriff's door opened and Naomi stepped out. From where he stood, Tommy could see she was a mess; mascara had run down her cheeks and her shoulders heaved as if she was crying. But then, as she began to walk toward him, something changed. She straightened up, her gait quickened, and a triumphant smile spread across her face; the sight of it made Tommy nervous.

He waited until she was only a couple of feet away before he stepped into her path, startling her so badly that she yelped.

"Jesus, Tommy!" she shouted. "You scared me half to death!"

"What were you doing in there?" he asked.

Naomi followed Tommy's eyes over her shoulder; when she turned back to him, her smile had grown thinner, more malicious. "I had an idea," she said gleefully. "A wicked one. Something that will be lots of fun."

"*What did you do?*" he demanded, the words coming out so brusquely that Naomi looked momentarily taken aback.

"I had a run-in with that fella you were talking about, the one who races cars and is sweet on your mother," she explained. "He got too rough with me, so I decided to return the favor."

Tommy saw that Naomi had failed to mention that she'd followed Drake to his car and thrown herself at him, *twice*. After she had slapped the driver for rejecting her, he'd finally had enough, accidentally knocking her to the ground. Tommy wondered if she'd ever willingly share these details with him; he doubted it.

"You're out for revenge," he said.

"Exactly. That's why I did *this*," she answered, stepping into the soft light of the streetlamp, tilting her head to give him a good look at her face. Tommy recoiled at what he saw; an ugly bruise bloomed at the corner of her mouth.

"But Drake...he..." Tommy stumbled.

Naomi laughed, short but loud. "After he drove off, I went back into the bar and convinced Chet Miller to sock me one." She frowned. "I told that idiot not to hit me very hard, but I swear he loosened a tooth. Hurts like hell."

"You had him hit you...*on purpose*?"

"It had to look convincing."

Tommy was stunned. "But...but why would you do that?"

"So I could blame it on McCoy." She smiled; doing so made her wince on account of her new bruise. "I went to Oglesby and told him that your mother's sweetheart forced himself on me and that when I fought back, he got rough." Naomi's voice rose, as if she was particularly proud of herself. "I was such a good actress that I think he bought every word."

"Did the sheriff say what he was going to do about it?"

"Arrest McCoy," she answered. "I just wish I could be there to see the look on his face."

"But it isn't true. You're lying," Tommy managed. He couldn't believe what he was hearing. All the time they'd been together, Naomi had talked about how important her looks were, how she was beautiful enough to become a model or Hollywood starlet; that she would allow herself to be hit, for her face to be marred, just so she could have her revenge showed how unhinged she had become.

"So what?" she answered with a scowl. But then her anger suddenly vanished and her eyes grew wide, like she'd had a brilliant idea. "You can help!" Naomi declared. She grabbed Tommy's wrist and began pulling him back toward the sheriff's office. "We'll tell Oglesby that you were there, that you saw the whole thing. Together, we'll make sure McCoy gets locked away for a *long* time!"

Tommy yanked his hand free. "I *did* see everything," he told her. "I was watching the two of you the whole time."

"Wait..." Naomi replied, stunned. "You...you *what*?"

"I saw you throw yourself at him. I know that *you* tried to kiss *him*. Drake didn't do a thing. What happened was all because of you."

"No, it...it wasn't like that—" she began, but Tommy silenced her.

"Stop lying!" he shouted. "I know what I saw!"

Just like that, something changed inside of Naomi, like

a light switch had been flipped. Gone was the shock at his revelation; it was replaced with a seductive stare, her lips pursed, all of her charms on display.

"I'm sorry you had to see that, but it wasn't what it looked like," she cooed, stepping toward him and brushing against his arm. "*You're* the only man I want. I was just having some fun, that's all. Nothing was going to happen. I promise."

But Tommy held his ground. "I don't believe you."

And so, for the second time in less than a minute, everything about Naomi shifted: her syrupy sweetness vanished in a flash, replaced with a bitter, nasty scowl, her eyes went narrow and hard, and her nose crinkled up as if from disgust.

"Then what are you going to do?" she snapped. "Run home to Mommy and tattle on me? Or are you going to be a man and do what I want?"

"I won't go along with this," he answered.

Naomi reacted with genuine surprise. "Maybe you don't understand what I mean," she snarled. "Either you go along with this and quit being so damned *independent*, or you and me"—she paused for emphasis—"are through."

Tommy knew he had a choice to make; either he stood up for what he knew to be right or he went along with Naomi's despicable plan. One meant an innocent man might end up behind bars. The other that he would never touch a certain beautiful young woman ever again. Surprisingly, it wasn't too hard of a decision.

He shook his head. "What you're doing is wrong."

Naomi laughed in his face. "So now the little boy thinks he's a man, huh? Well you're not! You're pathetic!"

And then, just like in the parking lot, Naomi lashed out. The slap stung, but Tommy took it without flinching or trying to stop her, just as Drake had done. Unfortunately, his reaction only made her angrier.

"Do you have any idea how many men in this shitty little town want me?" Naomi shouted. "As soon as I step back in my father's bar, there'll be a line waiting to buy me a drink, and here *you* are, stupid enough to toss me away!" With an especially cruel smile, she added, "You know what? Tonight I'm going to go to bed with the first guy who gives me attention. All those things I've denied you, all the fantasies you've been daydreaming about, I'm going to give to someone else."

Tommy knew that her words were meant to hurt him, to make him jealous enough to change his mind, but Naomi didn't realize that all she was doing was making him feel better about refusing to go along with her lie.

"Good-bye, Naomi," he said matter-of-factly.

Watching her walk away swinging her hips from side to side, Tommy couldn't help but think about how hard it had been to grow up without his father. He wondered how different a person he would be if Joe Sinclair had lived, if his mother's heart hadn't been broken. He only knew the man through stories told, but for some reason, Tommy thought that his father would have been damn proud of him...

* * *

"...but you'd already left your office so I came straight here," Tommy finished. "I didn't want Mr. McCoy to get in trouble for something he didn't do."

Clara had listened breathlessly to her son's story, hanging on every word. When Tommy had explained that Drake was innocent, she'd been unable to hold back a smile. Looking at Tommy as he answered each of the sheriff's many questions, Clara realized that he was no longer a boy, but on his way to becoming a man; Joe would have been proud.

"Well then, seems I need to have another talk with Naomi," the lawman said, tipping his hat back to scratch his head.

"Don't go too hard on her," Tommy replied, his feelings for the bartender's daughter still strong enough that he wanted to protect her, even just a bit.

"I reckon this means I'm free to go," Drake interjected.

Sheriff Oglesby nodded. "It's all right so long as you're not planning to leave town. I might have more questions."

Clara looked at Drake; when his eyes found hers, she knew just what he was thinking. Beginning with an innocent meeting, their lives had become entwined, moving forward together. There was still much to be done, many questions to be answered, plenty of details to be sorted out, from telling Tommy about their relationship, to getting Drake's garage up and running, and especially to settling matters with Eddie. But she felt hopeful, for the first time in forever.

Drake smiled. "I'm not going anywhere."

Chapter Twenty-Four

ARE YOU SURE you're all right?"

"Goddamn it! How many times are you gonna ask me that? What, do I look like I got one foot in the grave or somethin'?"

Drake wasn't sure if Amos wanted an honest answer. The mechanic was a mess. Deep, dark circles underlined his watery, bloodshot eyes. His skin was pale as a sheet and sweaty. Occasionally, his hand would shake, like that of a much older man. To make matters worse, he was as ornery as a bear that'd been woken two months early from its hibernation, liable to bite the head off anyone who wandered too close. Now that Drake thought about it, he realized that Amos had been steadily getting worse ever since they'd arrived in town.

"When this is over, let's get you to a doctor," he said.

"The only thing we're gonna do when this race is run is get the hell outta this town!" Amos snapped angrily in reply.

Drake frowned. Every time he tried to talk to the mechanic about his decision to give up racing, to stay in Sunset and start a new life with Clara, something got in the way. Just last night, when he had left Clara to be alone with her son, Drake had thought he'd finally have a chance, but when he'd gotten back to the hotel, Amos had been snoring loud enough to be heard out in the hall. So it'd had to wait, again... Not that there was going to be any surprise in how his friend would react; Amos would rant and rave until he was purple in the face. But Drake had made his decision. He wanted Clara. One partnership would end as another began.

So he and Amos would talk after the race, no matter what.

The dirt road was just as it had been the day of Drake's defeat, though it looked as if the trees that hemmed in the two cars had sprouted more leaves. Sitting in the Plymouth, he felt the power of the car's engine; it rumbled in his hands as they held the steering wheel. The Chrysler idled beside him. Its young driver looked cockier than ever, grinning like the cat that swallowed the canary, giving a short nod to Drake when their eyes met.

"He thinks he's got this in the bag," Amos observed.

"I suppose I gave him a reason to be confident."

"He can choke on it," the mechanic spat.

"You show his old man our money?" Drake asked.

"We wouldn't be here if I hadn't. Beatin' us made that bastard the cock a the walk. He's struttin' 'round like he's the mayor."

"The higher you climb, the farther you have to fall..."

"To hell with that mumbo jumbo," Amos growled. "Just make sure you get out in front before the curve this time."

But then, just as the two men began to go over their strategy, Drake noticed a familiar pickup truck pull up beside the track; Clara soon got out. When she'd asked him if she could come watch, Drake had readily agreed; after all, it might be the one and only chance she would have to see him race. The Chrysler's driver had attracted a much larger crowd, a couple dozen cars' worth, so it was nice to have someone besides Amos there rooting him on.

Unfortunately, his friend didn't see it the same way.

"Sweet Mary and Joseph!" Amos groaned when he saw Clara. "What in the hell's the widow doin' here? As if you ain't got enough on your mind!"

Fast as the pistons firing under the Plymouth's hood, Drake grabbed the mechanic's wrist, yanking the man closer as he squeezed tight; his patience with Amos had come to a sudden, angry end. "Watch your mouth," he growled, his voice as low as the rumble of the engine. "I've put up with your guff ever since we got to town, but I won't sit here and let you run Clara down. Do you understand me?"

Amos looked hard at him, his eyes wet and distant. "You done sayin' your piece?" he finally asked.

Drake answered by letting him go.

"Just win the goddamn race," the mechanic swore before walking away.

For the first time, Drake wondered if ending his partnership with Amos might be easier than he expected.

* * *

Clara stared at her reflection in the rearview mirror, wondering if she looked good enough. She'd tried on three outfits that morning, never completely satisfied, always wishing she were prettier. Eventually, she had settled on something casual, her favorite blue blouse and a pair of trousers, tying her hair back with a ribbon. She wanted to look nice for Drake, but not *too* dolled up, a delicate balance. Still...

"If you go home to change again, you're gonna miss the race." Tommy sat beside her in the passenger seat, leaning against the door and smiling.

"I just want to make a good impression, that's all."

"I've noticed the way he looks at you. He likes what he sees."

Clara blushed, though it was nice to hear a compliment from her son instead of backtalk or other harsh words. "Are you sure you don't want to wish Drake good luck?"

"Naw," Tommy answered, stifling a yawn. "It's not much fun being a third wheel. I'll watch from here."

"Suit yourself."

Outside, excitement for the race was steadily building. A crowd had gathered, pushing in among the trees and bushes lining the road. Everyone Clara met was familiar; most were friends or relatives of Ray Barks, Drake's opponent. She gave a few nods and words of greeting, but didn't allow herself to linger.

But even with everything that was happening, Clara's thoughts didn't stray far from her son. Last night, after

Drake had gone back to the hotel, she and Tommy had sat at the kitchen table and talked. When she had told him about his grandmother's accident, he'd been shocked, then angry at himself for not being around to help. He had even lashed out at Naomi, claiming that she'd just been using him for her own amusement; for her part, Clara said little, not wanting to add fuel to the fire. Instead, she'd put her hand on Tommy's and said that it was all water under the bridge; to her great relief, he hadn't moved away or disagreed. Maybe this really *was* a new beginning.

Drake wasn't hard to find. The Plymouth rumbled beside another sleek, powerful car, dappled sunlight sparkling off both hoods. He waved from behind the windshield. She gave him a smile as she approached, but it faltered a bit when she noticed Amos walking away, his back to her, his hands stuffed into his pockets. She wondered if he was leaving because of her.

"Are you sure it's all right that I'm here?" she asked as she leaned against Drake's door, her hands resting on the open window.

"Of course," he answered. "Why wouldn't it be?"

Clara almost said something about Amos—she'd never told Drake what the mechanic had said to her in the hotel lobby—but then thought better of it; she wouldn't want to distract him, not with the race about to start.

"Are you nervous?" she asked instead.

Drake shrugged. "Not really," he replied, then chuckled.

"What's so funny?"

"This," he said, wiggling his thumb back and forth between them. "It reminds me of the day we met, although we've switched spots."

Clara smiled at the memory; she couldn't believe how much her life had been changed that afternoon, all for the better.

"I'm glad you're here," Drake told her, placing his hand on hers.

"Me, too." She looked into his face and saw her own happiness reflected back at her. Right there, in his eyes, he was as open to her as a book; she could read about what had happened between them as well as what was to come, their yesterdays and tomorrows, but especially about their love. He grinned and some of his wrinkles vanished, although others appeared around his eyes; she found him devilishly handsome, with or without.

The other car's engine revved loudly, breaking the spell that had momentarily enchanted them, though Drake never let go of her hand.

"Are you here by yourself?" he asked.

Clara shook her head. "Tommy's back at the truck. My mother said she wasn't up to it, but I think she just wanted us to have more time together."

"How are things going?"

"I keep worrying that I'll say the wrong thing and it'll go back to the way it's been," she said, "but so far, so good."

"Maybe what happened with Naomi screwed his head on straighter. Would be nice if something good came out of that mess," Drake said, then grinned a bit mischievously. "Speaking of last night . . ."

Clara blushed like she was sixteen.

"Being with you like that," he told her, "it was like something out of a dream, only better."

Clara was certain Drake believed his words. But something still nagged at her, the thinnest thread of doubt. She motioned across the Plymouth's hood to the crowd. "Are you sure you want to walk away from all of this?"

"For you, I'd give up anything." With another sly smile, he added, "I suppose I'd even swear off sardine sandwiches."

"I'm honored," she played along, his humor putting her at ease.

"You should be," Drake joked. "After I've had a tin, about the only living things that want to kiss me are the neighborhood cats."

Once again, the other driver revved his engine, then he gave his horn a sharp honk. They looked up to see Amos and Felton Barks, Ray's father, standing in the middle of the road. From the way they were shooing people toward the trees, it was clear the race was about to begin.

Clara turned back to Drake. "Good luck," she told him.

"This is for us," he replied. "The money I stand to win goes toward getting you out from under Eddie's thumb for good. I promise."

Clara could no longer resist the urge to kiss him. She leaned inside the Plymouth and found Drake's lips; she touched them softly, letting them linger for a while before stepping back.

"Be careful," she said.

"Don't worry," Drake said. "I'll be back before you know it."

"Get in the goddamn car! Now!"

Sweet Woods raced out of the diner and down the sidewalk toward the Cadillac. He spat a half-chewed piece of toast from his mouth. He didn't know how many coins he had thrown on the counter to pay for his breakfast, but he didn't care, not after what he'd just heard.

"What's goin' on?" Jesse asked, leaping up from where he'd been leaning against the car, a cigarette dangling from his lips. "Did you hear somethin'?"

Sweet couldn't help but notice that while one of his men babbled questions, the other was doing just as he'd been told; Malcolm was behind the wheel, the engine roaring to life.

"Quit flappin' your gums and get in the car!"

Before Sweet had even shut his door, Malcolm was pulling away from the curb and accelerating down the street. Once his boss had pointed them in the right direction, he floored it, going faster and faster.

Jesse turned around in the passenger seat. "Is it Barstow?" he asked.

Sweet grinned, showing just a hint of teeth. "There's a race happenin'...right 'bout now..." he answered, his breath ragged from running. "Out in the woods...some little dirt road. Folks was talkin' 'bout it..."

"Could be them," Jesse agreed.

It was, Sweet was sure of it. He felt it in his gut. All the no-name, forgettable towns, the insult of having to chase after the drug-addled thief, it was finally going to pay off. Once they made it to the race, once he saw Barstow with his own two eyes, he was never letting the man out of his sight again.

Not until he had what was rightfully his.

Not until the bastard was dead.

This time, when the handkerchief dropped, Drake was ready, one hand on the Plymouth's gearshift, the other on the steering wheel. He pressed down on the gas, not so hard as to make the tires spin wildly in the dirt, but hard enough to blow off the line and take an early lead. Within seconds, the crowd was already behind him, not that Drake noticed. He couldn't hear anyone cheering. He didn't notice the wind whipping through the open windows. He didn't feel the vibration of the car. All he noticed was the track. Unlike the first time he'd raced the Chrysler, he was focused. Strangely enough, the reason was the same one that had previously distracted him.

It was because of Clara.

Before, she hadn't been there to watch but had been present all the same, at the edge of his thoughts, making his mind wander. But now, Clara gave him strength. It didn't matter that she was somewhere behind him; she was also waiting across the finish line, because a brighter future with her was what he stood to win.

Drake fluidly shifted the Plymouth from one gear to the next, taking the lead. Unfortunately, he still wasn't as far ahead as he'd hoped to be; the Chrysler hung close, half a length behind.

Just like in the first race, the Plymouth was on the left; farther down the track, the route curved to the right, meaning that if Drake wanted to win, he needed to be safely out in front before the final sprint to the covered bridge. He needed more and he needed it quick.

"Come on, girl," he coaxed. "Give me everything you've got."

The tires pounded over sticks, rocks, and ruts in the road. Trees and bushes whipped by in a blur. The engine roared like a wild animal, straining for ever greater speeds. Drake had the sudden hope that as grouchy as Amos had been, he still knew what he was doing under the hood.

Up ahead, he saw the curve approaching. Glancing into the side mirror, Drake sized up his lead, now at just less than a full car length, not much but enough to justify taking a risk. Slowly but deliberately, he eased the Plymouth to the right, hoping to force the Chrysler to slow, trapped between Drake and the woods.

"Back off," he said, staring in the mirror.

Suddenly, Drake felt a hard crack against his passenger-side rear panel. The Chrysler had fallen back, but not quick enough; the two cars had collided. Instantly, the Plymouth felt loose in his hands, fishtailing slightly and threatening to get away from him. With a practiced hand, Drake turned the wheel into the slide, backed off the gas, silently prayed that the wheels would regain their purchase, and held his breath as his heart crashed around in his chest. Seconds passed, but they felt like eternity. Finally, the Plymouth held the road and Drake jammed the pedal to the floor, the danger past. Amazingly, he still held his lead, now fully out in front.

"Yes!" he shouted at the top of his lungs, but then fell silent; this wasn't the time for celebration, not with so much of the race left to run.

Now firmly behind, the other driver pushed the Chrysler hard, as if it was a prized Thoroughbred. He feinted to his left before whipping around to the right, probing for an opening. For his part, Drake kept one eye on the road and the other on his mirrors, moving back and forth, blocking each attempt. He was calm, collected, and had been there before; he doubted his opponent, as skilled as he was, could say the same, and imagined he'd started to worry, sweating from more than the heat. Truthfully, Drake didn't give a damn about the other driver. All he wanted was to win. For himself, for his future, for Clara.

Up ahead, the bridge came into view. The Chrysler's actions grew more frantic and its driver even knocked up against the Plymouth's bumper, but Drake wasn't bothered; days earlier, he'd been in the same desperate position.

"Back off, kid," he said with a grin. "I know you may not want to admit it, but this race is over."

Amazingly, it was as if the other driver had heard him; the Chrysler suddenly fell back, finally accepting defeat. The Plymouth sped across the covered bridge, the roar of its engine echoing off the walls, the wooden planks singing beneath its tires, and Drake adding to the strange symphony by blasting the horn, celebrating and retiring at the same time.

He had won.

Chapter Twenty-Five

DRAKE DROVE THE Plymouth back to the starting line and again parked beside the Chrysler. The crowd had thinned and most of those who were left wore long faces, disappointed that their driver had lost; in contrast, Clara and Tommy stood just off the track flashing excited smiles. He waved, ready to celebrate, but then Drake noticed the other driver heading his way, the man's face creased by a deep frown.

"Aw, hell," Drake said, anticipating trouble; there were few things he hated more than a run-in with a sore loser.

He got out of the Plymouth, bracing himself for an argument or worse, but was surprised when instead the driver extended his hand. "That was one hell of a race you run," he said. "Makes me feel damn lucky I won our first go-round."

"Luck had nothing to do with it," Drake disagreed.

"With that car of yours and the way you handle it, you're going to win more than your fair share."

After he and the other driver had finished, Drake headed for Clara. On the way, he noticed Amos collecting their winnings from his nemesis. The older man's earlier bravado was gone; he looked heartbroken, like he might be sick, slowly counting out the bills as if he couldn't believe he had to part with them.

"That was incredible!" Clara congratulated him, beaming from ear to ear as her arms slid around his waist, pressing herself against his body.

"Not bad for my last race," he answered.

"Why would you stop doing this?" Tommy had wandered close, his eyes wide as he stared at the two cars. "If I could drive like that," he added, "I don't think I'd *ever* get out from behind the wheel."

Drake laughed. "I said the same thing when I was your age."

"So what happened?"

He looked at Clara and thought about how falling in love with her had changed so much, even how he felt about racing cars. Everything was different now, and he couldn't have been happier.

"When you get older," Drake explained, "you might be surprised..."

"Nuts to that!" the boy argued, making a sour face.

"Tommy!" Clara scolded.

"So how fast can it go?" he asked, ignoring his mother.

Drake couldn't help but notice the change in Tommy.

He remembered when he'd tried to enlist the boy's help to fix the garage door; Tommy had been quick to anger, itching for a fight. But now he seemed more relaxed, at ease with himself and his mother. Drake hoped it would last.

"Maybe you and I can take it out in the country and find out," Drake said to Tommy. Clara elbowed him in the ribs. "What? Just because I'm not going to race anymore doesn't mean I'm never going to get the itch to go speeding down a dirt road!"

Now all three of them laughed.

While Drake knew there was still unfinished business ahead, like his impending talk with Amos and settling Clara's issues with Eddie, he refused to be distracted. Nothing, and no one, was going to ruin this day.

"That's him, ain't it?"

Jesse pointed toward the track. Two men stood in front of the recently returned race cars; it appeared that they were counting money. Watching them, Sweet's heart started to pound. Though he was some distance away, there was no doubt in his mind that one of them was Amos Barstow, the same son of a bitch who had stolen his money and drugs and then led them on a wild goose chase through the backwaters of Missouri.

"It's Barstow, all right."

Jesse let out a sigh of relief. "Good thing we got here when we did," he said. "Any later and he might've given us the slip."

Even though Malcolm had driven like a bat out of hell,

they'd arrived too late to see the race. Cars and trucks had lined the road, were pulled down into ditches, and had parked between bushes, anywhere they could fit. Malcolm rolled the Cadillac slowly past as they looked closely at every vehicle, at each face, searching for the mechanic. Eventually, they'd parked and begun traipsing through the woods, ignoring the cheers and groans of disappointment from the crowd, working like hunting dogs on the trail, sniffing for the fox. When the race ended, some race-goers left, making their job a little easier. But it wasn't until Sweet saw the black Plymouth headed toward them that he allowed himself hope that they were on the right track. Soon after, Jesse had pointed.

Sweet popped a butterscotch candy into his mouth. He savored the sweet taste, his eyes never leaving Barstow. Then he pulled his gun from his waistband.

"Hey, now," Jesse cautioned. "Ain't we gonna wait till there ain't so many people around? We found him, so why not follow till we get him alone?"

Malcolm grunted; it wasn't clear whether he agreed or not.

Sweet didn't give a damn either way. He had been searching for the mechanic for too long to wait even one minute more. He thought of all the damage that had been done to his standing back in St. Louis, all that he'd lost, much more than just his money and drugs. It was time to settle up.

"Come on," he said. "Let's get what we came for."

*　　*　　*

"...seventy, eighty, ninety, and that makes two hundred..."

Amos grinned. He liked the way the bills felt in his hand, a tall enough stack that it had some weight to it.

"Pleasure doin' business with you," he said, not meaning it.

The other man stalked off, his shoulders slumped, his hands stuffed down in his pockets, angry and disappointed, a feeling Amos had experienced plenty of times, but he felt no pity; the man had crowed too loudly for that. Watching him sulk almost made up for Drake losing the first race. Almost.

Suddenly, a spasm began to shake his hand and he had to concentrate hard to quiet it. He needed morphine, bad. It was on his mind every second since he'd run out. One minute he was drenched with sweat, the next he was shivering so hard that his teeth chattered. He slept fitfully, sound asleep one moment but startled awake the next, couldn't eat, and got angry at the drop of a hat. He'd come to believe that if he didn't get a shot soon, he was going to die.

But somehow, even with all his suffering, Amos hadn't given in to temptation and stolen Drake's money. It was still there, buried in the bottom of his duffel bag. Three times now, he'd taken it out and counted the stacks, far more money than he held now, and considered leaving his troubles behind. But every time he had put it all back, ashamed at his behavior. In the end, his friendship with Drake had triumphed over his addiction, even if it had only been by the skin of his teeth.

Though he wasn't out of the woods yet...

Amos still needed the sweet kiss morphine gave him. He wanted it more than ever, and that was why they needed to get the hell out of this town and go somewhere he could score. With money in his pocket, he could buy whatever he desired. Maybe he and Drake would go to Kansas City. Maybe down to either Springfield or Joplin. Hell, he'd even go back to St. Louis if there was no other choice, although he didn't like the idea of getting too close to Sweet Woods. There was no telling what that lowlife would do if he caught sight of him.

"Good thing that ain't gonna happen," he mumbled.

But then, just as he was about to go tell Drake that it was time to head back to the hotel, get their things, and finally leave this godforsaken place, Amos saw three men walking toward him. He froze, his eyes blinking rapidly, thinking it a mirage induced by morphine withdrawal. But as seconds ticked by and the terrible sight remained, he knew that it was unbelievably, horrifyingly real.

It was Sweet Woods and his men. They had tracked him down. And so Amos did the only thing that made any sense to him.

He ran.

Amos hadn't gone five feet when he heard gunfire.

One moment, Clara was laughing at one of Drake's jokes, and the next she was being pulled to the ground, her knees hitting the dirt hard, unable to understand what was happening. A split second later, she realized that the strange sounds punctuating the early afternoon, loud enough to be heard above the crowd's shouts and screams, were gunshots. Lying on her stomach, dumbfounded, she watched as Drake yanked Tommy down, then moved himself between them and the danger, acting as a shield; Clara imagined he was moving on instinct, memories of his time at war telling him what to do.

What in heaven's name is happening?

It didn't take long to get an answer. Three men ran toward them, down the length of the crude race track. One of them was dressed fancier than the others, his clothes a style she had seen in a magazine at the drug store. His arm was extended, his finger squeezing the trigger of a pistol, causing the gun to fire.

"What are they doing?" Tommy asked, rising up to take a closer look.

"Keep your head down!" Drake hissed, pushing the boy lower.

All around them, people ran, trying to escape the chaos. Clara desperately wanted to do the same but was too frozen with fear to move. Instead, she watched the surreal scene unfold. It was only then that she realized the men were chasing, *were shooting at*, Amos. The mechanic ran as fast as he could, his arms and legs churning, breath bursting from his lungs in huge gasps, his face deep red from the effort.

"Are . . . are they after Amos?" she asked in disbelief.

Drake didn't answer, surely as shocked as she was.

Somehow, Amos managed to reach the Plymouth without being shot. Bumping against the passenger-side door, he pulled it open and slid inside just before a bullet slammed into the metal, while another smashed out the window, showering him with glass. Clara felt as if she was watching a movie, a gangster picture full of mayhem. When the Plymouth roared to life, she realized that Drake must have left the keys in the ignition. Seconds later, the car was on the move, its tires churning, shooting dirt and rocks everywhere. Fortunately for the mechanic, the men hadn't been able to reach him, but that didn't stop the well-dressed one from shooting out one of the Plymouth's taillights.

"You're dead, Barstow!" the gunman bellowed. "A dead man!"

"Back to the car!" one of the others shouted. "We can catch him!"

They turned and sprinted back the way they'd come, leaving chaos and confusion in their wake. But before Clara could start to make any sense of it all, Drake was on his feet, pulling her and Tommy up behind him.

"Where's your truck?" he asked insistently.

Too stunned to speak, Clara pointed instead, her arm shaking.

"Come on!" Drake barked.

All around them, people screamed and ran, ducking behind bushes and trees. Vehicles raced in every direction as their owners franticly tried to flee; a car sped right toward them, the driver wide-eyed behind the wheel, but veered away at the last second. Finally, they reached the truck.

"Give me the keys," Drake said.

Tommy handed them over. "Mom was going to let me

drive home," he explained, unable to suppress a smile, excited by the pandemonium. "Are we going after them?" he pressed, clearly hoping they would be.

Drake nodded, his face grim. They all jumped in the cab, Drake behind the wheel, Tommy at the other door, and Clara in between. When the engine sputtered to life, its weary pistons churning, it was a far cry from the power of the Plymouth.

"Who were those men?" Clara asked, finally finding her voice. "Why were they shooting? What did they want with Amos?"

"I have no idea," Drake answered, coaxing the truck out onto the road, "but I aim to find out."

Drake pulled around the corner from the hotel's front entrance and parked. Looking back over his shoulder, he could see the Plymouth sitting against the curb at an odd angle, as if it had skidded there. His hunch had been that Amos would return here, looking for somewhere to hide, the only place in Sunset he knew. Fortunately, he had been right. Still, he had no answers to the questions swimming around in his head.

A couple of other cars were parked nearby, some he recognized and others he didn't, but of those, he didn't know if one belonged to the mystery men; he hadn't gotten a look at what they were driving.

"Do you think they're here?" Tommy asked, still bubbling with excitement. He hadn't stopped talking the whole way back to town.

Drake shook his head. "I don't know," he answered. "Maybe."

"Then what are we waiting for? Let's go take a look!" the boy replied as he started to open his door.

"No!" Clara and Drake both shouted at the same time.

"It's too dangerous to go in there," his mother explained. "For any of us. The only thing we should do is fetch the sheriff. He'll know what to do."

"There isn't time," Drake disagreed. "By the time we brought him back, Amos could be dead. We can't take the risk."

"So what *are* we going to do?"

"You two stay here," he answered. "I'm going inside."

"Drake, no!" Clara shouted, grabbing his arm; her voice was full of fear and worry. "They have a gun!"

"I can't just sit here. Amos is my friend. I won't abandon him to those thugs." To soothe her, he added, "I'll be careful. I promise."

Clara still didn't look happy, but she gave no more argument.

Drake got out of the truck and squinted up at the hotel through the afternoon sun. From outside, everything was quiet, just another day, but who knew what was going on inside. Suddenly, he had a thought.

"Once I'm gone, turn the truck around so that it's facing toward Main Street," he explained. "That way, if we need to get out of here in a hurry, we'll be pointed in the right direction."

Clara slid behind the wheel. Unable to resist the urge,

and not completely ignorant of the danger he was putting himself in, Drake leaned down and gave her a gentle kiss; she didn't shy away from his affection, even with Tommy beside her.

"Be careful," she told him for the second time that day.

"I'll be right back," he answered.

Drake could only hope that he was telling her the truth.

Amos reached the top of the hotel's stairs drenched in sweat and breathing so hard that he felt faint. Panic gripped him tight, strangling his nerves. He knew that being here was a mistake, that he should have driven far away as fast as possible, letting this godforsaken place dwindle in the Plymouth's rearview mirror, but he couldn't leave. Not yet. Not without the money.

I need Drake's cash! I won't survive two days without it!

Digging into his pocket, he fumbled the key, dropping it on the floor. Once he'd finally retrieved it, he struggled to get it in the door; after he managed to insert it, he couldn't turn it in the lock.

"Goddamn it!" he swore.

When he heard it click, Amos shouldered the door open and made a beeline for Drake's duffel bag. It was right where the driver had left it that morning. Before they'd departed for the race, Amos had suggested that they check out of the hotel and take their things with them, but Drake had shook his head; he'd insinuated that there was something else they needed to talk about, but Amos had been too grouchy at that point to listen. Now the mechanic knew he should've insisted.

Rushing over, he snatched up the bag, clinging to it as if it was his salvation, which he supposed it was. But then, just as he allowed himself to hope that he would get away, Amos heard something that made his sweat go cold as ice.

"What room is Barstow in?" someone shouted down in the lobby. "Either you tell me, bitch, or I'll put a bullet between your eyes!"

Amos knew that voice from his nightmares. It was Sweet Woods. He and his men had caught up quicker than expected.

Instantly, the mechanic knew he was trapped like a rat. He couldn't go back down the stairs, and it would only be a matter of seconds before the bloodthirsty drug dealer would be coming up after him. Frantically, he looked around, desperate for a way out. Then he saw it. Just outside the window was a fire escape. In a different, more rational time, Amos might've checked to see if the ladder went all the way to the ground, but he was too panicked for that; frankly, plummeting a couple of floors and busting his head open on the concrete would be preferable to letting Sweet and his thugs get their hands on him. It would have to do. He had to get out of there.

To hell with Sweet. To hell with this damn town. And to hell with Drake, too.

He wanted to live.

* * *

As soon as Drake stepped into the lobby, he knew he'd made a mistake. Outside, he had peered in the windows, listened by the door, considered going around the back way, but he'd assumed that Amos had succeeded in giving his pursuers the slip. Unfortunately, he hadn't. Three men stood at the front desk, the same ones who'd tried to kill his friend. Every head in the room, including that of the hotel's terrified owner, turned to look at him. For a moment, no one moved. Then one of the men, the owner of the pistol, smiled.

"Well, well, well," he said with a chuckle. "Look who we have here."

Now that he was up close, Drake took a long look at the strangers. The colorfully dressed one was clearly in charge, his mouth as loud as his taste in clothes. The thinner one to his side kept looking from his boss to Drake and back again, as if he was a dog, eager to please. The third stood silently, his eyes hooded, his hands hanging loose at his sides, sizing up the new arrival; instinctively, Drake knew that if it came to a fight, this one would be the most dangerous. Still, he didn't recognize any of them. Strangely, they seemed to know him.

"Where is he, McCoy?" the leader asked.

"Where's who?" Drake responded, stalling for time.

"You know goddamn well who we want," the thinner one snapped, smiling, cocky and proud. "You want to keep breathin', you better answer."

"I don't know," he lied.

"Bullshit," the man in charge growled; he said it so angrily that the threatening, quiet goon took a step forward as if he anticipated violence.

"I don't know what's going on," Drake said truthfully, trying to defuse the situation. "What do you want with Amos?"

The two talkative members of the trio burst into laughter.

"Hilarious!" the thin one guffawed. "The nerve of you, actin' like you don't know what that son of a bitch took!"

"You been traipsin' 'round with him for weeks now," the boss added. "Drivin' hundreds of miles from St. Louis, and you expect me to buy that you ain't got no idea what he's been up to? What kind of fool do you take me for?"

Drake was beginning to suspect that *he* was the fool. For some reason, these men had come after them. What had Amos stolen?

"This has to be some sort of misunderstanding," he offered. "Just tell me what it is you think Amos has done and maybe we can—"

The flamboyantly dressed man pointed his gun at Drake and cocked the hammer. "The time for talkin' is over," he said. "Either you tell me what room the two of you are in, or otherwise, I'm gonna—"

But before the thug could finish his threat, they were all surprised by the sound of the Plymouth's engine roaring to life. Seconds later, they watched, stunned, as the race car peeled away from the curb, its tires smoking as it sped out of sight. Somehow, Amos had gotten past them.

Through those turbulent instants, Drake kept a cool

head. With the criminals momentarily distracted, he knew that this was going to be his only chance to escape. A hallway ran just off the lobby and toward the rear of the hotel. If he could just get around the corner, get back to Clara, he might be able to start piecing together what the hell was going on. And so, with the squeal of the Plymouth's tires still shattering the afternoon's quiet, he made his move.

"Hey!" the thin man shouted. "He's gettin' away!"

Drake thought that the goon's warning had come too late, that he was fast enough, that like Amos, he was going to make a clean break for it.

But he was wrong.

Just before he made it to safety, the leader, the criminal Drake had never met before today, pulled the trigger and shot him.

Chapter Twenty-Six

ARE YOU IN LOVE with him?"

Clara was so surprised by Tommy's question that she gasped. They had been sitting in the pickup, waiting for Drake to return. She'd been anxiously watching the hotel while her son drummed his fingers on the door. When he spoke, it was the first thing either of them had said since Drake left.

"I...It's..." she stammered, not because she didn't know the answer, but because she wasn't sure how to talk about it with her son.

Tommy turned to look at her. "With the way you kissed, I figured that things must be getting serious..." he said, offering a weak smile.

"They are," Clara acknowledged, speaking carefully, knowing that the situation was delicate. "Drake is a good man."

Her son nodded, but didn't speak.

Feeling the need to explain herself further, Clara said, "He's smart, kind, and funny. You'll see it, too, once you get to know him better."

"He seems like a good guy," Tommy added, his expression unreadable.

"He is," Clara agreed. But then she felt like she was selling Drake short, like even if she sat here for an hour, she wouldn't be able to tell Tommy about all the ways he had changed her life, how before the race car driver had arrived, her tomorrows were something to dread, rather than days to look forward to.

"I haven't felt this way in a long time," she finally explained.

"Since Dad died?"

Tommy's words silenced her. Tears filled Clara's eyes, but she refused to let them fall. She had already made her peace with Joe. Deep in her heart, she knew that he would have understood her feelings for Drake. It was time to face the future and quit clinging so tenaciously to the past. Now she had to convince Tommy.

"No one will ever replace your father," she began. "He will always be a part of both our lives. Nothing can ever change that." Clara paused. "But somehow, unexpectedly, I've found love again. Just when I was ready to give up all hope, Drake appeared, and while he can never make up for what we've lost, not completely, he can be the start of something new. The only thing I ask of you is that you don't turn your back on him. Give him a chance. That's all."

Tommy turned to look out the window. Slowly, almost imperceptibly at first, he nodded his head. "I'll try," he said.

It was then, as she was flooded with feelings of relief, that Clara's attention was drawn to a figure hurrying down the sidewalk toward them.

It took Clara a moment to realize that it was Amos.

The mechanic hobbled with a noticeable limp, his clothes drenched in sweat and his face as white as bone. He clutched a large bag to his chest, its strap swinging with every step. Passing in front of the truck, his eyes were focused straight ahead; he never spared them so much as a glance.

"Isn't that...?" Tommy remarked.

Clara didn't answer; she could only watch Amos go, too stunned to call out to him or honk the horn. The next thing she knew, the mechanic threw the bag in the back of the Plymouth, fired up the car's powerful engine, and disappeared in a cloud of burnt rubber.

"What was that all about?" Tommy asked.

In answer, Clara started the pickup.

Whatever was going to happen next would happen fast.

Drake leaned against the wall down the hall and around the corner from the lobby, cursing under his breath. He had paid a price for running. The bullet had punctured his biceps, tearing through his skin as easily as his shirt. Blood stained the fabric and dripped onto the floor. Drake knew that it could've been much worse; a couple inches to the right and he would probably be taking his last breath. But as bad as the wound hurt, he had a bigger problem: the door at the end of the hallway, the one he'd planned on using to make his escape, was locked tight.

"Come on!" the thin man shouted. "After McCoy before he gets away!"

Time was running out. Drake knew that he had only two choices: he could either bust the door down or stand his ground and fight, but the odds of surviving against three men, especially when they were armed, were slim to none.

Think, damn it! Think!

But then his salvation came from an unexpected source.

"To hell with the driver!" the leader barked. "I don't give a damn about him! I want Barstow!"

"But what about—"

"Move!"

The order was followed by the pounding of footsteps. Drake listened closely, his breath caught in his throat. As soon as he heard the slamming of car doors, he was off and running.

Outside, Drake found Clara behind the wheel of the pickup. She slid over as he got in, wincing in pain as he brushed his arm against the door.

"What happened?" she asked, staring at his blood-soaked shirt, her voice panicked. "Have you been *shot*?"

In answer, Drake threw the truck into gear and took off after the other cars. He concentrated on working the stick, the clutch, and the accelerator as smoothly as he could, but it still felt as if it was taking forever to increase their speed.

"Why are they after Amos?" Clara asked.

"I still don't really know," Drake answered, racing down Main Street; up ahead, he could just make out a Cadillac speeding toward the edge of town. "They claimed he'd stolen something from them."

"What?"

"They didn't say. But they seemed to think I was in on it."

"We saw him," Tommy said. "Your friend. The one those guys were shooting at. He walked right past us on the way to your car."

"He was limping like he'd hurt his leg," Clara added. "He was carrying a big duffel bag with him, but we were both so—"

"Amos was what?" Drake interrupted, his heart suddenly racing faster than the pickup truck.

"Limping," she repeated.

"Not that. What did you say he had with him?"

"A big bag."

Drake felt as if he'd been slugged in the gut. That bag was *his*. All the money he had saved over the years was in it. Thousands of dollars.

Amos was stealing from him, too...

Amos pointed the Plymouth out of town and pressed the gas pedal to the floor. He drove recklessly, drifting across the center line before overcorrecting, and took even the gentlest of corners fast enough to make the tires squeal. His poor driving made sense given how bad he felt: his hands, slick with sweat, trembled on the steering wheel; his guts ached, like they had been tied in knots; he blinked constantly, his eyes betraying him as the road wiggled like a worm on a fishing line.

"Come on, come on," he said to himself. "Keep it together."

In the end, the only thing that mattered was that he had the money. Somewhere, deep inside, Amos knew it was wrong to steal it like that, but what choice did he have? Morphine wasn't free. Sweet Woods and his men were right behind him. Without enough cash in his pocket, he was as good as dead. Though he hated to have done Drake that way, in his withdrawal-addled mind, he had already begun to rationalize his actions, to convince himself that his friend would understand, even that he was running away with Drake's blessing.

I'll make it up to him someday... We'll laugh about it...

Nervously, Amos looked in the rearview mirror. He had long since zoomed out of Sunset and was now barreling along a straightaway, the river out the passenger-side window. As he watched, he noticed something drawing steadily closer. After blinking a couple of times, the mechanic raised his hand to wipe sweat from his eyes and nearly drove off the road. But what he saw never changed. Tense seconds later, he understood that it was a car driving at high speed, kicking up a huge plume of dust in its wake. Just like that, all his hope vanished.

Sweet Woods wasn't about to let him go *that* easy.

* * *

"There he is!" Jesse shouted, so excited that he reached out to point, his finger pressing against the Cadillac's windshield.

Sweet smiled. He leaned forward over the front seat between the two men. His eyes narrowed, locked on the fleeing Plymouth.

"Son of a bitch didn't get far," Jesse continued. "As fast as we're goin', we're gonna catch him right quick!"

Ever since they'd rocketed away from the hotel, Sweet had been impressed with Malcolm's driving. He was strong and steady, his big hands clenching the steering wheel like a vise, and had quickly brought them to the Cadillac's top speed. The man knew how to negotiate turns by taking his foot off the gas and occasionally tapping the brakes. Even as Sweet watched, the distance between the two cars continued to shrink. Barstow might have been a whiz under the hood, but behind the wheel, Sweet would bet on his man any day of the week.

"Too bad about McCoy gettin' away," Jesse said, too worked up to keep his gums from flapping.

"Barstow first," Sweet replied. "Then we'll see about his driver."

There was a part of Sweet that wondered if Drake McCoy hadn't been telling the truth when he said he didn't know what Barstow had stolen. Over the years, Sweet had heard more than his share of lies, often while holding a gun, and there was usually something that gave the person away: eyes that couldn't stay in one place for long, a nervous twitch, or a shirt drenched in sweat. McCoy had shown none of these signs. Regardless, the driver was a loose end. Sweet had seen the splatter of blood on the hallway wall. McCoy had been wounded. It would be a simple matter to go back and put another bullet between his eyes; he'd put one into the old woman who'd been behind the counter, too, while he was at it.

The road rose sharply over a hill but then, after an equally steep descent, curved hard to the left. As fast as Malcolm was driving, there wasn't time to slow as he tried to negotiate the turn and the rear end started to fishtail. A second later, one of the rear wheels skidded onto the shoulder; rocks and loose dirt sprayed as the wheels spun. In that instant, a number of unfortunate possibilities loomed: they might flip, continue sliding down into the ditch, or even blow a tire. But amazingly, Malcolm kept them steady. Before Jesse could shout in fear, they were back on the road and again racing forward, the engine growling loudly as it tried to go as fast as its driver demanded.

"Jesus Christ almighty," Jesse swore. "That was close."

Sweet ignored him. "Stay on him," he ordered Malcolm. "Catch up and knock his ass off the road."

Malcolm did as he was told, closing the gap until Sweet could see Barstow's eyes watching them in his rearview mirror. As if to formally announce their presence, Malcolm drove the Cadillac into the rear of the Plymouth, giving it a solid bump.

"Hey, now," Jesse worried. "Be careful! We don't wanna—"

"Quit your bitchin'!" Sweet shouted. Grabbing Malcolm's shoulder, he said, "Wherever he goes, you follow! Drive *over* him if you have to!"

This was going to end right here, right now.

Clara watched Drake push the pickup as fast as its old engine would take them. The truck complained loudly, occasionally sputtering as its pistons misfired. Only a couple of days earlier, he'd *wanted* to drive it, curious about what the truck could do, had even called it a classic, but now Drake's earlier amusement was gone, replaced by raw frustration. Even though they raced out of Sunset, in comparison to the other two cars it felt as if they were crawling. The truck simply wasn't fast enough.

"Come on, damn you!" Drake complained, striking his palm against the steering wheel. "We're never going to catch them like this!"

Clara put her hand on his knee. "It's all right..." she said, recognizing the inevitable: Amos and his pursuers were going to get away.

"No, it isn't," he argued. Drake looked at her, his expression a mix of anger and worry. "Amos..." he began slowly, as if he couldn't find the words. "He stole...all of my money..."

Clara was stunned. "But...but how?"

"It was in the bag he was carrying, *my* bag," he explained. "It's most everything I've saved. There's a bit more in a bank in Illinois, but..."

Drake didn't finish, but Clara knew what remained unspoken. The money in his duffel bag was the future they'd both been counting on; it was how they were going to keep Eddie from following through on his threat to take away her house. All of their hopes and dreams were in danger.

"They're taking Baker's Road out of town," Tommy suddenly said.

"So?" Clara asked.

"It runs west along the river for a couple of miles, but then loops back toward town just before you reach Bill Shelton's farm," her son explained. "If we turn right after Walt Cornelius's place, the back roads will lead us right to them. We might even reach the highway ahead of them."

"Where's the turn?" Drake asked.

Tommy showed him and the pickup roared around the corner, spraying gravel. Clara bounced on the seat as her son directed Drake past recently plowed fields, over rickety bridges, and through dense woods. As they crested a hill, the valley opened beneath them and her eyes scanned the length of road that threaded through it; her heart beat faster when she saw two cars headed their way.

"There they are!" Clara shouted as she pointed.

"We're not going to get there in time," Tommy said with a frown. "They're moving too fast."

"We're sure as hell going to try," Drake said as he floored the accelerator.

Even as they rocketed down the hill, the truck's engine straining hard, Clara knew that Tommy was right; by the time they reached the highway, both cars would have already gone past. They were too late.

It would take a miracle to keep them from getting away . . .

Sweat dripped into Amos's eyes, but he was so focused on the other car that he didn't bother to wipe it away. Icy chills rippled across his skin, making him feel nauseous. His vision swam and his ears rang. He felt as if he was trapped in a nightmare from which he couldn't wake.

Once again, Sweet Woods's car rammed him; the jolt was jarring, hard enough to make his teeth chatter. This time, it caused the Plymouth to swerve wildly, forcing him to wrestle it back under control.

"Leave me alone!" he pleaded.

Amos glanced over his shoulder at Drake's bag in the backseat. If he could just get away, if he could find somewhere to buy more morphine, if he could rent a room, get a fix, sleep for a few days, everything would be all right, he was sure of it.

Because he was distracted, thinking about the drugs and the money he had stolen and bracing himself for another hit from the Cadillac, Amos wasn't paying attention to the road. He was driving fast, the Plymouth's speedometer buried. So when the sudden, sharp turn arrived, he hadn't seen it coming.

Even as Drake struggled to keep the pickup on the dirt road, he kept glancing at the two speeding cars. He could see that the Plymouth was going too fast as it approached the curve, the Cadillac right on its tail. He felt the sudden urge to cry out, to shout a warning to Amos, but it would have been futile. He was helpless to do anything but watch.

What happened next felt as if it occurred in slow motion.

Amos jammed down hard on the Plymouth's brakes, as if he suddenly realized he was in grave danger. Smoke billowed off the pavement as the tires screamed. But it wasn't enough. The car slid to the right, out of control, before flying off the road and over a steep incline. Incredibly, the Cadillac followed. Its driver had been too close, too intent on catching his quarry, and he hadn't realized he was being blindly led to his doom.

"Oh my God!" Clara shouted.

In his many years racing cars, Drake had seen plenty of crashes, but this was one of the worst. The Plymouth sailed through the air, landing on its undercarriage hard enough to blow out a couple of tires before bouncing toward a copse of trees. It rammed nose-first into a thick elm, its front end crumpling as if it was made out of paper; metal and glass flew everywhere. A heartbeat later, the Cadillac rammed it from behind, flipping over the Plymouth's roof to smash into the same tree. After all their furious racing, whipping down the backcountry roads, both cars fell silent and still.

Drake skidded to a stop at the bottom of the hill, a couple hundred feet from the crash. His heart felt like it was going to pound out of his chest.

"Stay here!" he shouted at Clara and Tommy before leaping out and running toward the wreck. He'd gone only a couple of steps before a fire erupted to life; Drake had no idea which of the car's gas tanks had ruptured, though it hardly mattered. In seconds, the flames grew, hungry, spreading until both vehicles were burning, sending black, acrid smoke billowing skyward. Drake had to shield his face, the intense heat like a wall. He peered into the fire, searching the cars for something, movement, a cry for help, but there was nothing.

"Amos!" he shouted at the top of his lungs, but he knew it was pointless; his friend was dead. No one could have survived that crash.

But then, just as he was about to give up hope, Drake saw the tall grass thirty feet from the wreckage begin to move. Without any consideration for his own safety, he ran to it, silently praying that he was wrong, that Amos had miraculously survived. Sure enough, someone was trying to crawl away, both battered and bloodied, his clothes singed as well as torn.

"I'm here, Amos!" Drake shouted. "I've got you!"

However, when he turned the wounded man over, Drake discovered that it wasn't the mechanic after all; it was the silent, dangerous-looking thug from the hotel. The man's mouth moved, but no sound came out. In his eyes, Drake saw no trace of viciousness, only confusion and fear. Even though the stranger had threatened to do him and Amos harm, Drake grabbed his arms and dragged him away from the fire. By the time he lay the thug down, the man was unconscious; a quick check revealed he was still alive.

Drake wiped his brow and stared at the blaze. Amos was dead. The Plymouth was wrecked. Everything he had spent years saving, almost all his money, was now nothing but ash. He glanced up at the truck; Clara and Tommy stood beside it, mesmerized by the fire. What was he going to tell her? Without his money, how were they going to build a future together? What hope did they have of getting rid of Eddie now?

Try as he might, Drake couldn't come up with a single answer.

Clara shivered in the wind, rubbing her hands on her bare arms, but she had no desire to get back in the truck. Dusk was fast approaching, the sun slowly settling for the night. Smoke still drifted lazily toward the sky, the sharp smell burning her nose. The fire department had long since come and gone, leaving behind two charred wrecks that had once been cars. The only survivor of the crash had been rushed to town in an ambulance; she didn't know what would happen to the remains of Amos and the other men. Right then, she couldn't bring herself to care.

All that mattered was Drake.

He stood with Sheriff Oglesby, talking about the crash. Clara was too far away to hear what was being said, but she guessed that Drake was telling the lawman the truth: that he didn't know why the men had been after Amos, not exactly, only that the mechanic had been accused of stealing something. Drake's expression was calm, he was nodding a lot, but Clara expected that he was torn up on the inside; even if Amos had robbed him of his money, they had spent years together traveling from race to race, under the Plymouth's hood, building a friendship as close as family. She worried how he would react to such a huge loss. Clara imagined that the worst part was that Drake would never have the chance to talk to Amos about his betrayal. He would die a thief.

And he took the money with him when he went…

Earlier, Clara had watched Drake walk the tall grass around the wrecks, hoping that his bag had been ejected as the survivor had, but he'd come up empty. Left with nothing but ash, she couldn't help but think of Eddie. How could they fend him off now? If the banker went through with his threat, then in addition to losing the Plymouth, Amos, and all of Drake's money, her home would be taken away. Once, she'd considered surrendering to Eddie's demands; now her love for Drake made it impossible. But what else could they do?

"Penny for your thoughts."

Clara jumped at the sound of Tommy's voice. She had been so preoccupied that she hadn't heard him approach. He hadn't said much since the crash, wandering up and down the ditches, watching from a distance.

She shook her head. "I'm just tired," she answered, then nodded toward the wrecked cars. "It's been a long day."

Tommy was silent for a bit, kicking rocks at his feet. "I've been thinking about something," he finally said. "What was in Drake's bag? Must have been important, as mad as he was that his friend took it."

Clara considered lying, but when she saw the way her son was looking at her, when she thought about their recent reconciliation, she couldn't.

Isn't his life in as much trouble as mine?

She took a deep breath. "There's something you should know…" she began.

By the time she'd finished, Clara had told Tommy everything. She explained that Drake had intended to help them, but that plan was now in jeopardy.

"It isn't fair," Tommy spat angrily.

"You'll find out that plenty in life isn't," Clara answered. "Sometimes, there isn't anything you can do about it."

"But he's blackmailing you!"

"Eddie doesn't see it that way," she explained. "He's in love with me and means to have me whether I want to be his wife or not."

Tommy balled his fists in anger. Clara was reminded of Joe; he would often rail away against things he found unjust, furious at a newspaper article or a radio program. Life father, like son, she supposed. But just like then, when Joe complained about there not being enough jobs to go around, the price of a pound of flour, or even about Hitler's march into Czechoslovakia, there was nothing that could be done. They were helpless.

"I've got an idea."

Clara turned to look at Tommy; for a moment, she thought she'd misheard. "There's nothing we can do now," she told him. "The money's gone."

Her son shook his head. "If my idea worked, we

wouldn't need it." From the look in Tommy's eyes, Clara could see he believed what he was saying.

"It's too late. We don't have—"

"Just hear me out and then decide," Tommy interrupted, his excitement showing. "Besides, what do we have to lose?"

Clara knew the answer: nothing. Amos's thievery and death had placed their backs against the wall. At this point any idea, no matter how odd or impractical, should be considered. After all, they needed a miracle . . .

"All right," she said. "Let's go talk to Drake."

Chapter Twenty-Seven

EDDIE STOOD IN FRONT of the large picture window and frowned. It looked miserable outside, the sky full of clouds the color of dishwater. This time of year depressed him. It was always raining and the mornings were cold enough to hint at the winter to come. Occasionally, he fantasized about moving someplace warm, somewhere like Florida, though he knew he would never leave Sunset; this was his home, where he and Clara would raise their family. He was lost in those thoughts, drinking a cup of coffee, when the telephone rang. Surprised, he looked at the clock; it wasn't even eight. Who could be calling at such an hour?

"Hello?" he asked tentatively.

"We need to talk." Immediately, Eddie recognized the voice on the other end of the line. It was Drake McCoy. His hand tightened on the receiver.

"What can I do for you?" he said.

"Cut the crap," McCoy replied. "You know why I'm calling."

"You've come to a decision..."

There was a moment of silence. "I have," the race car driver answered. "But that all depends on if your offer still stands."

"It does. The same as before."

"That's not good enough anymore. I want double."

Eddie nodded to himself; ever since the two men had met, he had been considering this possibility. "I already tried to give it to you."

"Not double *that*," McCoy said. "Twice the second amount."

"*Four* times the original offer?" he blurted.

"If that's too much..."

Eddie swallowed hard. He wasn't against paying such a hefty amount—he would've given most everything he owned to have Clara—but he was surprised that the driver was being so greedy. McCoy had flaunted his principles when they first met; Eddie wondered if something had happened with Clara to change his mind.

"All right," he eventually agreed. "Come down to the bank this afternoon and I'll get you your money."

"Not there."

Eddie frowned. "Why not?"

"Because Clara's working today, and even though I don't expect you to understand, I don't want to hurt her any more than necessary," McCoy explained. "She doesn't need to know what's happened until I'm long gone."

While Eddie would have enjoyed the triumphant feeling of watching Clara's face collapse as the race car driver walked out of her life forever, a part of him admired McCoy for wanting to avoid a scene. "If not the bank, then where?"

"The hotel. I'll be in the parlor at noon."

Before Eddie could say anything else, the phone line went dead.

Picking up his coffee, he took a drink but then spat it back out; while he'd been talking to McCoy, it had gone cold. But rather than refill it from the pot, Eddie chose something stronger, something fit for a celebration. With a glass of bourbon, he went back to the window. Suddenly, things didn't seem quite so gloomy. By the time night came, nothing would stand in the way of his life with Clara Sinclair.

She would be his, forever and always.

When Drake hung up the phone, Clara began to breathe again; the whole time she'd been in the kitchen, listening to his conversation with Eddie, her heart had raced.

"Do you think this is going to work?" she asked.

Drake nodded. "I do," he answered, though she wondered if he wasn't trying to convince himself as much as her.

Tommy's plan had surprised them both with its ingenuity; listening to him as he spelled it all out, Clara had wondered if spending so much time with a delinquent like Naomi had rubbed off on him. After that, Drake had made suggestions and they had stayed up most of the night finalizing what they would do. None of them had slept more than an hour or two.

But now, with a phone call, the ball had started rolling.

"What if something goes wrong?" Clara pressed, unable to stop agonizing over it. "What if he realizes we're up to something?"

"It doesn't matter," Drake answered. "Even if Eddie manages to sniff out our plan, then we're back where we started, stuck between a rock and a hard place. Tommy's right about one thing: we don't have anything to lose." Gently, he took her hand. "Just stick to what we talked about and it will all work out." He smiled. "Trust me."

Clara wrapped her arms around Drake's waist and held tight. She pressed her head to his chest and listened to the steady beat of his heart. Touching him like this, it was hard to believe all they had been through.

"I'm sorry about Amos," she told him.

Ever since the crash, Drake hadn't said a word about his friend, although it had been obvious he'd been thinking about the mechanic, wondering what had gone so wrong. All morning, his attention had wandered, no doubt replaying over and over again what they'd witnessed. After they'd decided on their plan to deal with Eddie, Drake had gone out onto the porch alone and sat on the steps, staring up at the cloudy sky. Clara imagined he was remembering races they'd run, conversations shared down country roads, laughs over beers; she'd watched from the window, but hadn't joined him, and eventually he'd come back inside.

"Me, too," he said. "But now isn't the time for mourning." Drake tipped her chin up until she was looking in his eyes. "What matters is you."

Clara rose on her tiptoes to kiss him tenderly, their lips barely brushing; if this worked, they could have a more passionate celebration later.

"You need to get ready for work," he told her.

She shook her head. "I can't believe I have to spend the morning with Eddie, acting like I have no idea what's going on."

"It's all part of the plan," Drake said. "Besides, I need to get going. I have things to take care of before the meeting at the hotel."

"Can I come with you?"

Both of them turned to see Tommy leaning against the doorway. There had been a time when Clara would've been horrified if her son found her standing in a man's arms, but not now; with all they had talked about, she knew Tommy understood what they could lose, as well as what they wished to gain.

Drake nodded. "Sure," he said. "I'd like that."

Watching them back the truck down the driveway, Clara thought that no matter what, one way or the other, things were about to change.

Forever.

Clara stood on the porch, finishing a cup of coffee. A steady rain had begun to fall, drumming on the roof above her head. In the distance, a deep roll of thunder rumbled. The weather matched her mood.

After Drake and Tommy left, she'd taken a shower, gotten dressed, put on a touch of makeup, and tried to ready herself to go to the bank. She still couldn't believe she was going to stand at her teller window, smile at customers, and pretend that she didn't know what was about to happen. She knew Drake was right, understood that it was part of their plan, but it made her sick to her stomach nevertheless. But she would go through with it, for all their sakes.

Behind her, Clara heard a floorboard creak; moments later, her mother appeared at the door. Christine had sat with them for most of the night, discussing how to deal with Eddie. She hadn't said much, but when their spirits lagged, especially Clara's, Christine had offered encouragement.

"Worrying never got anyone anywhere," she had said. "Besides, Eddie Fuller has always been an odd duck, even when he was a boy. Whatever bad comes from this, however he suffers, he'll deserve whatever he gets."

"Did you sleep?" Clara asked her now.

Her mother nodded. "A little," she said, but then yawned. "From the look on your face, I reckon I got more than you."

Clara smiled weakly. "I'm just so nervous. I keep thinking about everything that could go wrong. Drake tells me not to worry, but I can't help it."

"That's understandable," Christine said.

"Imagine what could happen if Eddie finds out what we're up to. He wouldn't rest until all of our things were out in the street. We'd be ruined."

"But Eddie doesn't want that," her mother disagreed. "All he wants is you, and he'll do whatever it takes to make that happen. His love will blind him."

"You sound like you think this will work."

"I do," Christine said, putting her arm around her daughter's shoulders. "But even if it doesn't, you and I have been through worse. Both of us lost our husbands. We raised our children largely on our own. We worked and scrimped to put food on the table. Even if we lose the house, we'll land on our feet."

Listening to her mother inspired Clara. She remembered the day, standing on this very porch, when she'd been told of Joe's death. Overwhelmed with grief, she had been unable to imagine a future without her husband, but she'd still managed to build one. Even if Eddie's vindictiveness put her on the street, she would still have Tommy and her mother. She would also have Drake. Together, they would build a new future, no matter what it took.

"Thanks, Mom," she said. "You've made me feel better."

"I'm glad," Christine answered. "Now get on down to the bank. It's time for you to get that rotten son of a gun off your back for good."

"Are you planning on marrying my mother?"

Drake tightened his grip on the steering wheel. Ever since he and Tommy had left the house, they had been busy. First, they'd gone to the filling station—if Eddie made a run for it, Drake wanted to make certain he had plenty of gas. After that, they went to the hotel and packed up the rest of his and Amos's things; a quick search of his dead friend's belongings revealed no clues to explain his thievery. Down in the lobby, Edna Gilbert offered her condolences for Amos but was thankful that the men who'd threatened her had met the same fate; when Drake told her that he and Eddie would be using her parlor that afternoon, her good humor vanished. After that, he'd telephoned his bank in Illinois, wanting to know exactly how much money he had left; it wasn't much, but it would get them by for a while if their gambit failed. Through it all, Tommy had been quiet, as if something was weighing on his mind. Now Drake knew what it had been.

"Someday," he answered, "if she'll have me." He paused. "Is this why you wanted to come along? To ask me that?"

"Partly," Tommy admitted.

"Do you have a problem with your mother and I being together?"

Clara's son shook his head. "No, I don't. I see how she looks at you and how even with all this craziness going on, you can still make her smile."

"I love her," Drake explained, knowing with all his heart it was true. "When we met, I knew she was the woman I'd been looking for my whole life. But I've worried you wouldn't be happy about it," he said, remembering their first encounter and how it had ended. "I'm not trying to be your father."

Tommy stared out his window, watching rainwater trickle down the glass. "I don't have many memories of him," he said. "I was so young when he died that I can't remember much. I'm not sure what you'd be replacing."

"I've spent more than twenty years *trying* to forget my old man."

"You have?" Tommy asked. "Why?"

"Because we fought like cats and dogs," Drake explained. "Nothing I did was ever good enough, so the first chance I got, I hit the road and never looked back. So even if I wanted to take your father's place, I'm not sure I'd know how. I suppose I'd have an idea what *not* to do, but that wouldn't make me much of a parent. What I'm hoping," he said, looking at Tommy, "is that we can be friends."

The boy was silent for a while, as if he was considering the offer, and then he slowly nodded. "I think we can do that."

"That's good to hear."

"Does this mean you'll teach me how to drive really fast?"

Drake laughed loudly. "We're going to need to get a new car first." Noticing Tommy's disappointment, he added, "Who knows? Maybe with some tinkering under the hood, this old truck might have a few good runs left in her."

"Don't hold your breath," Tommy joked; this time, they both laughed.

Turning down the street on which Clara and her family lived, Drake looked at the house through the whipping windshield wipers. If he made a mistake, if he underestimated Eddie, it could all be lost.

"Make sure that bastard gets what's coming to him," Tommy said, as if he had read Drake's mind.

For him, for Clara, for all of them, he was betting on it.

Eddie walked into the Sunset Hotel with a spring in his step. As usual, Edna Gilbert stood behind the front desk. When she saw him, she opened her mouth to say something, but Eddie strode past her and into the parlor without a word. Today, he wasn't in the mood for chitchat. He had far more important matters to attend to.

Drake McCoy sat at the same table Eddie had used at their last meeting. Without waiting for an invitation, Eddie took the seat opposite.

"I must say," he began, unbuttoning his vest, his stomach having grown a bit larger since his father's death, "I admire you not wanting Clara to see this."

The race car driver frowned. "Like I told you on the phone," he said, "I have no interest in being cruel."

"Just getting richer?" Eddie suggested.

McCoy shrugged.

"She seemed quite happy at the bank, smiling at her customers, going about her day like it was any other."

Oddly enough, it had been Eddie who'd struggled to stay focused on his work. Sitting at his desk, pretending to sort through papers, he kept going to his door to steal glances at her, daydreaming about the future they would soon share. With McCoy headed out of town, his pockets stuffed with cash, there was nothing left to keep them apart. Once, Clara had caught him looking at her. Quickly, her gaze had darted away, her discomfort obvious, which hurt Eddie deeply; her reaction strengthened his conviction to change her mind, to make her look upon him longingly, with love in her eyes.

"Did you bring the money?" McCoy asked.

Eddie nodded. He pulled another check from the inside pocket of his coat and pushed it across the table. "Eight thousand dollars."

McCoy picked up the check and looked at it. Eddie had expected the man to smile, pleased with the numbers. Instead, the race car driver frowned, as if something offended him. Then he ripped the check in half.

Eddie was so dumbfounded that he rose out of his chair. "What...what do you think you're doing?"

"It's not enough," the man answered matter-of-factly.

"But...but this is what we agreed to! You said so just this morning!"

McCoy shook his head. "I changed my mind. Now I want twelve thousand."

Eddie couldn't believe what he was hearing. His heart raced, his blood pressure rose, and he breathed so hard his nostrils flared. "This is...this is outrageous!" he shouted in a voice that hardly sounded like his own.

"Call it whatever you want," the driver answered, his face impassive, his voice sounding as if this was nothing out of the ordinary. "If it's too much, then I suppose I can stick around town a while longer. Folks here are real friendly."

Inside, Eddie raged. He hadn't bargained on McCoy

proving to be so greedy. Still, he *was* rich, wealthy enough to afford what the bastard was unjustly demanding. To Eddie, Clara Sinclair was worth any price. Whatever he had to spend to make her his, it was a price worth paying.

In the end, it was only money.

"All right," Eddie grumbled reluctantly. "Twelve thousand it is."

He sat back down, pulled out his checkbook, and started to write out the new amount. He was halfway done when McCoy interrupted him.

"I've got a question," he said.

Eddie's hand came to an abrupt halt, his pen making an unintended mark on the paper. Was McCoy going to make *another* demand?

"What is it?" he asked curtly.

"After you've paid me to go away, what will you do if Clara refuses to become your wife? What if she still rejects you?"

Eddie shook his head. This was nonsense. "She won't."

"But what if she does?" the driver pressed.

"Clara's smart enough not to make such a mistake."

McCoy chuckled. "I don't think you know her as well as you think you do."

"Don't tell me you're having second thoughts..." Eddie said.

The racer shook his head.

"Then why do you want to know so badly?"

"I'm curious."

Eddie licked his lips. "If Clara was foolish enough to

refuse what I'm offering, then I'd take away everything that matters to her."

"How?"

"How?" Eddie echoed, warming to his explanation. "Just how hard do you think it would be for me to go into the bank's records and make it appear as if Clara was behind on her house payments?"

"You've already told me this," the driver said. "What happens then?"

"Then I'll own her house and Clara will be out on the street, along with her son, her mother, and everything they own."

What Eddie left unsaid was that he hoped it wouldn't come to that; he wanted Clara, not her house. Threatening to take it was simply a means to an end. Regardless, he'd do it if she kept rejecting him. Though it would hurt him deeply, he would ruin her life. He wasn't a man to be trifled with.

"Isn't that illegal?" McCoy asked.

"Of course it is," Eddie snapped, growing annoyed at all the questions. "Truth is, Clara has never once been late on a payment, but so what? I can change that, turn it upside down, and no one will doubt me for a second."

"Because you're so important..."

"That's right. Banks *are* important, and the men who run them are powerful," he continued, thinking about all the times his father had failed to flaunt his authority, preaching to his son that he wasn't above the community; what complete hogwash! "Clara can claim that she's paid up until she's blue in the face, but it won't do her any good, and that's why she's going to do *exactly* as I say."

With that, Eddie returned to filling out the check.

"You're a real son of a bitch."

Once again, he stopped writing. McCoy's voice had been menacing, his words spat in accusation. Eddie looked up. The other man's face was twisted into a scowl, as if he was itching for a fight. Shockingly, so was Eddie.

"What did you call me?" he demanded.

"You heard me," McCoy answered. "I've spent an awful lot of years driving from one town to the next, most of them a lot like Sunset, and during that time, I've met all kinds of people. Some were rich, others poor. Some were educated, most were not. But I have never met such a spineless, manipulative bastard as you." The driver paused, letting a smile slowly spread across his face. "As long as I live, I'm going to be glad I played a part in bringing your life crashing down around your head. Just remember this: not everything is for sale."

Eddie stood quickly, so violently that his chair toppled over onto the floor. "What...what is this?" he shouted. "What are you talking about?"

"Turn around and find out."

Incredulous, confused, and more than a little frightened, Eddie spun on his heel just as two people stepped into the parlor. He suddenly felt ill.

Standing before him was Clara. Next to her was Sheriff Oglesby.

* * *

Clara couldn't believe what she'd heard. She and the sheriff had been standing outside the parlor, listening to Eddie and Drake's conversation. Several times, she'd wanted to rush into the room, to scream her outrage at Eddie, but every time she'd managed to fight down the urge, remembering what Drake had told her; until Eddie admitted to blackmailing her, until he acknowledged that he knew what he was doing was illegal, she couldn't show herself.

But it had been hard to hold back...

It hadn't been much easier at the bank. All morning, she'd struggled to act as if nothing was wrong, like it was just another day. The worst part had been catching Eddie staring at her with his goofy grin; she didn't want to imagine what disturbed fantasies were rolling around in his head.

As the clock neared noon, Eddie had left for his meeting with Drake; Clara had followed, dodging rain puddles as she hurried down back streets leading to the hotel. Sheriff Oglesby was waiting at the rear entrance; Drake had informed the lawman of their plans that morning. Edna Gilbert let them inside. Making their way to the parlor, they listened to Eddie incriminate himself.

Now, she no longer needed to keep quiet.

"How dare you?!" Clara shouted, her voice quavering with fury. She moved quickly, closing the distance between them, and slapped Eddie hard across his face; in the small room, the blow sounded as loud as a gunshot.

Eddie's eyes went as wide as saucers, not from pain but from shock. "Clara, wait...I didn't...I..." he stammered. "I never—"

Before he could lie, Clara hit him again. She reared back a third time, but the sheriff grabbed her wrist.

"Hold on," the lawman said. "No one's going to disagree that he had the first two coming, but that's enough for now."

"I don't know what you think you heard," Eddie argued, pressing his palm against his rapidly reddening cheek, "but I assure you that I wouldn't—"

"Stow it, Eddie," Sheriff Oglesby cut him off. "We've been standing outside the whole time. I heard every word loud and clear."

"Then you misunderstood! I didn't mean that—"

"Let's you and I go down to my office and have a talk," the lawman continued. "I'm particularly interested in one word: blackmail."

When they had come up with their plan, the intention wasn't to put Eddie behind bars but rather to render him impotent. Tommy had made the analogy that the banker's threat was like a loaded gun pointed straight at their heads; they needed to remove the bullets. But if Eddie ended up falling hard, if he went to jail, lost the bank and all his wealth, his life ruined, then so be it.

Suddenly, Eddie seemed to realize all he stood to lose. His panicked eyes found Clara. "I wouldn't have gone through with it!" he swore. "I love you! I have *always* loved you!"

Clara stared hard at him. She remembered all the times

he had approached her at her teller window, making pathetic come-ons, ignoring how she rejected him. She thought back to their talk in his office, when he'd proposed marriage and then threatened her with losing her home if she didn't accept.

Because of all that, she had no pity for Eddie Fuller.

"You have no idea what love is," Clara said matter-of-factly.

Her words made Eddie begin to lose control. His body trembled. Spittle wet his lips. Veins stood out on his neck. But when his fury overflowed, it was turned not against Clara but against the man he undoubtedly blamed for stealing her away.

"This is all because of you!" Eddie roared at Drake.

Completely unhinged, the banker lunged toward his perceived rival for Clara's love, intent on tearing the man limb from limb. Clara was so frightened she screamed. But Drake was as calm as he was behind the wheel of the Plymouth. Before Eddie could reach him, he was out of his chair. He sidestepped a weak attempt at a punch, and then drove his own fist into Eddie's stomach so hard that it lifted the man off the ground.

"Unfff," Eddie wheezed, the air violently driven from his lungs.

When he fell to the floor, he lay in a heap, his hands holding his midsection, rocking back and forth, heaving and retching.

The next thing Clara knew, she was in Drake's arms, holding him tight, thankful that it was finally over.

"Come on, now," the sheriff said as he pulled Eddie up onto unsteady feet. As the banker was led from the parlor, it sounded like he was crying.

Once they were alone, Drake asked, "Are you all right?"

Clara nodded. She was about to ask him the same when Edna Gilbert stuck her head through the doorway and said, "Looks like you got him."

"I hope so," Clara answered.

"Serves him right," the hotel owner remarked with a broad grin. "Standin' in the way of love like that. I hope when he's locked up, they lose the key."

Clara couldn't have agreed more.

Outside, the rain had stopped. Blue sky poked through the disappearing clouds; as the sun shone down, its light reflected off puddles, passing cars, and the wet sidewalks. Clara and Drake looked up, feeling the warmth of the afternoon, reveling in what had happened. Luring Eddie into their trap had been risky, but somehow everything had worked out. Now they were finally free to start their life together, to let their love bloom.

"Penny for your thoughts," Drake said.

Clara smiled. "I was just thinking about how different everything looks now that our troubles are behind us."

"I wouldn't go that far," he replied. "I lost my best friend, my car, and nearly all my savings, which means I can't open a garage."

"I suppose you're right..." she said, feeling a bit deflated.

Drake chuckled. He pulled Clara close, pushing hair off her cheek and looking deep into her eyes. "In the end, none of that is important," he explained. "What matters is that I have you. Together, we can do anything."

Clara believed him. Ever since their unlikeliest of meetings, her life had undergone one change after another: she had mended most of her troubles with her son, while Tommy had broken off his relationship with Naomi; Eddie's threat of taking away her home was no more; and even though her mother's memory continued to deteriorate, she no longer had to face it alone. But the most unbelievable change of all was having Drake by her side.

"I love you," she said.

He didn't answer with words, but instead leaned down to kiss her, making it clear that he felt the same.

"What do you say we go celebrate?" he asked when their lips parted.

Now *that* sounded like a wonderful idea.

Epilogue

October 1954

HAVE A GOOD EVENING. Stay warm!"

Clara waved to Roy Washington as she stepped out of the Sunset Bank and Trust and into the autumn evening. Darkness was coming fast, the days shortening. A nippy breeze stirred fallen leaves, swirling them around her feet and sending a chill racing through her; she stuffed her hands deep in her pockets, desperate for a bit of warmth. Still, as she quickened her pace down the empty sidewalk, her smile was as bright as summer. Her life was good.

Ever since Eddie had been hauled out of the hotel parlor by Sheriff Oglesby, everything at the bank had changed for the better. Roy, who had been fired shortly after Theo Fuller's death, was brought back to guide the bank through the turbulent waters Eddie had steered them into. An auditing of the books showed that Eddie had cost them tens of thousands of dollars—mostly out of sheer incompetence, but some funds had been embezzled to buy expensive clothes, drink, cigars, and other luxuries that had caught his fancy; that included the money he'd attempted to give Drake to leave town. For that, Eddie had been sentenced to thirty years behind bars. At his trial, Clara had expected him to protest his innocence, to complain that he was too important to go to jail, but he had barely said a word in his own defense, sitting with slumped shoulders, a beaten man. He would never bother anyone, especially Clara, again.

She walked past the post office, the grocery store, and the Sunset Hotel, where so much had happened last spring, before finally arriving at her destination.

The doors to Solomon Burke's auto garage stood wide open; inside, two men were bent over beneath an open hood, peering into an engine. Music was occasionally punctuated by the clang of a tool against metal.

Even though he couldn't possibly have heard her approach, Drake noticed her arrival. "Give me a minute," he said.

Clara nodded, stamping her feet in the chill.

Of course, this wasn't what they'd intended when Drake had first proposed giving up racing and staying in Sunset. But when all his money had been destroyed in the Plymouth's crash, his dream had been lost, or, at the least, postponed. Fortunately, he'd had no trouble catching on with Solomon; five minutes under the hood with Drake would have convinced anyone he was a good mechanic. Because he was easy to work with, as well as a good listener, he immediately fit right in. He still socked away as much money as he could afford to save; maybe he would someday open his own business, or he might even buy Solomon's. Either way, she knew he was happy.

Patting his boss on the back, Drake was done for the day. He pulled a handkerchief from his pocket and began to wipe grease from his hands; he never managed to get them completely clean.

"Sorry about that," he said. "I was never the best when it came to changing the distributor on a V8 engine. Amos had it down to a science."

It wasn't often, but Drake's old friend still came up in conversation occasionally. Miraculously, the thug who had been jettisoned from the Cadillac had survived his injuries. Once he could talk, he had explained that Amos was a morphine addict who'd stolen money and drugs from Sweet Woods, a small-time hood from St. Louis; he and the other tough had died in the crash that claimed Amos. For months after, Drake had sifted through his years with the mechanic, searching for something, some sign of his drug habit, but had come up empty. Clara suspected that there was a part of Drake that blamed himself for Amos's death; if he'd known about his friend's addiction, he could have saved him. So now when Amos was mentioned, it was always the good things, times on the road and under the hood, never anything that had happened in Sunset.

"So what's so important to show me that I have to stand out here in the cold?" Clara asked playfully.

Drake chuckled. "It wouldn't be much of a surprise if I just blurted it out, now would it? Come with me."

He led her around the back of the garage, past DeSotos, Chryslers, Oldsmobiles, and other makes, all in various stages of repair. True to his word, one of the first vehicles Drake worked on had been Clara's truck; after his long hours tinkering with it, the pickup ran better than it had in years, though it still occasionally sputtered to a stop if it idled too long.

"You'll never guess who brought in his car today," Drake said.

"Who?"

"Wilbur Marsh. That was his Studebaker that Solomon and I were working on." Drake shook his head. "He hasn't taken very good care of it."

"Did he say anything about Naomi?"

"Not a word."

One day, a little over a month ago, Naomi had disappeared from Sunset. Gossip around town was that she had hooked up with a man who'd come into the Marshland and decided to run off with him. Another rumor was that she was pregnant and had gone to live with relatives in Arkansas. For her part, Clara hoped that Naomi had decided to take a chance and gone to either New York or Hollywood to chase her dreams. Even though the young woman had caused her plenty of sleepless nights, Clara didn't wish her ill. She figured that Naomi deserved happiness, wherever it might be. Who knew, maybe one day there she would be, up on a billboard or on the cover of a magazine.

Drake suddenly stopped. "Close your eyes," he told her.

Clara did as he said and he took her by the elbow and led her a short distance farther.

"Open them."

A vehicle sat beneath a tarp. "It's a car," she jokingly guessed.

"Give the lady a cigar!" Drake shouted like a carnival barker. "But this isn't just any old car. This one is special."

With that, he whipped away the tarp with a flourish. Even with as little as Clara knew about cars, she recognized its make right away; it was a Plymouth. While it wasn't exactly the same as the one Drake had driven into Sunset, it had many of the same features: the curve of the hood, the shape of the headlights and side mirrors, and the black exterior. It had a few dents in its panels, some rust marring one of the wheel wells, and a crack across the passenger-side window, but it was a beauty all the same.

"I got it for a song," Drake explained. "Chris Gilliand didn't want it anymore, so I took it off his hands. It still needs a lot of work—the windshield wipers are busted, the trunk has to be forced open, and someone took a knife to the rear seats—but it's on its way to respectability. It might be an eyesore on the outside, but under the hood, it's a thing of beauty."

A sudden thought struck Clara, making her smile falter. "Is this because you want to start racing again?" she asked.

Drake laughed loudly. "No, it isn't," he answered. "That itch has been scratched. I'm done behind the wheel." He paused. "I was thinking that once I got it going, this might be Tommy's."

In the months since Drake's arrival, it sometimes felt as if Tommy had changed into a completely different person. Out from under Naomi's influence and with a strong male role model in his life, he was doing better than ever. Together, he and Drake had set about repairing the house; they rehung the fallen gutters, patched the roof, and had finally put the garage doors back up. Resuming an old tradition, all three of them had made almost weekly outings to the movie theater, indulging Tommy's newfound love of monster flicks. At school, Tommy's grades had started to improve and he'd made a few friends. He still had his moments of teenage rebelliousness, but that was to be expected; Clara didn't mind a little sass now and then, not so long as she had her son back.

Unfortunately, not everything with her family had gotten better. Christine's memory troubles plagued her more and more frequently. Just yesterday, she'd readied a load of laundry to hang on the line to dry; the problem was that it was pouring rain outside. She stumbled on names, forgot familiar phone numbers, blanked on addresses, and had even called Drake "Joe" once or twice; fortunately, he'd taken it in stride, never showing a hint of unease. Late at night, Clara often unloaded her worries to Drake. He always listened carefully, making the occasional comment, promising that they would do whatever they could to help Christine. Often, Clara thought about what he'd told her on the porch swing: that as long as they tried as hard as they could, that was enough. She still worried about her mother's future, but she knew they wouldn't let her go without a fight.

"So do you want to go for a ride?" Drake asked.

"It runs?" she replied.

"You better believe she runs." He opened the driver's-side door. "The other door doesn't open so hot," he explained.

Clara got in and slid across. Drake followed, put the key in the ignition, and started the Plymouth's engine; the rumble was familiar.

"Are you sure you remember how to drive a car like this?"

Drake grinned. "I couldn't forget if I tried."

While he drove around to the street, Clara couldn't help but think about how blessed she was to have met him. In the six months since Drake had unexpectedly given up racing and settled down with her in Sunset, she'd been blissfully happy. But as overwhelming as those first days together had been, what had followed was even better than she could have hoped. It was the day-to-day moments that made Clara fall head over heels for Drake: the way his hair was often mussed up; how he always tapped the wall just inside the kitchen door when he left after lunch; the unrecognizable yet pleasant tunes he whistled while he washed the dishes; but especially how he would surprise her with flowers or a note when she least expected it, just to tell her how much he loved her. Her heart still drummed faster every time she saw him, every time she heard his voice.

A week ago, Drake had proposed; Clara had tearfully

accepted. Sometime next spring, they would be married. Tommy had been as excited as she was, something for which she would be forever grateful; later, she learned that Drake had asked her son's permission for her hand. Their ceremony and reception would be a simple affair, with music and food, but she was already counting the days. Forever stretched out before them. Even after all the heartbreak that had battered her life with Joe's death, something wonderful had happened.

Love had changed her life. Again.

"So where do you want to go?" Drake asked, his free hand draped over the steering wheel.

"With you, I'd go anywhere," she told him. "As long as we go fast."

He chuckled. "That, I can most definitely do."

Whatever road they went down, they would drive it together.

ABOUT THE AUTHOR

Dorothy Garlock is one of America's—and the world's—favorite novelists. Her work has consistently appeared on national bestsellers lists, including the *New York Times* list, and there are over fifteen million copies of her books in print translated into eighteen languages. She has won more than twenty writing awards, including an *RT Book Reviews* Reviewers' Choice Award for Best Historical Fiction for *A Week from Sunday*, five Silver Pen Awards from *Affaire de Coeur*, and three Silver Certificate Awards. Her novel *With Hope* was chosen by Amazon as one of the best romances of the twentieth century.

After retiring as a news reporter and bookkeeper in 1978, she began her career as a novelist with the publication of *Love and Cherish*. She lives in Clear Lake, Iowa. You can visit her website at DorothyGarlock.com.